These days they reckon t...
hundred Usurper attempt...
per cent being successfu...
means is that 190 Usurpe...
have to agree, these are ...
Outside trying to get in. ...
the desperation of those who decide to go ahead with
it . . .

PETER MICHAEL

The Usurper

GRAFTON BOOKS

A Division of the Collins Publishing Group

LONDON GLASGOW
TORONTO SYDNEY AUCKLAND

Grafton Books
A Division of the Collins Publishing Group
8 Grafton Street, London W1X 3LA

A Grafton Paperback Original 1988

ISBN 0-586-20169-6

Printed and bound in Great Britain by
Collins, Glasgow

Set in Times

*To Kapok Michael
and to
Jack and Janet Rosenberg*

Part One

1

I don't know why they do it, the Usurpers. The old lady reckons they're 'morally wrong'. Don't know about that. I mean, morals: what use are morals these days? Morals don't get you a job now, do they?

I told Freddo when he asked me. 'Shall I, shan't I?' he said to me. 'C'mon, Demon,' he said; 'Shall I, shan't I?' I told Freddo what I thought, didn't I? Did he listen to me? 'The risk's too big,' I said. But Freddo always was a bit dense. 'You have to be smart to be a Usurper,' I said to him, 'and let's face it, Freddo, let's face it; you're not smart now, are you?' He wasn't. Everyone knew that, didn't they? That's why no one was too surprised when they heard the news. 'Too big a risk, Freddo,' I said, but Freddo never listened.

I heard the Nooz twice today. Nooz at Noon said that this week's Expo winner was seventy-two years old. You don't see anyone that old any more, eh? What a waste though; what a terrible waste. I said that to the old lady: 'Poor sod, what use is it to him?' I said, but Mum just smiled and said that it was never too late. Don't know about that neither. When you're dying you're already on the way out anyway, so what's the point? 'If I were seventy-two,' I said to Mum, 'I'd rather not win Expo at all!' But the old lady just tut-tutted and said, 'Chance would be a fine thing.'

I don't know about Mum; I think she might be going senile. Forty-five, she is; forty-five's not too early to go senile. Freddo's old lady went senile at forty, and no one so much as said a word. It seems to be getting earlier all

the time; soon it won't be worth living past thirty. Not
that it's worth it now; I mean, Freddo didn't make it past
twenty did he, and crying shame though it might have
been, who's to say that Freddo is not better off? Not me,
that's for sure, though it must be said that I haven't got
that many friends, and certainly not enough to have them
cop it, not even thick bastards like Freddo. 'Too big a
risk, Freddo,' I said, but he never listened, and now the
poor sod's dead. Ironic really, isn't it? Everything gets
more expensive by the day; has done ever since I can
remember (although some say it wasn't always that way);
everything, that is, except life. Life just gets cheaper;
each day it's worth just a bit less than the day before.
Except for the Working Class of course; they've got it
made.

I saw the Slut today. I hadn't seen her for a couple of
days. Two years it is now, and she still hasn't got used to
me calling her the Slut, although I don't see why she
cares. That's all she is, after all. 'My name's Gina!' she
screamed at me today. 'Can't you get that into your lame
brain?' I slapped her good for that; that's no way to talk
to your elders (Gina's only seventeen, but people think
she's older). I can, of course, remember her name very
clearly, but I prefer to call her the Slut, because it suits
her. Like the Knife; I couldn't think of the Knife with any
other name; I don't know that he was ever anything else.
Knife reckons Freddo got everything he deserved, being
unprepared like that. Deserved to cop it, said Knife, and
I can't help but think he must be right. Funny that; the
Knife is almost as dense as poor old Freddo, but he don't
half say some smart things sometimes.

I was pleased though to see the Slut, even though she
did scream at me; she really surpassed herself today,
coming out with some of the most disgusting sayings while
I was giving her the old prod. She's definitely getting

8

worse, is the Slut. When I first met her there was none of this obscenity business, although she did swear occasionally, but now, as soon as it's inside her, she's off. I don't know where she gets it from; admittedly it used to turn me on, all the things she'd say, but not any more. Now it's just disgusting. The old lady would probably say that the Slut had no morals, but what does she know about such things? The old lady probably hasn't had a prod in years.

The Slut was good though, warm and soft and wet. I like that feeling, warm and wet, and the cold sensation of the bricks against my palm, and the sound of the wind whistling down the Alley, and Gina moaning, up against the wall. Oh yes, she loves a prod does Gina, even though it is only ever in the Alley these days. But she knows I can't do it anywhere else, without the sulphurous fumes making my eyes water, my throat dry, and the feel of masonry and steel and tarmac; it's the only place I can do it, in the shadow of the decaying buildings, the only place that feels right. And Gina knows that, so she doesn't have much choice. Knife reckons she's got too much chemical crap in her already and that's what makes her so desperate all the time. I don't know about that, and I don't much care. Well, would you? Of course, old Freddo's had his last prod now; no more sticky-icky for poor old Freddo. I couldn't get him out of my mind. Usurpers, eh? I don't know why they do it I really don't.

It's a funny old town is Ilford, these days anyway. You see, I was in the Library again this afternoon, as usual, and found something very interesting. To me, that is. I mean, someone else might not give a monkey's, right? But to me, well, like I said, it was very interesting. Mind you I had to wait didn't I, what with the queue and all. Gets more crowded every day, does the Library, which is a good thing of course; anything to get them away from the Box. That's all the Slut does; watch the Box. I bet she

9

watched it as soon as she got home, after the Alley; she once suggested I give her a prod while she watched it. That was stupid of her, knowing how I feel. She never suggested it again, of course.

So, what I found in the Library was these postcards; different shots of Ilford taken through the ages, with old-fashioned cameras and stuff. Well, it was a shock. There was a picture, for instance, of Ilford Hill, up by where the main intersection was, taken in 1922, and there was a tram, with rails and overhead cables and everything. Sepia it was, being an old photograph, but you had to hand it to them because the quality was top-ho, as the Knife would say. I mean, clear and clean as a whistle; you could even see the faces of the people walking along the street, and the cobblestones. I was impressed I can tell you. All sorts of photos there were. A colour one from 1960 showed the High Street with shops and traffic, cars and big red buses like in the museum; very busy, with people shopping. (I had to laugh at that one, of course.) On the left-hand side you could make out the Angel Inn in the days when it used to be a pub. Apparently, according to the librarian lady, they never had brothels in those days, at least not out in the open like. Just goes to show, doesn't it?

There was another one, too, of a place called Valentine's Park, which looked like it must have been down by the telephone exchange; what we now call the Waste. Funny to think that people used to go for a stroll around there, taking the dog for a walk and stuff, and feeding the ducks. Yeah, there even used to be ducks swimming around the pond. No one in their right mind would go walking around the Waste these days, not unless they were looking for trouble. That photo was dated 1986, which I calculated as being around about the time Dad was a kid. I wanted to ask him if he could remember being a kid and going to Valentine's Park and school and stuff, but I knew there would be no point. Dad has a great memory, but only for things that never happened; of course, that's the only sort of memory worth having these days, and I must admit I quite envy the old sod. Not that it would be much use to me, what with me wanting to know what it was really like. I suppose that's why I bother going down to the Library. Sometimes I think I must be the only one not Jobbing in that place.

I was hoping that they might have some copies, especially of that Park photo, but they didn't. Pity.

The librarian lady was very nice; not at all like your average Working Class snob, but she's got a very unusual job, hasn't she? I mean, how many Workers do you know who mix with us? Not many, right? So I guess it must make her more human. Mind you, she still wore the old spray gun, cocked and at the ready, but you can't blame her; I'd do the same in her position. Still, she was nice; looked lovely, and I would have loved to have gotten a bit closer, give her a good sniff. Once, about a year ago, I was the last to leave the Library before it closed. She pressed the button on her console to open the steel doorway that leads to the compound outside and then to her personnel carrier. She should never have done that with me still there, but she knows me quite well and I suppose she was a bit casual. Anyway, she hit the wrong button, and her glass barrier slid back. At first she didn't realize, because for a second she just stood there, her back to me, with nothing but air between us. She must've felt a draught as she suddenly whirled round. She went rigid with fear; I mean, I thought she was going to wet herself there and then. We just stood a metre apart, looking at one another. Looking back on it, I guess she was thinking: 'He can kill me. Right now.' The ridiculous thing was, all *I* was thinking was: 'I can smell your perfume,' and lovely it was too. Just think, a job there on my plate, and all I could do was sniff! She leaped forward so fast that I jumped, and then she hit the right button. The glass slid back, and I watched her, grinning like an idiot. She ran off down the steel passage.

It was on the way home that I met Knife. I hate the walk home; it's always raining, and all the old buildings become sort of stained and dirty in the rain. I always walk along the road bit, where the cars used to drive. I can still remember seeing cars along that road when I was a little kid, but there hadn't been any in Ilford for years, except for the personnel carriers taking the Outside Workers to and from the Wall, and, of course, the Snorters.

I saw the Knife from several yards away. He was hanging around outside the Angel, nipping in and out of the doorway, and as usual he was smoking a J. I'm never sure with the Knife, whether or not he smokes tobacco. He's a fool if he does, what with the price. The fact that you can still get two years for possession wouldn't worry the Knife though; he just doesn't care. Still, if I were him, I'd stay on the safe side and stick to grass, especially in public.

'Hey, Demon,' he said as I approached. 'Tell me the plan.'

'No plan, Knife. What are you doing?'

'Usual,' said Knife. He was cleaning his nails with a long, silver blade; it must have been eight centimetres long, but no more than one centimetre wide at any point, and it had a long black handle.

'New blade?' I said, realizing too late that it was a mistake. Knife had knocked my feet away and had me on my back before I had time to take a breath. He kneeled on my chest, jammed his left forearm against my throat. He held the sharp edge of the knife so close to my right eye that my eyelashes brushed against it each time I blinked.

'Look Demon! Surgical steel! Do you know how long I've been looking for one of these?'

'Tell me, Knife, tell me,' I said nervously, trying to sound enthusiastic.

'Six months, Demon; and now I have it. Watch this!' He took his forearm away (which was a relief, I can tell you), pulled out a hair from the back of my head, held it vertically between two fingers and gently swept the knife across it, lopping off the top.

'Beautiful, eh Demon?'

'Absolutely!' I said, genuinely impressed; he was a Master with a blade. The Knife leapt to his feet, reached forward and pulled me up. As I caught my breath, Knife brushed the dirt and water off his black leather trousers, put the knife back in the inside pocket of the matching leather jacket and lit another J.

'Drag?' he said, offering the J to me. I could smell cannabis on his breath.

'Tobacco?' I asked quietly.

'Oh Demon, tut-tut!' said the Knife, grinning widely and displaying his blackened, decaying teeth, destroyed because of his other all-consuming passion. 'Where would I get tobacco from?' he said mockingly. 'Just grass, Demon, just grass. Here.'

'Just wondered,' I said meekly. You could never be too sure with Knife. I took a deep drag from his J; the hot smoke burnt the back of my throat and I coughed violently. My head reeled; nicotine.

'You bastard,' I said, tears streaming down my cheeks. The Knife threw back his head and laughed; his short, spiky jet-black hair quivered slightly as his head shook in short, sharp spasms. I could see the smooth, glistening cheeks and neck, smooth as silk. Shaving close was the only decent thing he did with his blades; no one has as smooth a face as Knife. When he finally stopped laughing,

13

he put his arm around my shoulders and patted me on the cheek. It was funny how he could be both gentle and threatening at the same time.

'Sorry Demon,' he said. 'I couldn't resist it.' I smiled. What else could I do? Knife was the only close friend I had, and I was pleased; he was not the sort of guy to have as an enemy.

'Seen the Slut lately?' said the Knife, blowing smoke into the rain-soaked day.

'This morning. She's getting worse, Knife; one day she'll say the wrong thing at the wrong time, and I'll do something bad to her. I know it'll happen.'

'I have an idea, Demon,' said the Knife, waving his finger at me, and tapping his foot excitedly; he always tapped his foot when he had an idea. 'I have an idea, I have an idea,' he said again, reaching into his jacket. He pulled out his new steel blade, and waved it around.

'I'll cut her tongue out. Then she won't be able to say nothing! I can even do it while you're giving her the old prod; I'll wait until you're up her, then as soon as she says it, as soon as she says the wrong thing, swish, swish!' He waved the knife back and forth very quickly. 'No more tongue, Demon, eh? Then you can prod her in peace; it's difficult to scream without a tongue, Demon; just think what you could do in the Alley knowing she can't scream?' The wild, crazed smile had returned to his lips, and his breathing was deep and heavy. I swallowed air, gave a sniff.

'Let me think about it, Knife,' I said, unconvincingly I expect. It wouldn't do to say no straight out, not with the Knife all excited over his idea and all. Of course, I could never give the okay; that's how we differ, me and the Knife: I can't stand blades. It's not the blood; I'm used to that; you see it all the time, not that I enjoy it. No, it's

14

the cutting, the slicing, that I hate. But that's how the Knife gets it on, isn't it?

'I'll let you know,' I said. 'Gotta be going now. See you later, eh?'

'Sure,' said Knife, and put the blade away. 'Hey, Demon,' he started as I was walking away. 'Have you got any, you know . . .' I smiled, reached into my pocket.

'Catch!' I said, as I threw the Knife a small slab of chocolate. He caught it with one hand, snatching it out of the air. There was nothing, but nothing, that the Knife loved as much as chocolate.

'You're okay, Demon, you're okay.'

'See you, Knife,' I said cheerfully, and walked down the High Street towards the intersection at Ilford Hill. I turned right, and speeded up a bit, wanting to get out of the rain; past the old station with its busted windows and rusting gates, and then left into York Road and the terrible stench from the river. I gagged; I could never get used to that smell.

It was just ten minutes' walk from the Library to home, and the only person I had seen was the Knife; even down by the river, you could see, there was no one. But I wasn't surprised; after all, you don't see anyone on the streets these days do you?

2

The old man and the old lady were in the living room, watching the Box as usual. Dad was recently classified, or rather, certified, AW (that stands for Addicted Watcher) so he doesn't even have to do food collection now; all he has to do is tune in to the old Console (I reckon it should be 'ConSoul'), morning to night, and Sign In once a month. Ever since Social made Consoles available to everyone, he doesn't even have to go up to the Office; he just Signs In through the Console. Still, he's happy, I suppose – not that you can tell with AWs.

Apparently, according to the Knife's old man anyway, there was a time when nobody had Consoles; everyone had a Box, of course, but it wasn't connected to the Computer, or the Telephone. Some people had their own personal Computer (which I find very hard to believe), and used them to play games on and things. Funny to think of people playing games on a Console, don't you think? They had to pay for them in those days, but then again, in those days, most people had jobs (which is another thing I find very hard to believe).

'Gina called,' said the old lady without turning around.

'What did she want?'

'Shh!' said the old man. 'Not now! It's "Quiz-Biz"; I don't want to miss anything!'

'I'll tell you later,' said the old lady. One day, I thought to myself, I shall hurl a brick through the Console, just so that I can see them both flip. If you've ever seen an AW on withdrawal, you'll know what I mean. I'd do it, just for the fun of it.

'What did she want?' I said, louder this time, and walked around and stood in front of the Box. Dad started to cry.

'Now you've done it!' said the old lady. 'Look what you've done. He missed the answer! Why do you always have to upset him like that?' She never took her eyes off the Box. I reckon the old lady will be certified soon.

I walked up the stairs to my room and fell on the bed. The rain was pitter-pattering against the window. It had been a mistake to go home – too dark in the room, what with the clouds and the rain and all; too dark to read. And Lights On wasn't for another five hours. The 'Conservation of Energy (Minimal Appliances) Order' passed last year is the limit, really. I resent it more than any other of the daft rulings, because it means you can't boil some water for a cup of tea, and you can't turn the lights on until an hour after dark. But you can keep the Console on every hour of the day and night, and the bloody thing uses up a hundred times as much juice as a light bulb. This geezer at the Library today was saying how we are now in a 'period of stagnation', but he was wrong. Things are changing every day, because every day things are getting worse. We're no more stagnating now than we were ten years ago when the last shops and pubs closed down for good, not that I ever went into a pub, being only eleven years old at the time. The only shop of any sort is the Hyper, and everyone has a free Console, courtesy of the Social Security, with a Box showing twenty-four-hour, non-stop, visual sedation. Nobody ever has to go out if they don't want to, except for food collection, that is.

But, of course, nobody cares much any more, do they? The Working Class don't care; they've got it made. And the AWs don't care, as long as they've got their Console and a bit of food in their guts. And people like the Knife

17

don't give a monkey's about anything. As long as he can find a new blade every now and then, get a bit of illegal tobacco once a month, and slice someone up occasionally. In a strange way, the only ones who care are the Usurpers, and even then they only care about themselves. But at least they try I suppose. Still, I wouldn't be a Usurper; too big a risk.

Nooz at Morn said that we could expect two more days of heavy rain. They announced that all the Offices would be phased out by year's end, and everyone would be able to Sign In through the Console. Tube travel is going to be restricted to alternate days, as of Thursday, which makes no difference to me, because I hardly ever use the Tube these days. Come to think of it, I don't know anyone who does. What's the point? West End's Inside, and the suburbs are all the same; why waste time going to another place if it's just as grimy and empty and lifeless as Ilford? Oh yes, and they said that the Work Rate was holding steady at twelve per cent, so we could expect a recovery by August. Recovery! What a joke, eh? Funny thing is, they believe it.

The Usurper Toll was only 146 this week, probably because of the rain; it's always less in January and February. If Freddo had listened, it would only have been 145. You have to be smart to be a Usurper, and we all know that Freddo was a long way from being smart. I mean he never spent much time in the Library; I'm not even convinced that Freddo could read. His old lady once told me that he always slept through the Prime Ed. programmes on the Console when he was a kid, and I know for a fact that he never watched Second Ed. because that's when I first got to know him. If Freddo had been a kid at the same time as my dad, when they had schools and stuff, Freddo would have been the sort to bunk off. Even if through some miracle he pulled it off, Usurped, and got his target, he would never have lasted. They would have taken his Card off him within a week, as soon as they realized he wasn't competent; them's the rules: one week to prove yourself, then if you're no use, you're out. Natural Selectivity my arse! In one week you've got one dead Worker, one would-be Usurper now Street Scum, and no one doing the job. It's just pragmatism – good word, eh? I learnt it in the Library last week. They can't stop the murders, so they wrap them up in rules and regulations, red tape, and, hey presto! it's 'Natural Selectivity'!

And even if you can do the job, you get no Passport until you've been there for a year. Even those who get their target, and prove competency, most don't last the year, as they're so vulnerable. They've never been inside the Wall, and they don't know how to act, see? Fish out of water, as the old man would say, so they're prime targets themselves. It was on the Nooz last year how one job with the Central Office of Information changed hands four times in three months!

I wanted to know what the Slut wanted, but I couldn't be bothered to call her. If it was important, she'd call back, although I couldn't imagine what the Slut could find important, unless the Box was on the blink or something, and she wanted to come over. Too bad if that was the case.

I thought about the poor old bloke who won Expo this week. Rough justice is what I call it; live your whole life in hope of getting a Passport so you can get out of this Godforsaken country, and then just as you're about to take your final breath, bingo! The Slut keeps talking about where she's going to go ('Africa's the spot; wild animals and beaches and hot weather . . .') if she wins a Passport, and I laugh, not because it's funny, but because it's so pitiful. She doesn't understand. There's this book

19

in the Library, see, called *Statistics*, full of weird and wonderful facts and figures, all sorts of things. My favourite is the one about getting struck by lightning. 'The odds of getting struck by lightning during a thunderstorm,' it says, 'are approximately ten million to one.' What with the number of people holding Expo Lottery tickets (even Dad's got some – had them for so long, his are still called Premium Bonds) and the average holding being somewhere between fifty and sixty, I worked out that Gina is one hundred times more likely to be struck by lightning than she is to win a Passport. I haven't told her that yet; I'm saving it for another time. I'll tell her while we're having a prod, just as she's about to come; that should shut her up for a while. I can hardly wait.

'Jim! Jim!'

'What do you want?'

'It's Gina,' said Mum, 'on the phone. She wants a word.'

'Coming,' I said. That's as good a word as any, I thought to myself as I ran down the stairs; Gina would appreciate that one. I took the phone from the old lady, and looked at Dad. He was getting all upset again; the phone's attached to the Console, see, so I had to turn the volume down on the Box so I could hear properly.

'Hello?'

'Hello, Demon. Where you been?'

'None of your business. What do you want, Gina?'

'Your cock,' said Gina, so loudly that I'm sure the old lady heard.

'Not on the phone, you filthy slut!'

'Jim!' said the old lady, trying hard to be shocked. I turned my back on her and faced the wall.

'It was good this morning, wasn't it, Jim? You needed it this morning, eh boy?'

'You've got a filthy mouth, Gina. Now what did you call about?'

'Lucy's got hold of a bottle.'

'Congratulations to Lucy,' I said sarcastically, although I knew Gina wouldn't understand. 'Where did she get it from?'

'She bought it, didn't she. Luce hasn't been eating for two weeks, you know, since the business, so she bought a bottle. She wants to know if you and the Knife want to help us out with it?'

'My God, you crazy bitch . . .'

'Jim!'

'Shut up, Mum! Firstly you know I don't drink that shit, Gina, and – '

'I just wanted to see you is all. I bet the Knife would be interested.'

' – and secondly, do you and Lucy want to end up in pieces? You've seen the Knife when he's had a few. You must be mad.'

'You're just limp, Demon. I'll call Knife myself then.'

'Don't be a fool Gina . . .'

'Bye, Demon. We'll be at the Waste after Lights On if you decide to join us.'

'Gina!' But she'd already hung up on me.

'You shouldn't talk like that!' said the old lady, tut-tutting away.

'Turn it up again, Jimbo,' said the old man, on the verge of wetting himself. 'Please boy, turn it up!' I looked at him then, poor old sod, and her, ranting away; pathetic it was.

'Ah, do it yourself!' I said, and slammed the door behind me. I ran back up to my room and sat at my desk, staring out of the window on to the blank wall across the alley just a few yards away. Rough justice, that's what it is. Here I am, Jim Demon, citizen, surrounded by half-

21

wits and misfits, nymphos and nutters, murderers, muggers and morons, all living a life they don't want, with people they don't like, in a world they don't understand. And for what? Don't ask me, friends, don't ask me, because I haven't a clue. Sometimes, in fact most times, I wonder why I bother.

3

I suppose I should have left her to it; I mean, I've seen the Knife with a bit of vodka inside him, and it's not a pretty sight. Let her face the music alone, teach her a lesson so to speak. But I didn't, did I? No, I had to go; the Slut is too stupid to know what she's doing half the time, so, just to be on the safe side, I decided to go along. After all, the Waste is only ten minutes' walk away.

Lights On was about Seven-O, so as soon as I'd finished eating, I grabbed a torch and a box of matches, and took off. Like I said, it's only ten minutes' walk to the Waste, in the opposite direction to the Library, but it might just as well be the other side of the world.

As you hit Northbrook Road you say goodbye to street-lights. Now then, I'm no fan of walking along Northbrook Road in the dark, so I lit the torch. Don't ask me why, but I get this strange feeling whenever I light it. There's something really ancient and primeval about fire held in the hand like that, having to use it as both a guide and a weapon. So I feel like I'm going back in time, whenever I see the flames curling round the cloth, and feel the thick, heavy wood in my hand; beechwood, I think, but I couldn't say for sure.

There was a bit of a wind that night, blowing the flames about this way and that, and you could see the shadows dancing around on the road, odd shapes, strangely in tune with this primitive feeling that was surging through my blood. I could have fought like that, you know, if something attacked me, a wild beast or something; fought with my bare hands, with my fear and hatred, with my lust for survival. Light the torch and you feel alive, that's what it seems like. Not that there are any wild beasts in Ilford, apart from the dogs and the Street Scum of course, but even they don't fight much these days; too weak, too feeble.

Shadows in doorways, flickering lights in windows; it was dark, too dark to see clearly; too dark to know if the bundle in the gutter was a dead baby or just some old rags; dead baby, more likely; you can always find a use for old rags these days. Too dark to know what lay ahead. And if the Scum attacked, what then? All alone, in this blackness; I know what would happen then. The lights in the windows would all go out, that's what; nobody wants to see a massacre on their front doorstep if they can help it; too much of a responsibility. Help? That's a joke. And if you're losing, better to cop it than be left half alive in the gutter, limbs scattered across the road, because you'd just lie there, alone, until your last breath freed you. Even in daylight, they wouldn't help you; too busy watching the Box. Besides, the AWs (and don't under-estimate how many there are along Northbrook, eh?) can't tell the difference between real and make-believe. They see at least a dozen gory deaths on the Box every day, so what's another one outside their front door worth, right?

As for the Snorters, well, who wants to see Snorters these days? Elitist fucking stormtroopers driving round in their custom-built torture wagons. But they only ever hang around the Wall these days; you'd never see one in Ilford, unless there was a tobacco bust on, in which case you'd better be out of sight. See, the Snorters love a fight, and, to be fair, they never take sides; they just move in and crack *everyone's* skull. Freddo's old man was a Snorter in the days of the Metro Police, but that was back when there was no such thing as a Wall or a Work Rate. See, they expressed the rate the other way round; as the number of people *not* working. Funny that. Fancy there being a time when the Work Rate was fifty or even sixty per cent! Some say that, once upon a time, the Work Rate was as high as eighty, but that's just crap. Still, people need their myths and fables don't they? Just like Freddo's old man's old man, who reckoned that when he was a kid there were thousands of Snorters, and they never carried shooters or spray guns or nothing! Mind you, he also used to say how there were Blacks in London, how they were allowed to wander around like everyone else. Can you imagine walking along the High Street and seeing some African wallah wandering around in his grass skirt with a bone through his nose and a parrot perched on his shoulder? Freddo's old man's old man went senile at forty-seven though, and I think that just about explains everything.

As I approached the Waste I suddenly started thinking about the postcard in the Library of Valentine's Park, and of the green railings and the iron gate that used to be locked at nights (or so the librarian lady said) and of the pond and the ducks and the trees, most of which must have been killed off by the sulphur, and it seemed sort of sad that it was all gone, turned into the town dump, the Waste, with all its crap and rubbish and filth, and the Winos and Derros and Scum. You had to watch yourself in the Waste; I was pleased the Knife was going to be there, because, if nothing else, you could feel safe with the Knife around. Lucy and the Slut would be thankful for that, stupid bitches. You can't afford to mess around in the Waste; anyone with sense knows that.

They were there all right, standing by the Ruin, the Slut holding a small torch, both of them giggling like a couple of kids.

'Well, well,' said the Slut. 'Seems you're not so soggy

after all, eh Demon? I was just saying to Luce, wasn't I girl, how I thought . . .'

'Shut up, Gina,' I said, sharp like. I wasn't in the mood for her nonsense. 'Hello, Luce,' I said to the other one. 'Heard you had a spot of bother.' Lucy looked at the ground and shuffled about. She was small, no taller than my shoulder, I'd say. Pretty little thing too, with long blonde hair and a tight, boyish shape to her. But she was not much better than Gina when it came down to facts; two abortions already, the second only a fortnight ago. And to think: only fifteen years old.

'I'm okay, thanks, Demon. I got a bottle.'

'Yeah. The Slut told me. What you want to do that for then, eh?'

'Wanted to, didn't she; you don't have to have none . . .'

'Shut up, Gina; I was talking to Luce, not you.' I eyed the Slut up and down. I had to admit it, she looked good. Long black hair swept back, a low-cut top which revealed plenty of her substantial bust, and a short leather skirt; she had slip-on sandals on her feet. Gina was undoubtedly dressed for the occasion; I knew she wouldn't have any underwear on. But I wanted to make sure didn't I?

'Come here then,' I said, and gave a little jerk of my head.

'Why; what do you want?'

'Just come here.' She walked towards me slowly; her breasts bounced slightly as she moved. No bra, that was for sure.

'You shouldn't talk dirty on the phone,' I said, and slipped my hand up between her thighs. No pants; just warm and soft.

'Here, get off! What a dirty trick!' said the Slut and pushed me away.

'Just checking,' I said and smiled. Lucy giggled, then

26

looked back at the ground embarrassed. 'Seen the Knife then?'

'Right behind you.' I turned around and saw the Knife's face pressing up against mine. Something sharp was pressing in my stomach. I reached down slowly and grasped his wrist, pulled it away from my gut and held it up; the thick, heavy blade glinted evilly in the torch light.

'I wish you wouldn't do that,' I said, but the Knife just laughed. 'And why aren't you carrying a torch?'

'C'mon, Demon; I can take care of myself,' he said, rotating the knife slowly in his hand. 'Besides, I can see in the dark; you know that.' That was another strange thing about the Knife; although I could never really prove it, I believed it to be true; the Knife could see in the dark.

'So, where's the bottle then?' said the Knife, looking towards the girls.

'Here,' said Gina. 'This is Luce. Say "Hi", Luce.'

'Hi,' said Luce meekly.

'Well hello there,' said the Knife, licking his lips. He looked at me for a moment, and I saw his eyes glinting; the same evil glinting that had come from the blade. 'Fine, fine,' he said; his foot started to tap rhythmically. 'To the Cave, methinks. Right?' There was this hollow in the ground, in the side of a small hill; we called it the Cave because I guess that's what it looked like. It took us just a few minutes to walk over to the Cave via a path cleared through all the junk. I walked ahead with the torch; the Slut walked behind me, occasionally making a grab for my waist. Then Lucy, clutching her bottle tightly. The Knife came last, but I didn't know what he was doing. I could have made a good guess as to what he was thinking though.

In the distance we could hear a few Derros shouting and screaming; probably a fight about something or other, and I thought I heard a few Hounds howling although it could have been the wind. I wanted it to be the wind; I could deal with a few Winos and Derros, but wild dogs was another matter. I knew I was safe with the torch, but knowing something and feeling it are two different things, don't you think?

We settled into the Cave, sitting on the floor in a line, with our backs to the dirt; me, Gina, Lucy and then the Knife. I stuck the torch in the ground by the entrance to the hollow, just out of the wind, where it flickered irregularly.

I didn't really know what I was doing there, though. The night air was cold and damp, the Cave was only just big enough to seat the four of us comfortably (and I hate cramped places), and the sky was overcast; no moon, no stars; as dreary a night as I could remember. I looked at my companions and wondered what they were thinking. Knife whittling away at an old stick, sharpening it into a giant blade; the Slut, sitting with her legs slightly apart, giggling; Lucy, her legs drawn up close to her body, clutching her bottle to her as if it were a little child, trying to protect it from the cold. I once heard a woman on the Box describe a Presenter she didn't like (the one who reads the Nooz and introduces the programmes on Second Ed.) as 'one dimensional'. I hadn't previously known what she meant.

'So, where's the bottle then, eh?' said the Knife, sticking his blade in the soft earth.

'Here,' said Lucy, reluctantly letting go of her bottle and handing it across. The Knife unscrewed the top and threw it away.

'Won't be needing *that* now, will we?' he said. He put the bottle to his lips and took a long swig. He pulled the bottle away from his mouth, belched loudly, and thrust it towards me. 'That's better. Here you go, Demon. Get some of that down you; takes away your worries, eh?' and then he laughed; Gina giggled.

'Give it to the Slut,' I said, pushing the bottle away.

'He doesn't drink,' said Gina. 'Makes him go all limp.'

'Watch it, Gina!' I spat the words at her; she wasn't going to talk that way tonight.

'Is that so, Demon?' I knew the Knife was trying to bait me. This time, Lucy laughed. I wasn't going to argue with the Knife, because he might have left, and I wasn't happy about hanging around the Waste without the Knife there. So I grabbed the bottle, held it to my lips, threw my head back and took a long swig. The foul-tasting spirit burnt the back of my throat and I thought I was going to scream. But I kept drinking several seconds longer than the Knife had done; I wasn't going to have the Slut make a fool of me.

'There!' I said, throwing the bottle at the Slut and wiping the tears away on my sleeve. I looked at the torch and found it difficult to focus on it. I wiped my eyes again; the flames were a bit clearer then.

Gina drank heavily from the bottle, as did Lucy, which surprised me, because, like I said, she was only a little thing. The Knife repeated his performance and then it was back to me. The bottle passed swiftly from hand to hand, and it wasn't long before it was empty. The liquor hit Gina very quickly, and she started getting all silly and giggled a lot, and whereas Lucy and the Knife seemed to find this very amusing, it just made me angry. However, even my mood lightened after a while; the Knife started to tell some story or other about how he once caught his old man giving the old lady a prod, and I must admit, the way he told it, it did sound very funny.

I guess by this time we were all a bit drunk. We smoked a couple of Js too, so that may have helped things along a bit; you know how it is, especially when you haven't had any drink for a long time. And I remember seeing the Slut sitting there with her legs apart and her breasts heaving up and down as she laughed, and I wanted suddenly to be in the Alley with her up against the wall, and it must have been while I was thinking of this that Lucy and the Knife took off and disappeared out of sight, so of course I leant over towards the Slut and that's when she grabbed my crotch. I pushed her down in the dirt and pulled off her top while she pulled up her leather skirt, and I closed my eyes and tried to imagine that I was in the Alley while the Slut got my jeans down.

I don't know how much later it was when we heard the scream (I hadn't finished yet, that much I do remember), but I leapt up, grabbed the torch and ran outside, trying to pull up my jeans with my spare hand.

'What was that?' screamed Gina, following me outside. I looked around holding the torch high, but saw nothing at first. 'Look, behind you!' said Gina and I turned to see shadowy forms on the hill, no more than ten metres away. I ran over to where the Knife was standing. He began laughing quietly, and shaking his head; I saw the blood drip off his blade and run down his hand and on to the ground where Lucy lay naked, silent and still.

4

I think it very decent of the Knife to have been so forgiving, considering how hard I hit him. I put it down to the alcohol of course, which presumably was also responsible for my hysterical reaction.

When Lucy recovered consciousness and we found something with which to bandage Knife's hand, we decided to call it a night. Lucy was still a bit shaken as we walked back – not surprising as that was precisely what the Knife had intended by waving his blade in her face while they were having a prod. Of course, the Knife's idea of a bit of fun is very different to mine, but each to his own, right? I still contend that he got off lightly; his reactions are astonishing under normal circumstances, but he's less adept when he's been drinking – hence his own cut hand. I mean, it could have been a major artery, right?

We said goodnight at the Exchange; Knife took off at a fast pace, while the Slut decided to walk Lucy back home, which I suppose indicates that Gina does at least care about her friends, which is a rare thing these days. Me? I walked back pretty fast myself, and I guess the excitement and the alcohol took their toll, because I slept very heavily that night, and wouldn't you guess, I woke up with a hangover.

It was the next day that I saw Kate for the first time. I had spent the morning down the Hyper doing food collection with the old lady; I can't pretend that this is my favourite occupation, but it has to be done. The Hyper is what I call a really depressing place, what with the queues and the thousands of people and the empty shelves and everything. I thought about the picture of the High Street with people shopping; it must have been pretty good to have had a choice of what to buy, all those different shops with clothes and food and shoes, and places selling tobacco and stuff. But in the Hyper, well, what sort of choice have you got there?

In the afternoon I went down to the Library, and that's when I saw her, sitting alone with a stack of books so high you could barely see the top of her head. Intriguing it was; I mean, you see plenty of guys down the Library, but how often do you see a woman, eh? And she was working hard, you could see that. I wondered why I'd never seen her before. Anyway, I was asking the librarian lady about whether there were any more postcards of the Park, when this girl stood up and stretched. What a sight it was; beautiful, that was the only word for it, and that's a word you don't often hear these days. Slim, womanly body, dressed in jeans and a thick heavy sweater, sort of blue and brown. Shoulder length light-brown hair, prominent high cheekbones, blue eyes, bright blue, and these warm, wide, sensuous lips. Well, it'd been a long time since I had noticed a woman, but she was something special. So I told the librarian lady not to worry about the postcards, and walked over to where the girl was working, and stood a couple of metres away, just watching. It was a few moments before she noticed me.

'Do you want something?' she said. Her voice was soft and sort of melodious, not harsh and trashy like the Slut's, and she had this refined kind of accent, not unlike the Working Class, I thought. I wasn't sure what to say then, and felt a bit clumsy just standing there, so I walked over and picked up the book that rested on the top of the pile.

'This book,' I said, weighing it in my hand. 'I was, er, looking for it.'

'It's not easy to find,' said the girl. 'You can use it if you like; I don't need it for the moment.'

'Thanks,' I said, then asked politely: 'What are you doing?' She looked up then; she really did have the most lovely eyes.

'Jobbing,' she said. She must have registered the look of surprise in my eyes, because she smiled.

'Usurper?' I said quietly, and somewhat surprised.

'Aren't we all?' she said, and laughed. Well, I wasn't sure how to react to that, so I didn't say anything for a while. I must admit, I found it difficult to imagine this pretty, refined girl sticking a sharp knife into someone's gut and taking their Work Card. I mean, apart from anything else, there was the risk!

It must have been six years since they passed the Security of Employment Act. The one Act of Parliament that everyone in the country knew about. The title always tickled me. I can imagine some little geezer in Westminster or wherever – one with a protected job, of course – thinking it up, and giggling. 'Cos, of course, it legalizes *insecurity* of employment. Any day you could go up to the library, go to the first desk, and there you'd find it, the 'Security of Employment Act'. It was compulsory reading for anyone taking Jobbing seriously. I looked through it once, just as a matter of interest. Section 1: 'Security of Employment' – just like the government to make sure their protected status was in the first section. Then Sections 2 to 5, the 'Exceptions to Security' – in other words, who could be murdered and how. One for one, that was the rule. If you accidentally killed someone other than your target, you were as good as dead yourself. Then Sections 6 to 8: 'Protection of the Employed' – how the target could kill or maim anyone 'reasonably suspected' of being a Usurper. I won't go through all the rest, the stuff on competency, examinations and so on, just Section

14. The one that every Jobber, and even a lot of others, knew off by heart. 'A qualifying person' – that is, once you've killed your target and survived a year in his job – 'shall be entitled, upon application to the Secretary of State for Security, to an Exit Visa.'

That was it. The thing everyone, at least all those with any ability left to think, wanted. Out.

These days they reckon there are, on average, about two hundred Usurper attempts every week, with less than five per cent being successful. To you and me, what that really means is that 190 Usurpers get killed every week. You'd have to agree, these are not good odds if you're on the Outside trying to get in. It also tells you something about the desperation of those who decide to go ahead with it. Usurpers are not, on the whole, stupid people. On the contrary, those who take Jobbing seriously – which is the only way to take it – are pretty bright. They only have a week to show they can do the target's job, often with the target's ex-workmates making life as difficult as possible. Would-be Usurpers spend most of their time in the Libraries, Jobbing; that is, researching and learning the job of the target. Of course, not all jobs can be learnt from books; the basic ones can (although there's not too many of those), but the majority are all up West and what they call 'Technologically Advanced', and no amount of reading is going to help you there. However, there are a few that any bright, educated person could probably succeed at; for instance, those Workers that have to compile and read the Nooz for the Consoles, or the Prime Ed. teachers who do the kids' education programmes.

I looked at the girl and tried to imagine what sort of Jobbing she was doing; I would like to have asked, but of course, you don't do that sort of thing, not with a complete stranger.

34

'Not me,' I said, shaking my head. 'I'm no Usurper; too big a risk.'

'Oh yeh?' said the girl. 'Read that book; you'll soon change your mind.'

I looked at the title: *The Impact of Technology on Occupational Structure in Post-Industrial Society*, by Henry Jordan.

'Looks old,' I said. 'I mean, I thought it was more recent,' I continued quickly, not wanting to give myself away.

'Twenty-two years,' said the girl. 'Just think, twenty-two years ago he knew what was going to happen. But did anyone listen to him? Read it; like I said, you'll change your mind.'

'Fine,' I said, not wanting the conversation to finish. 'By the way, my name's Demon; Jim Demon.'

'Demon?'

'Demon.' She shrugged, and held out her hand.

'Kate Mason,' said the girl. 'Pleased to know you.'

I shook her hand. Her grip was firm – more like a man's, I thought, but then I'd not shaken hands with a woman before. What a strange girl, I thought. Sort of different, independent, or perhaps it was just confident?

'You from round here?' I asked.

'Not far.'

'I've not seen you here before.'

'Oh?'

I could see that she was a bit impatient, and wanted to go back to her work, so I thanked her for the book and walked over to an empty desk, from where I could keep an eye on her. I opened the book to the first page and made out as if I was reading it; I didn't even understand what the title meant, but I hadn't wanted to show my ignorance, so I hadn't said anything. I saw the word 'Occupational' so I knew it must have something to do with jobs, but I had no idea what. I looked across at the girl, Kate, and smiled. Why did she say it would change my mind? How daft; it would take more than a book to change my mind.

The rest of the afternoon I spent thumbing through the book and thinking about Kate and how different she was from the Slut. I tried to imagine what was going through her mind, how she was preparing herself, how she intended going about it. It wasn't easy to kill another person. Morally, I drew the line at that one. I accept entirely, morals don't get you jobs, but to plan a murder, right down to the last detail, and then to execute it, and your target, well, you had to want a job an awful lot for that. I can understand the principle; the Working Class have got it made, after all; big comfortable houses, luxury cars, loads of money. And up West they had all sorts of things; nightclubs with music and fancy food and drinks, and cinemas where they showed classy films from other countries on a screen like a giant Box. Freddo even reckoned that tobacco was legal inside the Wall, but I don't know about that. Most importantly though, Passports. The Working Class could go wherever they liked. Jetplanes flew daily from the Airport to all over the World, and even the lesser Workers could cross the Channel to New Canada to see Paris and the like, while the really top nobs flew to really distant places like Greece and Babylon.

No doubt all *that* was worth killing for in theory. There ain't no problem about killing as a concept – you see it every day, and no one could describe me as squeamish. What bothered me was the *fact* of it. You were killing someone's father, someone's husband. And if you put a geezer's dad on one side of the scales, and a steak dinner and a foreign film on the other, as far as I was concerned: no contest.

I started to read bits of Henry Jordan's book, primarily because I had nothing else to do, and here's the funny thing; it *was* pretty interesting, even though I had to struggle a bit with some of the words. Seems like Jordan was one of those sociologist boffins, and the 'Preface' pretty much told the rest of the story.

The aim of this discussion is to establish in exact terms the extent to which employment and the structure of occupation within the post-industrial society are affected by the introduction of new and progressive technologies into the primary and manufacturing industries, and to forecast the sociological and economic effects that this will have on society as a whole.

Since Mattheson and Webb's *High Tech Prognosis* (1992), the first long-term study to attempt to predict the likely sociological changes in post-industrial Britain, a number of supervening factors, principally political (both domestic and international) and legislative, have altered the scenario in a number of significant respects. It is the intention of this work to analyse critically how Mattheson and Webb's prognosis has stood the test of time, and to make alternative suggestions as to how occupational shifts and sociological changes will affect the structure and quality of life in the next 25 to 30 years.

Now, although I cannot say that I was particularly fond of Jordan's style, which was a bit ponderous to say the least, I have to admit that I found myself unable to put his book down. Funny isn't it, how sometimes you read something, and it just sort of 'clicks'? Well, Jordan's book was full of ideas and stuff which did just that. I read on with interest, and found the chapter on 'The Quality of Life' particularly fascinating, in a disturbing sort of way. For instance, this bit.

. . . which in time leads to a selection of proposals for improving the quality of life, such as: continuing education, available as a right to all members of society, and to be taken at any time; income maintenance to free individuals from the sort of economic insecurity which might lead them to desire economic growth above improvement; more structured leisure, and a wider range of opportunities for enjoying it; and, most importantly, the liberation of individuals from the necessity of doing some particular and undesired job. The beginning of total automation, started in the twentieth century, has removed the need for human labour on the production line and in the primary industries; in mining, agriculture and so on. The final necessity is to educate the masses that the Judaeo-Christian work ethic is no longer tenable. This, however, is where the problems begin . . .

You can say that again! So what went wrong, Jordan, old boy? I mean, people haven't worked down mines since the end of the last century, the same with factories. As for the economic security bit, well, we all get dole, don't we? And no one stops you from educating yourself, what with the Libraries and the Tert. Ed. and Further Ed. programmes on the Console. By this time I was more than a little intrigued, so I carried on reading, unaware that Kate had left. There was a chapter about trends in occupations, full of statistics, facts and figures that I couldn't really grasp, although I think that the gist of it was summed up at the end of the chapter. I got the impression that Jordan was warming up for his finale.

The most significant occupational categories will therefore be the professions; engineers, scientists and technicians. Society will be dependent on information and its analysis for its maintenance. The critical activity will be the codification, analysis and retrieval of information. Power will reside in those who can control this function. We can therefore expect to see a continuation of the trend whereby formal political power wanes at the expense of the new technologies in executive positions.

The technocratic elite. As far as I could understand it, that was just Jordan's expression for what we call the Working Class, or at least the vast bulk of them. If so, Mr

Henry Jordan was not only a sociologist, he was something of a prophet. It was, however, his final words that put the lid on it for me, so to speak:

The advanced technologies will alter the classical concept of the four factors of production, at least insofar as primary and secondary production is concerned. Tertiary (service) industries will continue to employ labour, but on a scale drastically reduced by the absence of wealth and a numerically small privileged class. In the post-industrial society, 'labour' will effectively be eliminated from the equation; 'information' will become the critical factor. The political implications are that there will be born – there is already forming – a technocracy, an elite of technocrats. The class distinctions already evident will be more far-reaching and divisive than any before seen in Western civilization. For those not fortunate enough to be technocrats, there will be an unprecedented decline in the quality of life. Security measures to separate the 'Haves' from the 'Have-Nots' will be vital.

So that's what happened, eh? I had to take my hat off to Henry Jordan; there was a man who really knew what was going on. I wondered how many people had read Jordan's book, and if they had realized what it meant. Kate obviously did, and no doubt saw it the same way I did. It had all been foreseen; not an accident, not a mistake. It was predicted, and no one did a damn thing to stop it. For all I knew, they had wanted it to go this way. The more I thought about it, the surer I became. And here was I thinking all this time that I was just unlucky! Poor old Jim Demon; born outside the Wall and destined to live his whole life in ignorance.

I opened the book again to find out more about the author. Inside there was a dedication, 'To my dearest Marie'. Not much use. I looked at the dust jacket, and found a small black and white photo of Henry Jordan: thin face, deep, narrow eyes, aquiline nose. The blurb said that he'd been twenty-four when he wrote the book, which meant that there was a good chance that he'd still be alive and kicking. I wondered what had happened to him. Had he been swept away by the tide of his own prophetic vision, drowned by the weight of his own wisdom? Or, perhaps, seeing the wind of change, had he equipped himself suitably, and now resided in a plush mansion inside the Wall, an integral part of the power structure he had foreseen?

I slipped the jacket off the book, taking care that nobody saw what I was doing, folded it carefully, and put it in my pocket. I wasn't sure why. I just did it. For the first time in years I was interested in something. It was as if someone had pressed a button deep in my head, and now, if I listened carefully, I could hear a quiet, purposeful hum which hadn't been there before.

5

The following day I woke up early; earlier than usual that is. I hadn't intended to, it just happened; and although I could not have explained why if someone had asked me, I was feeling pretty good. The previous evening I had told the old lady that I didn't want to talk to anyone, especially the Slut, and that if she phoned the old lady was to say that I wasn't home. Sure enough the Slut phoned twice; I don't think she believed Mum, but it didn't matter much. Anyway, like I said, I felt good that morning, so I went down to the Library rather early. Now, whether this was because I wanted to see Kate Mason again I couldn't say, but I think this must have been in the back of my mind, because as soon as I arrived I walked straight to the desk where she had been sitting when I'd last seen her, and sure enough, there she was, surrounded by books and Jobbing hard.

'Hello, Kate,' I said softly, so as not to surprise her.

She didn't look up until I had repeated my greeting.

'Oh . . . yeh . . . hi,' she said, returning immediately to the book in front of her. I got the distinct impression that I wasn't wanted. Still, I thought, give it one more go.

'Shall I leave this here?' I asked, holding out Jordan's book.

'If you like,' she replied, not even looking up this time. 'You can hang on to it for the moment – I shan't need it today.' Then: 'I don't suppose you've read it all since yesterday anyway.'

Was there a hint of sarcasm in her voice, or was I

imagining it? 'I've finished with it,' I said firmly, and turned to go. I got a step away when she slammed shut the book she'd been working on, and swore lightly under her breath.

'I don't for one minute suppose that *you* know anything about firearms?' she asked.

'Hand guns you mean?'

'Yeh,' she said, her voice registering interest for the first time.

'Could be.'

Then she looked at me, hard, eyes like slits, weighing me up. I could hear her mind ticking over, as clear as if sub-titles had flashed up on the desk in front of her: 'Is he bullshitting?' Then: 'Of course he is! How could a bloke like him . . . ?' Her face changed to one of scorn – I was about to be dismissed – but then it changed again. 'What if he *does*?' said the sub-titles.

I suppose you're also thinking I'm a bullshitter, right? As my old man would have said in his younger days, when the thought of winning Expo wasn't the only thing that put a bump in his trousers, giving it the mouth? Trying it on to get a classy blonde bint up against the wall in the Alley? Just shows you how wrong you can be. Okay, I accept that I wasn't completely unimpressed by the shape and movement of what I could see lay beneath Kate's pullover. What's more, had she needed an expert on astrophysics I might still have been tempted to chance my arm and pretend I knew what it was. But it just so happened that I did know something about guns. Obviously I'd never actually seen one, not up close like. Since when Dad was a kid all the licences had been withdrawn. But, like most kids, I loved gunfights on the Box. Unlike most kids, when I wasn't watching the Box I had my nose buried in a book. So one day I'd gone to the

Library to see if I could find any books on the subject. I'd had the idea that maybe I could make one. Well, I was only eleven, right? Anyway, there was a whole section on the history of armaments, from cross-bows right up to nuclear bombs. Of course, there was nothing from the last fifty years or so, nothing on any of the fancy weapons used by the Snorters, but the old ones, the stuff James Bond and Billy the Kid used, they were there. I'd learnt why and how guns worked, and also a bit about the theory of shooting. So I smiled at Kate, knowing what I knew, and knowing that she didn't. She smiled back, and nodded slowly.

'Okay, mate,' she said, and stood up. 'I could do with a break anyway.' She stretched, just like the day before, and my heart rate doubled to a fast gallop. There was no doubt about it: she was a cracker. She grabbed her jacket, slung it over her shoulder, and walked off. I stood watching her lovely backside as she threaded her way through the desks. She paused and turned back to me.

'Coming?' she called, ignoring the half-a-dozen angry glares of the people disturbed around her. I smiled and nodded and followed her out.

She was waiting for me on the steps.

'Okay, John, fancy a coffee?' she asked.

'It's Jim,' I replied.

'Course it is. Anyway, do you want a coffee?'

'Where?'

'There's a Vendo just round the corner.'

'Yeh, I know it.'

She slipped her arm through mine. 'That'll do then,' she said, and we walked off across the road.

Kate motioned for me to sit down at a table while she fetched two coffees from the machine. There were probably no more than a dozen or so people in the Vendo, but then again, it was still early; most people don't bother getting out of bed until midday these days. In the evening it was usually packed, since it was just about the only place to go. The kids would bring tobacco sometimes, which was bloody silly as it just tempted the Snorters to come and break some skulls. Tobacco busts always started at the local Vendo. There was no alcohol of course, just tea and coffee and Coke, but there were plenty of tables and chairs and music pumping out of the loudspeakers after Lights On. There was also an old darts board in the corner that wasn't used much due to the number of accidents, what with innocent bystanders getting punctured every now and then, which I consider a great pity, since there is surely no better game around than darts.

'They used to have people in places like this to serve you your drinks, you know,' said Kate as she returned with the coffees.

'What? Why?'

'Like Jordan said in the book, before they automated everything. The Vendo machines were just part of that, taking jobs away. They still have old-fashioned cafés up West, where you sit down and have your coffee brought to you.'

'How do you know?' It sounded very unlikely to me.

'It's no secret, Jim. The Working Class just tend to keep things like that to themselves.'

'What's wrong with machines?' Now that seemed like a pretty reasonable question, but I could see by the way Kate frowned that she thought otherwise.

'It's all to do with "Quality of Life", right?' she replied, as if not expecting me to understand, which shows you that she wasn't all that dim, 'cos I didn't.

'I don't see how it makes any difference. I mean, you brought me my coffee, right?' Kate sighed. Seemed like I had said the wrong thing.

'What interested you in Jordan's book?' she asked.

44

'Ah . . .' I said, trying to think quickly. Nothing came to mind, so I had no choice but to come clean. This will blow it out good and proper, I thought.

'I'd never heard of it before yesterday. I saw you sitting there, and I needed an excuse to talk to you.'

She shook her head, and smiled, but nicely, like she really meant it. 'That figures,' she said.

'Look,' she said, her voice becoming softer, 'I can't explain it to you, Jim; it's all part and parcel of the same thing. Being served in cafés, going to restaurants and choosing what you want to eat, real food mind, off a fancy menu, having it brought to you; going dancing in flashy nightclubs, dressed up in beautiful clothes and looking really tops, or watching people performing plays, you know, acting in a theatre, and being able to drive back to a big, plush house with a garden, in your own car. That's all wonderful, but it's what it signifies that is really important. It's freedom – freedom of choice about where to go, what to do, what to eat. That's the real difference between Outside and Inside; we may be outside the Wall, but we're the prisoners.'

I had to think about that for a while, because I hadn't quite seen it like that before. I mean, I knew the Working Class had it made; that's what everyone said, but I don't suppose it had ever dawned on me what that really meant. The way Kate put it, I had to admit, made me think about it from a different angle.

'I bet you haven't been more than five Ks from Ilford in any direction. Just imagine being able to get in a Jetplane and fly across the seas. The South Pacific, Jim,' she said, becoming quite enthusiastic. 'Beautiful islands with white sand and palm trees with coconuts, and clear, warm water and blue skies and sunshine all day . . . it all exists, Jim; it's all there. But not for the likes of you and me, Jim Demon, not for the likes of you and me; the reason is standing in the corner there dispensing luke-warm coffee that tastes like it's been drunk once already.'

Now, I don't suppose Kate meant this literally for one moment, and that a Vendo coffee machine was the reason why I wasn't floating around the South Pacific on a wooden raft munching coconuts, but there was no doubt about it, it was an interesting way of looking at things. I too had seen pictures of other countries, but it's difficult, if not downright impossible, to imagine that they really exist outside books or the Box. I mean, walk down Ilford High Street on a cold, wet, windy day in March and try thinking about islands with white sands, palm trees and sunshine, and you'll see what I mean. Can't be done, right? Perhaps for that reason I'd never really thought about getting out. But Kate had obviously thought about it a lot. That made me feel uncomfortable, as though she was ahead of me, more advanced, and I'd never felt that with a woman before. From the moment I'd met her, I'd had the feeling that she'd been in control of the situation – except for those few seconds in the Library when she'd asked me about guns. Even then, I'd somehow lost the initiative almost immediately. Maybe that was the reason I made the mistake of helping her out with her gun problem, just to prove I wasn't a complete dildo, and that's where all the trouble began. Still, as the old lady would say, I'm getting ahead of myself.

I glanced at Kate, and was surprised by the expression on her face. It had changed completely from one of bored disinterest to animated excitement. It was flushed, and her eyes shone. At that moment she was the most beautiful woman I'd ever seen.

'So you're going to Usurp then?' I said. It seemed such a shame. She looked up, and her face went all sort of hard again.

'Damn right I'm going to Usurp.' She slammed her fist

on the table, becoming angry. 'Why should all those things be denied to me? I'm twenty years old, which is twenty years too many wasted in this cesspit waiting for something to happen, tuning into the bloody Console day in, day out, waiting for the day when they certify me AW. Life's too short to waste this way, Jim, it's just too damn short.'

'Could be even shorter if you Usurp.'

'It's better than sitting around this place doing nothing and growing old. What do you do, Jim?'

'Do?' I repeated, somewhat shocked, because this was a really strange question to ask, not something you heard in your average conversation.

'Yes, do; in the Library, at home, on the streets; what do you do? You come to the Library but you're not Jobbing, so you must be there for some other reason, true? I mean, do you write?'

'Write?' Now you may begin to think that I was not participating fully in this conversation, but bear in mind that we had only been in the Vendo five minutes and I was not the least familiar with this line of questioning, which I can only describe as bizarre. Do? Write? Where did she get these notions from?

'I don't do anything,' I said outright. Now, under different circumstances this would have sounded fine, but somehow the words hit the air and sort of froze there, suspended in front of me.

'Damn right! The fact is, you do nothing to justify your miserable existence! Like everyone else you walk around in a daze, a mindless moron just trying to pass the days; you fill your gut with tasteless, useless food that you have to collect at the Hyper because you've got no choice; you smoke a couple of Js and douse yourself in poisonous vodka to take away the pain of living, to kill the endless hours between waking and sleeping. You got a girl, Jim?'

'Well, er . . .'

'Good for a quick prod over the Waste, is she?'

'Now wait a minute . . .'

'No, Jim, no more waiting. Not for me. My time is almost up; I'm not prepared to take the shit any longer. How much dole do you get? Twenty-five Credits and ten New Sovs a week? And where does it go? What's left when you've paid for food collection, bought an ounce, saved the remainder for a pair of jeans? Even a food server up West gets two hundred Sovs a week! Lord knows what a Presenter gets. Life's too short, Jim; grab the chance while you can. You've read Jordan's book, you know now. It was all planned this way, so that a few people could lead a decent life, a life of luxury, while the rest just rot away, and you're the poor sod who has chosen to suffer! Don't you see, Jim? Grab your chance before it's too late!'

By then there were a lot of people all looking strangely at Kate, and it must be said, she looked pretty wild, so I couldn't blame them. They stopped looking as she calmed down. I was at a bit of a loss to know what to say.

'Freddo tried to grab it, but he wasn't smart, or prepared, and now he's dead.'

'Well I don't know about Freddo, whoever he was, but I know this much; I *am* smart, and I *am* prepared, and I'm going to make it.'

'And if you don't?'

'Then at least I will have died trying; at least I will have given it my best shot. And if I do make it . . .' but she never finished the sentence.

So we sat there in the Vendo in silence. And I looked around at the other people, sitting there drinking their coffee and smoking their Js, and I had to admit that Kate had a very good point.

48

'Dreams,' she said at last, gazing around at the others. 'Where are their dreams? Where are yours?'

And it's a funny thing, because I considered this carefully for a few moments before I realized that I couldn't tell Kate where my dreams were, because I didn't know; I mean, I had absolutely no idea . . .

6

Our morning chats became quite an institution, which was a bit of a surprise frankly, as I didn't think she'd be interested in a 'mindless moron'. But the next day she was at the Library, and after a couple of hours she came over and asked me if I'd like a breath of fresh air, so out we went. That became the pattern. Every day we'd go wandering off somewhere, Kate doing the talking, and me listening. I never realized that a girl could talk so much – let's face it, the Slut's vocabulary was about two hundred words, and most of them were dirty – yet the funny thing was, I enjoyed just listening. Interesting though: she never said anything about herself, only about her ideas about the world. She avoided questions about her family and where she lived, and she made it very plain that anything about her Jobbing was out of bounds. I once asked her why she'd wanted to know about guns, and she just put a finger on my lips and smiled. Still, we had enough to talk about. I mean, I thought *I* was quite a thinker, but that girl didn't stop. There were even periods – short ones I'll admit – when I was forced to concentrate so hard to understand her that I stopped thinking of giving it the prod. After all, I'm a normal lad, and Kate was no bucket of fish in the looks department. Another odd thing was that whenever I thought about doing it with her, I couldn't imagine it happening in the Alley. Looking back on it, although I wouldn't have admitted it then, I felt just a little grubby about the location of my hours of passion with the Slut.

So Kate put her arm through mine, and we walked and

talked. I loved it. After a while I began to get the impression that she did too. It wasn't all smooth and easy though. Kate Mason was nothing less than a bona fide smartypants, and she would often leave me behind. 'Technological determinism' and 'social mobilization' were a bit beyond me. Not that I'm a complete dummy, as you may have realized by now. I read plenty, and understand most of it. Also I have quite a knack of tying together odd ideas which most people don't realize are connected. I just have this problem of expressing myself clearly, see?

Without doubt the biggest problem revolved round the question of the Usurpers. Now I have never actually opposed Usurping, as you know, but looking at it logically, to my mind it simply doesn't make sense, not on the available odds. Kate says 'This life is shit! It stinks!' and she's dead right. If even half of what she says about Working Class life is true, fifteen Ks away from me are people living in paradise. But just because I live in a cesspit doesn't seem to me to be a good reason deliberately and consciously to kill one of them. Especially as there's a twenty to one chance that the only person who's going to end up dead is yours truly. I mean, I loathe this miserable pointless existence as much as the next person, but I figure it's better than no existence at all. Seeing as I can't change the system, I reckon I'm better off 'walking around like a mindless moron' as Kate puts it, than not walking around, period. And that's what we would argue about, because Kate would say I was apathetic and gutless (which is patently untrue, don't you think?) and destined to end up as an AW as a result. 'It's not life!' she said on many occasions. 'It's a living death!' And perhaps she was right. But Freddo tried it and lost, and the thought of Kate having her head blown off in a Usurper attempt really sickened me. That was the other reason why hanging round Kate was not always easy. I knew that one day she wouldn't show up, that her desk at the Library would be empty. And that night on the Nooz there'd be pictures of her lying on some Working Class floor in a pool of her own blood. That's how I began to realize that I was getting involved with her. I mean I really liked her, and that was a first for me.

It was after one of these discussions about Life, the World and Everything. We'd been talking about Usurping in general, and strayed on to the forbidden area of Kate's Usurping in particular. As usual, I had been defending my position of 'Nothing is worth murdering for', and, as usual, she'd been disagreeing. Finally, angrily, she came out with her 'It's my life!' line.

'So that gives you the right to throw it away?' I asked.

'If I choose!'

'Wrong!'

'Why?' she challenged. 'What does it matter if I decide to relieve the government of the responsibility of feeding me for the next thirty years?'

'Your death doesn't just affect you; it affects others too.'

'Oh, yeh?' she said derisively. 'Who the hell cares?'

'I do.'

That made her pause. She stopped in front of me, and came up very close.

'You big, dumb, ugly idiot,' she said, and took my face in her hands and kissed me, right there, on Ilford High Street. And that's when I realized (and believe me, this is a tough admission) that I was In Love with Kate Mason.

Now before you have hysterics, and dismiss this as the foolish ramblings of an infatuated youth, let me put you straight. Jim Demon does not, repeat, *not*, go around falling in love. I am not, in case you hadn't noticed, the romantic sort, a fact which made my diagnosis all the more startling. I mean, I simply was not used to thinking about a girl – other than carnally – every night, just before going to sleep. Nor had I ever felt my heart speed up at the sight of a fully-dressed girl, as though it was trying to make up for lost time.

I would have liked a second opinion as to what was wrong with me, but there was no one I could talk to about it. Can you imagine the Knife's reaction if I had bumped into him in the street and said, 'Hey Knife, guess what? I'm in love!' It doesn't bear thinking about. As for the old folks, well, forget it. So I kept it to myself, and continued seeing Kate as often as possible, never letting on how I really felt, and in a strange way, hoped the feeling would just fade away so that I could return to normal.

The Slut was a problem of course, wanting to know why I never called and didn't want to see her, so I told her I had an infection. 'What, again?' she said, full of sympathy. 'I suppose I'll have to call the sodding Doc!' and then she hung up. But she was a minor problem compared to the everyday difficulty of keeping control of my emotions. One minute excited and breathless, the next miserable, or just wandering around looking dopey, as if someone had borrowed half my brain and forgotten to leave a note. Let me tell you, if you've never fallen in love, don't bother. Aching like that for someone is a lousy feeling, like when you're hungry and can't find anything to eat; just lousy.

Then, one day, I arrived at the Library a bit later than usual. The old man had been ill during the night. I'd always ignored his coughing – he got through so many Js a day – but he'd begun to cough up blood. Then he had some sort of fit. Mum called me in. I thought he'd had it. His eyes were rolled back, he had blood and foam on his lips, and his whole body was bucking and twisting like a fish out of water. Suddenly he lay still. The old lady went hysterical, thumping him on the chest, calling 'Arthur!' at the top of her lungs. 'Come back!' she was screaming, 'Don't you die, you bastard!' and then, which surprised me no end, 'I love you!' I had no idea she loved the old git. Anyway, he came round after a bit, and went to sleep. Mum got the Doc on the Box. He just said, 'Epileptic fit. Be round tomorrow' and disappeared.

So when I arrived I was feeling even more thoughtful than usual. Kate was waiting for me at the door. She had no books with her.

'Where have you been?' she said, quite snappy. 'Never mind. I need your help.'

With that, she grabbed my hand, and dragged me out of the Library.

'Where are we going?' I asked.

'The Waste.'

'What? What for?'

'You'll see.'

We walked in silence along the empty streets. It was cold, and it was drizzling, and the water began to work its way into my right shoe. When we got to the Waste, Kate set off across the nettles and piles of rubbish as though she knew where she was going. It occurred to me that I hadn't come equipped – no knife, no torch, no weapon of any sort – and that faced with a gang of Derros, we wouldn't stand a chance.

'Just a minute, Kate . . .' I started.

'Come on,' she insisted, without looking round. I shrugged, and followed her, keeping my eyes on the ground. Within a few paces I found what I was looking for, an old spanner lying by the side of a pile of rusting metalwork. It wasn't much use, but it would do in an emergency. I kept a few paces behind Kate, trying to listen for any sounds other than the rustle of our own footsteps and the sighing of the wind. The drizzle seemed to muffle sounds as well as cut down visibility.

Kate came to a slight dip in the ground. It looked as if it had been used as a site for bonfires, as the vegetation was shorter, and the area was clear of rubbish. On the far side of the dip was one of the few remaining pieces of fencing still erect in the Waste. On top of it, at regular intervals, were spaced six tin cans.

I pointed at them. 'What . . .' I said.

'I came here earlier,' said Kate, her back to me. She was reaching inside her jacket. She turned to me, her right hand still out of sight. She came up to me and looked at me closely, as if deciding on how I would take something she was about to say. For the first time, I realized her cheeks were flushed, and her eyes bright and excited.

'You are going to help me, aren't you?'

Well, I wasn't going to say no, was I? She was only two inches from my face, and looking as beautiful as I'd ever seen her, even with little puffs of steam coming from her pink lips, and drops of water on her eyelashes.

She didn't wait for an answer. She took her hand out of her jacket. In it was a brown felt bag with a drawstring tying it closed. She opened the bag and took out a shooter.

Now, as I've said, I'd never seen one in real life before. The government had collected them all up when the licences were withdrawn. This one must have been about a hundred years old, but there was a smell of oil and cleanness about it which told me that someone had looked after it. God knows where she got it from.

Kate was looking up at me, smiling, proud, I think. So my reaction probably came as a bit of a surprise. I hit her. Not very hard, but hard enough for her to spin round, on the side of her face. She looked at me in astonishment.

'What was that for?' she said, holding her cheek.

'You're actually going to do it, aren't you? You're actually going to kill someone? Someone's father, or mother, or sister!' I was really shouting at her. She seemed to recoil with every word. I don't really know why I was upset all of a sudden. I'd known she was serious right from the start. Maybe it had something to do with the old man, or the fact that I loved her and I couldn't tell her.

'Yes!' she spat, recovering herself. 'I'm not going to live on a dunghill for the rest of my life! Just over there,' she said, pointing in completely the wrong direction, 'are human beings. Real human beings, living their lives with some sort of dignity. I would rather die than live the life you lead – no future, no hope, just living death.'

She was saying I was a coward. For the first time I wondered if she was right. She saw she had hurt me by that last line, and she stepped up to me again and spoke softly.

'You've got brains, Jim. Oh, I know you say you haven't, but you see things clearly. It's all right for someone like the Knife, but how can you *choose* to live like this when you know there's more? Why don't you help me? Together we stand a much better chance. We could both make it through – there's no reason why we shouldn't *both* find jobs.'

'You mean "both murder someone" don't you?'

She didn't answer at first. 'Then get lost!' she said, turning her back on me. She walked away from me towards the centre of the clearing. She raised her right hand, cocked the gun, and aimed at the tins on the fence. She was about to get a surprise. She was holding the gun in front of her chest, with her arm bent. She pulled the trigger and fired. The recoil knocked the gun upwards out

56

of her hand, and she found herself sitting in the mud. I had to laugh, she looked so surprised.

'What's so fucking funny?' she scowled, without getting up. She seemed on the verge of tears. Then she too began to laugh. 'Oh, Jim, I've got twelve magazines, only twelve, and I'll need a hundred before I can shoot straight. What's worse, I can't get the clips in or out; I can't get the bloody thing undone!'

I walked over, picked up the gun, and wiped the mud off it.

'I suppose if I don't show you, you'll only shoot yourself, won't you?' I said. She scrambled to her feet.

'Can you teach me? Do you know how? I don't believe it, can you really? Oh, Jim!' she said, and she threw her arms around me.

It was four hours later, just as the light was beginning to fade, that I dropped her off at the corner of the road she said was hers and walked back home. In all modesty, I don't know if it was brilliant tuition, or the fact that the girl was a natural, but once I got the gun working it only took four magazines before she was hitting five tins out of every six. I suppose I should have expected her to be good at that too.

7

The next morning I got up early again. After taking something to eat I popped in to see the old man. He was propped up in bed, eyes fixed on the spare Console that I had set up for him in the bedroom. He was quite talkative, and, for someone who didn't take his eyes off the screen for the entire time we spoke, he did pretty well to string three sentences together, in a row, all on roughly the same subject. I went downstairs and as I passed the front door I heard a sharp noise coming from outside. Have you ever had that situation when your body reacts even before your mind has actually thought it through? I was out of the door, having undone the safety grille and three locks, and running up the road before it had consciously registered on my mind what the noise was. Gunfire, and it had come from the Library. There was only one person in Ilford who I knew had a gun; and I was the stupid prick who had taught her how to use it.

It was as I turned the corner that I saw the commotion. There must have been two hundred people running around, screaming and shouting, at least three torture wagons, and dozens of Snorters in their black leather uniforms. Their guns were drawn, and suddenly a warm wave of hope washed over me; it could have been their gunfire. I stood on the corner, undecided. It was never wise to be within a mile of a Snorter bust. Their jobs were not protected; any approach was usually interpreted as 'reasonable suspicion' of Usurpation, and was answered by gunfire. In the last tobacco bust in Ilford twenty-two

58

unarmed civilians had died. I looked across the sea of frightened people, all with their arms above their heads, to show that they were not armed, and saw the Snorters begin to form up in two columns on the Library steps. Two Docs came out of the building, carrying a stretcher. Kate! I knew it was Kate! I dashed into the crowd, raising my hands as I did so. I was shouting I think, I don't remember clearly. I know I was crying, because my vision was blurred, and I kept shaking my head to clear my eyes. All I could think was: It's Kate. I then understood why she had spent so long in the Library, day after day, right in front of the librarian, the Working Class lady with the Passport to paradise.

The stretcher was out of sight in the ambulance before I could reach it.

'Who was it? Who was it?' I yelled, grabbing the person nearest to me. I shrugged them off without waiting for an answer, and pushed my way up the steps. I must actually have barged straight into the last Snorters as they came down, but I didn't care. I made it into the reading room. There was a group of people standing round the glass cubicle, strangely quiet compared to the chaos outside. I followed the line of their gaze. There was the librarian wiping blood off her desk, cool and calm, like it was the sort of thing she did every day. I felt a hand on my arm. I turned round. It was Kate.

'Sprayed him in the eyes, then shot him in the head,' she said flatly. She was looking at the pool of blood on the floor. I grabbed her by the shoulders and made her face me. I wanted to control my breathing before I said anything. She looked at me questioningly, and I guess she then saw the tears.

'Jim?' she said. She reached up and wiped my face wonderingly. 'You . . . you didn't think . . .' and then she smiled, shook her head in disbelief and held me, hiding my sobs in her arms.

I lay back with my hands behind my head, and watched Kate brushing her hair. Now the fact is, in all the reading I've done, I've never bothered with poetry. It didn't seem to have anything to do with me, Ilford, the Wall, Snorters and the Console. I expect that the Working Class understood it, but not me. Then I watched Kate at the dressing table in her bedroom, the silhouette of her breast, her soft arm reaching up and brushing downwards, her hair glinting in the candlelight (we'd been busy at Lights On, and then decided to help the economy by sticking to the candle) and the smell of her perfume on me, and I thought, maybe Wordsworth and Co. did have something to say after all.

She had taken my hand without a word, and led me out of the Library. We walked swiftly back to her house, me still confused, and wondering what had happened to the tough, cynical Jim Demon that I had been a month before. Before I met her, I wasn't afraid of anything, understand, *anything*. Except closed-in spaces that is. And dogs. And Street Scum, but then anyone with any sense is frightened of those, right? But those things aside . . . Now I meet this crazy girl who thinks too much for her own good, and I'm actually *crying*! Love's like an illness – it makes you weak. Now I know how that bloke Samson felt, poor sod. So what with thinking about crying, and poetry, and how much I love Kate, I'm not really paying a lot of attention to what's going on. As we go past her parents' room she says 'He's away, and she's AW; she won't come up' but I'm still not with it. Only once the curtains are drawn, and she begins taking off her jeans, do I start paying attention. She pulled her thick sweater over her head, and my heartbeat took off like a greyhound out of a trap. She stood, naked, looking at me, and I knew I would never go back to the Alley.

'Well?' she asked. 'Are you just going to stand there?'

'I love you,' I said, the words emerging from my mouth unbidden.

'I know,' she replied. 'Come and show me.' And I did, although it took the rest of the day.

Kate asked me to stay the night. Now I know I'm twenty-one, emancipated (in theory at least; in fact there's only one party to vote for, and so I don't bother) and master of my own destiny and all that, but the fact is I'd never stayed out overnight before. Very few people who had homes did – too dangerous you see? Houses didn't often get attacked, but it had happened, and in Ilford too. A gang of Street Scum would descend on the place and pull it apart, and take anything or anyone they fancied. No one would lift a finger to stop them. Once it was Lights On, the Snorters were nowhere to be seen. They were supposed to be a fucking police force, and they didn't go out after dark! Safe and cosy inside the Wall, right? So people with property to protect made their own arrangements. The old folks depended on me to do the locks and grilles and so on.

Anyway, I wanted to stay, so I called them. Mum answered, and I could hear Dad whining in the background about not being able to hear the cartoon. There was a long pause at the other end when I told her.

'Who you with?' she asked.

'A girl. I've not told you about her. Her name's Kate.' There was another long pause.

'You know Dad's still not himself. Well, she must be quite important, Jimmy, if you want to stay, so we'll see you in the morning.' She was all right, was Mum. She despaired of me ever 'settling down' as she put it, and so I suppose she thought this could be it. In fact, her making it easy for me like that made me feel as though I should go home. If I did stay, I'd never hear the last of it from the old lady; she'd be talking registry offices from Seven-O till Lights On.

I helped Kate settle her place down for the night, and we went back to bed. We took the spare Console with us. We were going to watch an old horror movie in bed. We were talking through Nooz at Ten when I saw something on the screen which distracted me. Kate saw that I didn't have my whole attention on her, and she reached over and snapped it off.

'Now look here, Jim Demon! It's not every day I take some bloke into my bed, especially . . .'

'Hang on!' I said, cutting her off. I reached across her, not entirely oblivious of her breasts brushing my arm as I did so, and switched the Box back on.

'That face . . . did you see it? Come on, you pile of junk!' I shouted at the screen. It was an old model, and it took time for the picture to focus. The face had gone, but the news reader was still talking. I turned the volume up, and ignored the thumping on the wall from her parents.

' – has today been promoted to Minister for Social Planning. Mr Jordan takes over from Ms Marie Fowler who disappeared in unexplained circumstances last month. No word has yet been heard of Ms Fowler and the Ceepee are now discounting the earlier rumours of a kidnapping plot – ' Kate had turned it off again, but I'd heard enough.

'Did you hear that? It's him! Didn't you see his picture? He's older, of course, but it's him!'

'Who?'

'Jordan! Our 'Enery. Henry Jordan!'

'No, I'm sure you're wrong . . .'

'I'm telling you it was him. I'd recognize those eyes

62

anywhere.' I turned to Kate and grabbed her hand. 'You must have seen him.' Kate took her hand away.

'Don't be so bloody silly, of course it wasn't.'

I looked carefully at her but she avoided my gaze.

'Kate? What's up? Kate?' She got out of bed and put on her dressing gown. 'I don't know what's got into you, girl. We were only saying the other day that we wondered whether he was still around . . .' She stood with her back to me, staring at the floor. I got out of bed, and put my arms around her.

'Come on, come on back to bed. I don't know why you're so upset, but it doesn't matter. I'm sorry I mentioned it.' She didn't answer. I shivered. She turned round to face me, and shoved me backwards on to the bed, and then jumped on top of me. I didn't pursue the point, something I was later to regret. Still, I had my hands full, didn't I?

8

I woke up the next morning quite late, and feeling great. I was alone in the bed. I listened carefully, but there didn't seem to be anyone else upstairs. I didn't really want to call out. I got dressed and went downstairs. I could hear Mr and Mrs Mason quarrelling in the living room. I looked into the kitchen, but I had the feeling that Kate wasn't in the house. I was opening the front door, when a man's head poked out of the living room.

'You Jim?' he asked sharply.

'Sometimes,' I said. I mean, it was a pretty daft question. How many other geezers were going to be coming out of Kate's bedroom that morning? Come to think of it I didn't want to examine that too closely. Kate had never spoken about anyone else, but you don't know, do you?

'Suit yourself,' he said, as he disappeared. His head reappeared round the corner. 'If you are, there's a letter on the table for you.' The door closed and he resumed his bickering with his wife.

I went to the table by the front door, and picked up an envelope, with 'Jim' on the front. My good mood evaporated as I read. Kate had gone.

'When a prisoner was going to escape, he used to say he was going "over the wall". Well, Jim, my love, I'm a prisoner and I'm going over the Wall. One way or another I'm going to escape. For what it's worth now, I love you too.'

I put the letter carefully back on the table and let myself

out. I started walking home. All I can remember is that I felt numb. Oh yes, there was something else. That hum in the back of my head. It was an octave higher in pitch, and twice as loud.

9

'Sounds like a pretty daft idea to me, Demon; you sure your head's okay?'

'It's not daft to me, Knife. Will you help me or not?'

'Maybe.'

'What do you mean, "maybe"?'

'What makes you think you can find her for a start?'

'Don't you worry about that; I'll find her.'

'Okay, suppose you do. What do you think she'll do?'

'What?' I was getting pretty exasperated. Knife didn't usually question me like this.

'You think she's going to throw herself into your arms? Think about it, Demon. You are the enemy now. She won't want to come within a mile of you in case you try to Usurp.'

'Don't be ridiculous, she's in love with me.'

'But she still left.'

'That's not the point,' I shouted, part of me realizing he was right. 'Either you're going to help me, or you're not, in which case I'll go alone.' I turned and stormed off down the street. Knife came after me and caught me by the arm.

'Hey, hey. Don't get so upset,' he said, turning me round. 'We can't have you getting yourself killed, can we?' He patted my cheek, not altogether affectionately. 'So, calm down, right?'

I nodded. 'I'm sorry, Knife. I'm just a bit uptight, you know?'

'Yeh, I can see. But that ain't the way to get in. That's the way to get yourself killed,' and he gave a sharp slicing action with his finger across his throat, and gave his gap-toothed grin. We both laughed, and the tension was broken.

'Have you been in before?' I asked.

'Maybe,' he said. He clearly was not going to be forthcoming, so I changed tack.

'What do you suggest I do?'

'You go to the Library a fair bit, right?'

'I did.'

'Yeh, well,' he continued, ignoring my self-pity, 'next time, check out the maps and plans. We want a map of the West End.'

'They're all pretty old, Knife, the maps that is. Nothing more recent than forty years at a guess.'

'Just see what you can find, eh? Up West hasn't changed much I bet.' He winked, and walked off.

'Hey,' I called after him, and threw straight at him what I'd had in my pocket. With one fluid, graceful motion, Knife turned, stepped to one side, and caught it ten centimetres from his face. A slab of chocolate.

'Spot on, old son,' he said. 'I'll see you after Lights On.'

I don't know why I went straight to Knife when I decided to get into London. I just thought that if anyone I knew would be able to help, it would be him. He seemed to know things that no one else did and, what's more, he could see in the dark. Had I known then what the venture entailed, I would have thought twice. I went directly to the Library.

Now, one thing that has to be said for Ilford Library is that when they built it (or rebuilt it, according to the plaque, in 1985) they made it relatively easy to find whatever you want. The 'Maps and Plans' section was pretty extensive, and contained maps from all over the world, including a number of fairly detailed ones of Ilford and the surrounding areas. The notable exception was London. I must have spent two hours looking at every single map of England, and then I went on to Europe just in case something had been misfiled. Nothing. Just as I had given up, I looked up, and there, on the wall above my head, was a map of Greater London. I cursed myself for being unobservant, and went to have a closer look. The Wall was marked clearly. Everything within it was blocked out in red ink. No detail at all, and no bloody use. I went to the librarian and asked her. I don't really know why I didn't start with her. She knew, like everyone else, that most of the 'regulars' were Jobbing, so it wouldn't have been a strange request. But I had my principles, see? I *wasn't* Jobbing; I wasn't planning to kill anyone, and I didn't want her to think that I was. Anyway, she suggested that I look in all the books on London, but she told me straight out, there wouldn't be anything. The government had had them all removed years ago. She was right. Another two hours, yielding only junk. It might have been that word that put me in mind of all the rubbish lying in the cellar back home, I can't say for sure. Whatever it was, I remembered all the old cases and chests, full of papers and books and stuff that the old man had thrown down there over the years. I went straight home.

I was surprised to find the cellar so dry, recalling how in previous winters it had always flooded at the first sign of rain. There were no lights down there – I had stripped out the wire for the alarm system on the back door – so I had to take a torch, which was not the safest of things in the circumstances. The ceiling was so low I had to stoop, and there was old paper, and curtains and so on every-where. Now then, as I have mentioned previously, cramped places do not agree with me. Put simply, they scare the living daylights out of me, as the old man would have put it. The thought of the torch going out made me sweat, even with the cold.

Most of the cases were full of old newspapers and magazines, yellow, crumbling and with tide marks on them. Many of them fell apart as I opened them. I'd have to clear the place out soon, or there really would be a fire. The torch started to splutter, sending shadows dancing around the walls and, I must admit, I started to panic. I picked it up and rested it on an old metal chest. On the floor behind the chest was a book. I picked it up, and there, underneath, was what I had been looking for.

'Perfect,' said the Knife, examining the map carefully. 'Absolutely perfect.' Now my opinion was that a torn and battered bus map printed in 1976 was far from perfect, but I couldn't help but feel pleased, what with the Knife being so enthusiastic. The Knife pulled a black marker pen from inside his jacket, and drew a sort of oval shape on the map.

'What are you doing?'

'This line is approximately where the Wall is, see.'

'You know where it is off by heart?' I said, amazed.

'The closest point to us is this place here: "Bank",' he went on, ignoring my question. 'The last stop on the Tube is Liverpool Street . . .' he pondered. 'Once inside the Wall, all we have to do is follow this road . . . "Holborn", for a K or two, and then . . . bingo! The West End!'

'Wait a minute,' I said, puzzled. 'You told me to find a map of the West End. But that's only part of London, isn't it? What makes you think she'll be there?'

'She was your bird, Demon; didn't you ever listen to anything she said?'

'Course I did. What are you on about?'

'Never mind, old son. Just think back to what she was reading about and trust me.'

'Knife . . . ?'

'Forget it!' he said sharply. I looked carefully at him. He turned to me and looked me straight in the eye.

'Let's get one thing clear, Demon. If I help you with this, you will do exactly as I say, without question, and without argument. I am not going to get myself killed on account of some woman you've fallen for. Do you understand?'

I felt as though I had been suckered. I'd always taken Knife at face value: fast and tough, yes, and unpredictable. Maybe even a bit of a psycho. But not too well equipped when it came to the old grey matter. In the last few days I'd begun to realize that his blades weren't the only things that were sharp.

'Okay, Knife. Whatever you say.'

'Fine,' he said, and smiled his awful smile with genuine warmth.

'Just one question though, and it'll be the last. If you think this'll be so dangerous, why are you helping me?'

'Let's just say it'll be an interesting way to spend a few days.'

'Days! You expect us to stay there overnight?'

'Well, if you reckon you can find Kate amongst three million people in a couple of hours, fine. Otherwise we'll be there a bit longer.'

It was just as well he was coming, you know. Despite my bravado, I hadn't a clue how to find Kate. I told Knife, and thanked him for his help.

'Don't thank me yet, Demon. Still,' he added, 'we aim to please.'

10

I hopped from foot to foot, as quietly as possible, trying to keep warm. It was Eleven-O, and the streets were completely deserted. I'd been waiting outside Gants Hill Tube for only three or four minutes, but already my fingers were becoming numb. I was where Knife had told me to be, in the doorway of a shop – this one had once been a 'Dry Cleaners' – you could still make out the faded painting on the wooden fascia – with an unobstructed view of the entrance to the Tube. There was total silence. Even the wind, which had been blowing all day, had now gone, and it was as still as a corpse. The only light was the illuminated sign above the Tube, which cast a yellow pool on the pavement. I was on the other side of the roundabout, in pitch blackness. A movement caught my eye a few yards from where I stood. It was a small animal, a rat probably, scavenging through the grass which grew in the gutters and in the patchwork cracks across the tarmac.

I thought about the task ahead. I had been unable to resist asking more questions – I told Knife that it could be dangerous if I didn't know what to do, especially if we got separated – and he relented. One thing he wouldn't tell me though, and that was how we were going to get through the Wall. He simply said: 'By Tube', which I took to be a joke. The Tube line stopped at Liverpool Street. Coming out of the station you could see the Wall before you. It had been built during the last years of the twentieth century. The idea had been put forward, so they said, of rebuilding the original London Wall, which had existed when the town was fortified. Tourist attraction, they said, historical. What's more, it would employ engineers, designers and builders for twenty years, they said, which, as you can imagine, was very popular. Of course, it wouldn't actually conform to the original site of the wall throughout its length, because London was so much bigger than when the original existed. So they built it. The old man's brother, Uncle Sid, worked on it for a bit, before he died. None of them realized they were building their own prison; they were to be locked away on the *Outside*, while the only freedom lay within. I don't suppose I would have understood it either, if it had not been for Jordan's book. It was only a short step to add the guards, the electronic equipment, cameras and all, and floodlight it at night, to turn it into a fully-fledged fortress. Still, it wasn't completely impregnable. Of the 146 Usurpers killed in that week, 15 were killed on the *Inside*. It was generally thought that they got in using forged Work Permits, although I doubted it. On entry, all Permits were screened, and if the information encoded on the Permit did not tally with the person presenting it, you'd had it. No matter how clever you were, you couldn't forge a card without the electronic equipment; and I'd never heard of any Usurper getting hold of that, let alone knowing how to use it.

I heard footsteps approaching the station from the opposite direction. They were bold and loud, most unlike those of the Knife, but I watched intently anyway. I was beginning to learn not to be surprised by anything he did. It was him! He'd told me to look for a person in a hat. There he was, Homburg on his head, carrying a black bag, and looking for all the world like a Doc on a late call! The figure silhouetted against the light seemed to hesitate for a split second, more of a falter in its step which might have gone unnoticed by anyone else, and I stepped out of the doorway and crossed the road. Knife disappeared into the station. It had been my idea for us to go separately. I thought it might look suspicious for both of us to get on the last train together.

As I put a coin in the machine, and the automatic barriers slid back, I could see the Knife at the far end of the platform. I sauntered down towards him. There was no one else in the entire station, but there were the cameras. The train arrived, and we both got into the first carriage. The Knife sat down. I stood with my back to the glass partition. We had practised this a number of times. In my position I partially obscured the seat in which Knife sat from the camera mounted in the top corner of the carriage. Knife bent down, as if to tie a shoelace. He fiddled for a few seconds, and I heard the sound of metal on metal. Suddenly, the lights in the carriage went out. I leapt over to Knife, and he drew out of his doctor's bag two bundles, one of which he threw to me. In the light from the adjoining carriage we both dressed in the blue polyester overalls of Tube maintenance men. I pulled a cap out of my pocket and put it on, while Knife hung a very official 'Not in Use' sign on each of the doors. He then checked that the light on the camera monitor was out, and sat down.

'So far, so good,' he said. 'We've got about twenty minutes to go through the next bit. Come and sit down. Good. Now, you asked me how we were going to get through the Wall. I'll tell you.' He pulled a piece of paper out of his pocket.

'This is a plan of Liverpool Street station. It is, as you rightly said, the end of the Central Line. Here are the stairs leading to the exit, and here's the connection to the District and Met, which goes out to Upminster. Here,' he said, pointing to the left side of the plan, 'is the continuation of the Central Line on the other side of the Wall.'

73

'What? What do you mean, "continuation"?'

'Exactly that. Before the Wall went up, and they bricked up the tunnel, this train went all the way to the West End; all the way, Demon.' He smiled in triumph.

'Are you sure? I mean, it seems too easy. Why doesn't everyone know about it?'

'Because it's a well-kept secret. That's why I didn't tell you before we set out. I wanted to be sure you didn't tell anyone.'

'Thanks for the vote of confidence.'

'Sorry. I hope you understand.' I didn't in fact, but there was something more important on my mind.

'If the tunnel's bricked up, how do we get through?'

'Well, Demon, it's a funny thing, but wouldn't you just know it? There's a service shaft running from one end of the tunnel to the other. We don't need to get through the Wall at all; we're going underneath it.'

'But surely they must know about it?'

'Possibly. But if they do, they obviously don't consider it to be dangerous to them, as it's not guarded.' He smiled mysteriously. I let it pass.

'Is this the way Freddo tried to get in?'

'Yes, but don't panic. He wasn't caught in the tunnel. He was shot on the streets, two Ks away from the station.'

'But they might have followed him . . .'

'Believe me, they didn't.'

The rest of the journey passed in silence. The Tube slid silently through the empty stations, automatically passing those where no one wanted to get on or off. It stopped once at Leytonstone, but no one approached our carriage. We pulled into Liverpool Street. Knife retrieved the two signs and reconnected the power. The doors opened, but we stayed inside. Knife counted off two minutes, and then, as the doors closed, we stepped out on to an empty platform. The service hatch that led to the shaft was located behind a ceramic map of the Tube system. I loosened two screws as quickly as I could, Knife doing the other two. The map swung away from the wall, and revealed a small doorway, about a metre off the ground. I stood watch while Knife set to work on the lock with a piece of wire and one of his thinnest blades, and within a few seconds the door swung inwards. He then refixed two of the screws holding the map, leaving them sufficiently loose to enable us to get into the shaft, and with us inside, he pulled the map back into place with a piece of nylon fishing line. The entire procedure had taken two and a half minutes.

We were in a very low, very narrow shaft, which, as Knife closed the door behind us, descended into complete and total blackness.

Which was, of course, when I started to panic.

11

'But I can't breathe!'

'Calm down, Demon. It's only fifty metres or so.'

'For God's sake, light a torch!'

'Don't be ridiculous, you can't light a torch in here. Now pull yourself together!'

'You don't understand, Knife; I can't; I can't!'

'If you don't keep your voice down, I'll make *sure* you can't breathe – only on a more permanent basis.'

'I've got to get out, I've got to get out!' I said, trying to get past him to the door. And that's when he hit me. Firmly, squarely, right on the jaw. Being able to see in the dark has its advantages in situations like that, and the Knife's accuracy, judged in retrospect, was remarkable. It worked too, because, although still terrified, I had my fear under control.

'Right,' said Knife, as I tried to feel if my mouth was bleeding, 'just keep your head down and crawl as quickly as you can. I'll go ahead so you won't have to worry about bumping into anything.' And off he went, scuttling away into the black. Believe me, when I say 'black' I mean *black*; I couldn't see my hand in front of my face.

I heard Knife moving further away from me. For a few seconds I remained where I was, and then the fear of being left alone overcame the fear of what was ahead.

'Wait!' I called, and scrambled after him. The shaft felt rough under my hands and knees. I saw that the overalls had more than one purpose. As I panted, hot, rusty air scorched the back of my throat. I could feel the roof of the shaft pressing down on my back. With every movement, it seemed lower. The tunnel was getting lower!

'It's your imagination,' I heard myself say, but I didn't believe it. The walls began to close in. Any second, and I would be trapped. I forced myself on, willing each step, fighting back the rising tide of hysteria . . . knee . . . hand . . . knee . . . hand. The roof pressed my head down almost to the floor, forcing the breath out of me. At the back of my mind I registered a high pitched whine. I felt a sharp slap across my cheek.

'Shut up!' hissed the Knife, his voice coming out of the black only centimetres from my ear.

'We're there,' he whispered. I heard Knife open his bag and take something out. I then heard screws being turned, and then, with painful but joyous suddenness, light spilled into the shaft. Two more screws, and there was a square of light in front of me, about a metre square. Knife peered cautiously out, and in one movement, rolled out of the shaft, landing on his feet. A few seconds later his head appeared, framed in the entrance, and he beckoned me to follow him. I climbed down gratefully.

To our left lay a short length of tunnel, ending abruptly in a concrete wall. To the right I could see the lights of a platform. There were people on it. Knife made a move in their direction, but I held his arm. He looked at me questioningly. I held up my hand for him to wait. I had felt a movement of air coming through the tunnel. A piece of paper skipped and hopped towards us down the tracks. Then, at the far end of the platform, there appeared the headlamps of a train. I pulled Knife back towards the shaft. We pressed our backs against the wall. The train swept towards us, decelerating fast. It stopped within two metres of where we stood, the glare from the headlamps blinding us. Of course, there was no driver in it, the entire system being run from Computer Central,

but even if there had been, we were still in our maintenance overalls. The doors of the train opened, and we ran
swiftly to the platform, jumped on to it, and joined the
passengers as they got off. No one even looked at us.

'So I told her, if that was her attitude, she could go
without me,' I said. There was a momentary pause, and
then the Knife caught on.

'That's what I'd have done. I don't blame you for one
minute.'

We continued this nonsense all the way down and past
the barriers, even though there was no one to hear it for
part of the way. We climbed the last steps, and emerged
into the street.

'Nice one, Demon,' said Knife, 'I knew you'd be all
right in a pinch.' I wasn't listening. We'd made it. I was
inside the Wall, and in one piece. And somewhere out
there was Kate.

'Er . . . Knife?' I said after a while.

'Yes, mate?'

'Any suggestions as to what we do next?'

Knife smiled. 'I thought we might go and visit a friend
of mine.'

'You've got friends on this side of the Wall?' I asked,
incredulously.

'One or two,' he said, 'one or two.'

Part Two

12

There I was, minding my own business, and this tall ugly bloke comes over and starts chatting me up. Pretended he wanted a book, which gave it away right from the start, 'cos he didn't look as though he could read. So I blinded him with science and told him what it was about. His mouth opened and closed a few times like a goldfish and then he sloped off to fake reading it. Still, I should do him justice, he *was* game: he was still pretending to be engrossed when I left the Library. I almost felt sorry for him.

The walk back took over an hour 'cos I decided to skirt round Romford Road: I didn't want to bump into Trevor for a while, and I knew he'd be looking out for me.

It was Lights On as I walked in. Mum was asleep in front of the Box. She woke up as I closed the door.

'That you, Katy?'

'Yeh, it's me.' Things are looking up. That was the second time she'd recognized me that day. She was AW – and bad with it. Registered eight years before when I was only twelve. In the last two years she'd faded fast. Normally she thought I was one of the characters in the soaps she watched. The rest of the time she looked straight through me.

'Make us a cuppa, dear,' she asked, reaching for the volume control on the Box. That would be it for the night. She'd fall asleep there and wake up the next morning and not even know it was a different day. I made her a cup of tea and left it by her side. I wanted to know where the Prick was, but I knew I wouldn't get a sensible answer. I went upstairs to my room, locking the door behind me. I needn't have worried: he either didn't come back that night, or decided that he was too tired.

I woke up just before the alarm at Seven-O. I got out of bed and went to the window. It was freezing in the bedroom. My breath came in clouds of steam and there was condensation running down the few remaining glass panes. It was still dark outside. I planned to slip out of the house early and get to the Library before it got too busy. I still hadn't solved my gun problem and I wanted time to do some research without any nosey parkers asking questions.

I pulled on my jeans and pullover and crept along to the bathroom without putting on the lights. I began to splash my face with cold water.

'You're up early,' said a voice behind me. I knew immediately who it was, but I couldn't help jumping. He always moves so silently, as if he's on oiled castors; 'Sebaceous Sid' is another of my names for him. 'Went to bed early too,' he said softly. I looked at him quickly in the mirror. He was wearing his overcoat, and his skinny bare legs stuck out the bottom like twigs.

'Yeh,' I said, chatty as I could. 'Tired, wasn't I?'

'Shame,' says he.

I wasted some time wiping round the sink. He was standing in the doorway and I'd have to squeeze past him to get out. I folded my towel carefully over the rail still hoping he'd move, but he'd found something interesting on the palm of his hand, and he wasn't moving anywhere. Tits or bum? I thought. Tits.

''Scuse,' I said, and eased past him with my back to him. His hands went round me to my front, and squeezed. I could feel his erection through his overcoat. I had to give it to him; that was one thing about him you could

82

always bank on, if you follow me. Come rain or shine, morning, noon or night, it was always up. Hence: 'the Prick'.

'What's the hurry, Kath? It's still dark out. Why don't you stay for a bit? It's warm in my room. Got some firewood last night.'

'Sorry, Sid,' I said, removing his hands gently. 'Got a lot to do today. Tonight maybe, yeh?'

I escaped to my room and shut the door. I leant back against it, listening. The corridor was silent, and I imagined him staring at my door, wondering if he should press the point. Then I heard the floorboards creak, and his door closed. Jesus! One of these days . . . Trouble was, as much as I desperately wanted to castrate the creep, I didn't dare do it. He looked after Mum, and he really was quite kind to her, making her meals and so on. God knows why. I suppose it was all right in the beginning, when Dad first left. Mum was still mostly there. Came back from the Hyper one day with him. He'd carried her shopping, would you believe it? Came in for tea, and stayed nine years. But what kept him there after Mum's lights went out, I really had no idea. It wasn't just my presence and his hard-on, although that had something to do with it. He really seemed to care for her. So, for the moment, I'd have to let him have his occasional fumble. I used to lie back and think of London. At least it stopped me wanting to puke.

I gathered up my notes and left the house. I'd grab a coffee at the Vendo after I'd done a couple of hours. Dawn was just breaking as I hit the main road. There was a thin mist coming from the direction of the canal which deadened the sound of my footsteps. I reached into my bag. The knife was there. I sharpened it every night, like a religious ritual, just before going to bed. I had thought of carrying the gun, but I didn't want to risk it. Too valuable. People would kill for it, no question.

Got to the Library just as it was opening. Smiled at the librarian. We'd never spoken, but there was something between us. I was the only girl Jobbing there. Sure, there were other girls in the Library, but more often than not they were just looking to make a few extra New Sovs up against the wall round the back. So maybe she respected me or something. Maybe I reminded her of herself before she Usurped, who knows? Anyway, she always gave me a smile, and the books I wanted were always available, and that was all I was interested in.

I started where I'd left off the day before. I had to find something on the design of the gun 'cos I couldn't get the bloody thing open to change the clip. I suspected something was broken inside. It wouldn't have surprised me if that bastard from Seven Kings had swindled me. He certainly screwed me, that's for sure.

I spent two fruitless hours as the Library gradually filled up. Just as I was losing my patience, the lanky geezer turned up at the desk looking like a lost puppy. I tried to ignore him, but he kept on.

'I don't for one minute suppose that *you* know anything about firearms?' I asked. I wasn't being serious. About the only thing he knew about guns was that they went bang!

'Hand guns, you mean?' he replied.

I looked up at him. 'Yeh.'

'Could be.'

I studied him carefully for the first time. He was tall, very tall, around one metre ninety, thin but muscley. He had a lop-sided sort of face – none of his features were the right size. His nose was too small and his mouth too wide, and he had large, deep-set eyes, but the overall effect wasn't bad. Not horny, understand, just okay. I looked at the eyes. They flicked up from my chest where they had been lingering. Yeh, I thought, just another dirty old man. I was about to look down again when he smiled, and suddenly I wasn't so sure. His eyes showed no embarrassment, just amusement. That, and confidence. Maybe . . . just maybe . . . I smiled back.

'Okay, mate. I could do with a break anyway,' I said, getting up. And off we went.

13

Turned out he wasn't that stupid after all. He had this funny roundabout way of speaking, and he did come out with the strangest things every now and then, but you could tell there was real intelligence there. Rare, that. I began to believe he might really know about guns, 'cos he knew about a lot of stuff I'd never heard of. A real bookworm. Within a few days I found myself opening up to him in a way I'd not done with anyone before, except with Dad that is. Still, I was careful. After that first mention I never spoke about guns at all. Had to be really sure if I could trust him first. I wondered if he'd raise the subject, but the only time he did I made it clear that it was not open for discussion. He just nodded and bided his time. That was another thing I liked about him: he was patient. I saw the way he looked at me. He was hot, real hot, but he never pounced or nothing. It was as if he, sort of, well, *respected me* I suppose. Looking back on it, I realize that I didn't value that the way I should. I thought he was just weak, which shows you how wrong you can be.

After a couple of weeks I decided I couldn't wait any more. I went over to the Waste, found a good spot, and set up some tin cans as targets. I had already used four rounds, and I didn't know how many had been in the clip when I got it. I stood about twenty feet away from the tins, aimed and fired. The gun flew up out of my hand and I was thrown backwards into the mud. I looked back at the cans: all still there. Okay, I thought as I got up, there's no point wasting any more. We'll see if Mr Demon's just bullshit or not.

He was late arriving at the Library. Great, I thought, just when I need him, he's probably gone and got himself wasted. I waited on the steps for about half an hour. I really began to get quite worried; he was later than he had ever been. Then I saw him come round the corner and breathed a sigh of relief. Even from that distance I could see something had happened. He looked as miserable as hell, his shoulders drooping, his long loping gait slow and thoughtful. Still, I had no time for that: this was *it*, my last hurdle was about (hopefully) to be overcome. His problems would have to wait.

'Where have you been?' I said. 'Never mind. I need your help.'

I grabbed his hand and ran down the steps.

'Where are we going?' he asked.

'The Waste.'

'What? What for?'

'You'll see.'

He tried to talk as we went but I shut him up. I needed to concentrate on how I was going to do this. We got to the Waste, and I led the way directly to the clearing. He was sharp, I'll give him that; he noticed the cans immediately.

'What . . .' he said, pointing at them.

'I came here earlier,' I answered. I reached inside my jacket, and then paused. I turned and looked at him carefully. He returned my look, confused, wary, but still like a big ungainly puppy-dog.

'You are going to help me, aren't you?' I asked in my most helpless of female voices, and took out the gun. I undid the pouch and showed it to him. I looked up, and the bastard hit me! I was so surprised that I just stood there, holding my cheek.

'What was that for?'

'You're actually going to do it, aren't you? You're actually going to kill someone? Someone's father, or mother, or sister!' he screamed. I was astonished. The geezer was off his bloody chump! All those civilized conversations about technological progress, sociology and Usurping. They'd just gone in one ear and out the other.

'Yes! I'm not going to live on a dunghill for the rest of my life! Just over there are human beings. Real human beings, living their lives with some sort of dignity. I would rather die than live the life you lead – no future, no hope, just living death.' I thought that was quite good considering it was unrehearsed, but I wondered if I'd gone too far. I changed tack again.

'You've got brains, Jim. Oh, I know you say you haven't, but you see things clearly. It's all right for someone like the Knife, but how can you *choose* to live like this when you know there's more? Why don't you help me? Together we stand a much better chance. We could both make it through – there's no reason why we shouldn't both find jobs.'

'You mean "both murder someone" don't you?'

It occurred to me then that I'd really misjudged him. He was dead serious. A real 'Conshie' – a conscientious objector. God knows how he'd survived in Ilford as long as he had. He just didn't understand what I was on about. Come to that, I wondered if he'd understood a single word of what I'd been saying to him over the last weeks. Maybe I'd been right all along: all he'd been interested in was my fanny.

'Then get lost!' I said, turning away from him. This was it. I had one last card. I raised my hand, cocked the gun, and aimed at the tins on the fence, pulled the trigger and fired. The recoil knocked the gun out of my hand and I feigned falling backwards heavily, landing on my arse. He laughed.

'What's so fucking funny?' I said, also beginning to laugh. 'Oh, Jim, I've got twelve magazines, only twelve, and I'll need a hundred before I can shoot straight. What's worse, I can't get the clips in or out; I can't get the bloody thing undone!' I threw in a couple of sobs for good measure.

He walked over, picked up the gun, and wiped the mud off it. I wasn't sure what he was going to do.

'I suppose if I don't show you, you'll only shoot yourself, won't you?'

'Can you teach me?' I said, wide-eyed. 'Do you know how? I don't believe it, can you really? Oh, Jim!' I said, and threw my arms around him. I should've got a bleedin' Oscar.

14

My heart was pounding so hard I was afraid I would wake Jim, but he slept on, as peaceful and innocent as a baby. Poor bloke. I almost felt I'd miss him. I tiptoed out of the bedroom and along the corridor. I went downstairs to the cellar, picked up the rucksack that had been packed and ready for the last two weeks, and checked over my equipment one last time. Then I crept to the front door and left. I thought about going back to take a last look at Mum. I decided against it – she wouldn't even notice I was gone. And as for the Prick – well, I had nothing to say to him, 'cept 'Goodbye'.

The journey to Dagenham Marshes would only take about an hour, but I wanted to be in position with plenty of time to spare. I took the cycle out of the back garden, and set off. It had taken me nearly two years to find all the parts for the bike. Found the frame rotting over the Waste and scavenged over the whole of Ilford for the rest; cleaning, polishing and oiling down in the cellar, until I was confident it would not let me down.

I cycled quickly, but without pushing myself. I was going to need all my strength for what lay ahead. The rucksack on my back didn't bother me, even though it must have weighed fifteen kilos. Until I had met Jim I had been running six Ks a day with it.

I first saw the maintenance barge when I was in my teens. It was just after Dad left. A group of us used to go out to the Marshes rambling when it was hot. Sometimes if the weather was real good we'd stay out all night. Had a boyfriend called Trev. He had this special trick with his tongue and I thought he was the real thing. Mum used to complain I was going wild. She was probably right. Anyway, one time we were out, mid-afternoon. I'd found this bay thing, where the bank sloped gently into the water. Persuaded the others to help me clear all the junk from the edge, and we used to sit there staring out over the reeds. No fish, of course, and you wouldn't want to get in the water. They used to say it would rot a body away within an hour, but I never believed that. Still, never tried.

We were sitting having a smoke, when I heard a noise from the other side of the river. It was a boat, and it was coming towards us. We scattered like sheep, thinking it was Snorters. None of us had seen Snorters on boats before, but everyone knew there were river patrols where the Thames entered the Wall, and the thing coming towards us was equipped with searchlights and machine guns. I hid behind an old jetty, and watched it approach. It was a barge. Its sides were armoured and it had a little turret, like I'd seen in pictures of submarines. It chugged past me, and I could hear its engines slowing. It finally stopped at the pier next to the electricity station, only a few metres past where I crouched. I scrambled along the path and through the reeds to where it was moored. The hatch opened with a clang, and up popped a head. It looked as though it belonged to one of those pirates you see in films, like what's-his-name, Robert Newton. It had a grizzled beard, a funny hat, and an eyepatch. The owner of the face was singing to himself, and was paying no attention to the security procedures which I'd seen all Outside Workers go through. He didn't even look around him, but was looking down, inside the turret, where it looked as though he'd got his feet tangled.

'Blast and dammit,' he cursed, 'will you come out of it!'

Then up past his legs scrambled a hound! I almost wet

myself. I thought: I'm done for. The only dogs I'd seen before were enormous mangy things that would rip your throat out given half a chance. This one looked quite different. It had a sleek and glossy coat, and a chain around its neck, and it certainly didn't look dangerous, as it padded around in all directions along the top of the barge. It even went up to the pirate geezer and licked his face! I'd heard you could tame them, but I'd never believed it.

The pirate was trying to get out of the turret. He swore again, and then lifted up his eyepatch, looked around him, put it back in place, and climbed out. I snorted – I mean he looked so fucking ridiculous! He looked over to where I was hiding. I ducked down further into the reeds, lost my balance, and fell into the water with a splash. I stood up, coughing foul water, and found myself looking directly into his face. I don't know which of us was more afraid. He backed off from me, and fell with a bump on his arse. The dog started barking and raced towards me, and I fell back in the water. The pirate recovered himself first.

'Captain! Come away from there!' he shouted. The dog backed off, circled once or twice, and came back to the edge of the deck. His master also came over, and reached out a hand to me.

'Come on, Miss, give us your hand. Can't have you drowning – or poisoned more like.'

I reached out my hand, and he hauled me aboard, coughing and spluttering. I stood there, retching, and the sailor disappeared back down the turret.

'Don't worry about Cap'n Hook, he won't bite,' he called back, sounding tinny from the bowels of the barge. He reappeared in a moment with a towel in one hand and a glass in the other.

'Here, dry yourself off, and drink some of this.'

I grabbed the towel and frantically began to rub my face and hair with it.

'Am I done for?' I asked. 'Won't my body start rotting 'cos of the water?'

'You won't rot,' he answered, 'but you'll be pretty sick unless you drink *that*,' holding out the glass to me. I hesitated.

'Don't worry. It's just water with an anti-bacterial pill in it. Standard issue, "Drinking, disinfectant, swallowing Thames, for the use of".'

I hadn't the slightest idea what he was talking about, but I took it anyway. My mouth tasted like a sewer. The drink was sweet and clean, and I felt a lot better. Now I had the chance to look at him more closely. He was about fifty, with a bushy beard, and sparkling grey eyes. He had a lined, weatherbeaten face, brown, like tanned leather, and he was about as tall as I was. The only fifty-year-olds that I had come across before were more dead than alive; almost all AWs, and every one of them pallid and frail. This sailor looked fitter than anyone I'd ever seen.

'Cap'n Sam Crocker, at your service, Miss,' he said, holding out his hand, then changing his mind and saluting, and then offering his hand again. I had to laugh. What a dickhead!

'Miss Katherine Mason, at *your* service,' I said, and shook his hand, smiling.

'And this,' he said, turning to the dog, 'is Captain Hook, First Mate of this vessel. Say "hello", Cap'n.' The dog approached me, and raised its right front paw, wagging its tail.

'Hi,' I said, saluting the dog from a safe distance.

'Now, Miss Mason, what causes you to be out swimming in the muck?'

'We were out rambling when your boat came along.

93

The others all ran off, but I was curious, so I stayed to have a look.' There was a pause.

'May I ask you a question?' I asked.

'Surely.'

'Aren't you, well, frightened of me? I might Usurp you or something.'

He laughed. 'You think I should be afraid of you killing me? How would you do that, pray?'

'I don't know. I might push you overboard, and drown you, or something.' That made him laugh even more.

'That's if you didn't drown first,' he said.

'I mean . . . I don't want to kill you or nothing . . .'

'I'm pleased to hear it,' he said.

'. . . but I thought you were supposed to take precautions, just in case . . .' I ended rather lamely.

'Well, firstly, I've got a protected job, so it wouldn't do you any good at all. And secondly I'm the only lighterman cum electrician cum plumber in the entire country, to the best of my knowledge, and so you couldn't do my job. There's no books on it, no classes you can take. Would you know how to service that pile of junk?' he asked, pointing to the electricity station, 'or keep this tub afloat? Of course not.' I shook my head.

'No,' he mused, more to himself than to me. He shook himself out of his reverie. 'Well, I must be getting at it before the tide turns. *Meggie* will never make it back against the tide. I'm afraid I shall have to ask you to step ashore, Mademoiselle,' he said, becoming formal again.

'Certainly, chief,' I replied, and he held my hand as I stepped on to the iron pier.

'If you walk to the left at the end of the pier, you'll see a path through the reeds. That will take you back to where your friends are still waiting.'

'Are they still there?'

'Oh yes. Two lads, and another lassie, but not half as

94

pretty as you,' he said. 'There's not much that escapes me.' I began to walk down the pier. Then something occurred to me, and I turned back.

'How often do you come out?' I called.

'Once a month, the first Tuesday of each month,' he called back. I waved in reply. As I walked back down the path, I could hear his singing again, each chorus punctuated with Cap'n Hook's barks.

After that, I saw Captain Sam as often as I could get out there on my own. I could only go in the summer, as it was a two-hour walk to the Marshes, and two hours back, and I wouldn't risk being caught out in the open after dark. But when the sun rose at Five-O and didn't set until Nine-O, I could spend the whole day out there. I would sit on the pier, waiting for the familiar sound of *Meggie*'s engines put-putting towards me. Captain Sam would drift in with a bump, the hatch would fly open, and the dog would bound out and jump into my lap, licking and woofing and all that. I never really felt at ease with it, but I didn't want to offend the old man. He was my one and only contact with the Inside. We'd sit on the deck, eating his sandwiches and talking. I wanted to know what it was like inside the Wall, but more important, I had to find out about Dad. The second or third time I met him on my own I asked.

'You ever heard of a John Mason?'

'No. Can't say as I have.'

'He's tall, dark, like me, blue eyes. About forty.'

'Where would I have met him?' asked the Captain.

'I dunno . . . Inside somewhere.'

'Why? Who is he?'

'My . . . my father . . .'

He paused, and looked carefully at me. I couldn't meet his glance.

'I'm sorry, Katy, but, you know, I don't meet many

95

people. I live on the *Meggie*, you see. Only go ashore for provisions.' He smiled, and patted me on the leg. 'I'm sure he's there somewhere.'

I hated him for that, for being nice, for treating me like a kid. I knew what he was thinking. Mum had said it often enough.

The day Dad had left I'd been stayimg over at a friend's. I got back the next morning and he wasn't in. That wasn't unusual, as he often went off for days at a time. I always imagined he was Jobbing somewhere out of the area so Mum wouldn't find out. But he didn't come back. After a week I asked Mum if she knew where he was. She just slapped me round the face and started crying. I got nothing out of her for a week. I even started walking round some of the places where he used to hang around, looking for him. Then, one night I got back, and she was in the lounge with some geezer. There was an empty bottle on the floor and they were both drunk. I screamed at her.

'You just wait till my Dad gets back! He'll beat the living daylights out of you!'

'Oh, God, listen to her!' she said, staggering to her feet. She weaved her way towards me, wagging her finger at me as she spoke.

'Don't you understand, you stupid little cow? He's gone! Left! He's buggered off to that little tart in Bow! That or he's been topped coming back one night down the Waste! He ain't coming back!'

'He is! I don't believe it!'

'Well you better bloody believe it, girl, 'cos you're gonna have to start looking after yourself.'

'He's Usurped!' I shouted. She stopped for a second, as if she'd not heard me properly.

'You what? Usurped! Get that, Frank,' she said, turning to the bloke, 'she reckons the old fart's Usurped!' She

96

laughed. She tottered back and collapsed on to the couch. 'That's rich,' she said quietly. 'Usurped. He couldn't Usurp an old paper bag . . .'

I didn't care what anyone said, I knew. Dad wouldn't have just left, not without telling me. I knew he was Inside somewhere, doing some swanky job, living the life of Riley. From that day I made up my mind to get Inside, no matter what, and find him. But I'd need to find out everything I could about the place if I was to get Inside and stay in one piece. That was where Captain Sam came in. Even if he was a complete nutter, he still knew more about the Inside than anyone else I'd ever met.

Trouble was, as far as the Captain was concerned, there wasn't much difference between inside the Wall and outside. He'd always been able to come and go as he pleased. Like he said, he was the only lighterman cum whatever in England, so I suppose they put up with his daft antics, his false eyepatch and everything. His life was made up of voltage meters, diesel engines and piston rings, and, of course, Cap'n Hook. Still, he was able to tell me about the Thames, the Palace of Westminster, the Tower of London, and the docks. I heard about the restaurants at St Katharine's dock, where the technocrats sat drinking wine and being served food on summer nights, about the shops, one in particular at a place called 'Knightsbridge' where it was said you could buy anything in the world; and about the houses, where even the most modest had an electricity supply which was on the whole day! And one day, blushing and shy, the Captain brought out from behind his back a present for me. I opened this beautiful patterned paper, like I'd never seen before, and inside was a pink scarf. It felt like gossamer, and the Captain told me it was silk. I threw my arms around him and thanked him from the bottom of my heart, and I really meant it. I hadn't been given a present since I was a kid. I never let Mum see it – wore it every day. It was a token of what life still owed me, and what I would one day claim.

The scarf was at the bottom of the rucksack, folded carefully, and wrapped in plastic. It was the only non-necessity I had taken with me. The dawn was just breaking as I arrived at the jetty. I dismounted and hid the bike in the reeds. Whatever happened I would never need it again. But after having done so much work on it, I didn't just want to leave it lying in the open for anyone to find. I opened the rucksack, and stripped off. The problem was going to be keeping my clothes clean and dry. I guessed that my clothes were bound to stand out a mile on the Inside, so I chose the nicest ones I had to wear. I folded them up as neatly as I could, shivering. Then I got into my wet-suit. Of all the equipment I had made or scavenged, I was most proud of this. I had read about them in the Library, how divers could keep warm by having a thin layer of water around their bodies which retained body heat, and was only replaced gradually with cold water. I had looked everywhere for something out of which I could make such a suit, with no success, until I split the cushion of Mum's favourite chair. As she bawled at me, I looked at the material. It was shiny on the outside, and I knew it was waterproof from the number of times Dad had spilt his tea over it. The inside, however, was spongy. I scoured the Waste, and soon found what remained of a settee made with the same covering. I stripped it off, and made some trousers with it. They worked! The only trouble was that the seams all split when I swam. So I got some nylon fishing line and sewed them all up again by hand. Perfect! I then made the tunic, with rubber zips from two old pairs of wellingtons to attach it to the trousers. It wasn't completely waterproof, and it didn't look like the one-piece suits I'd seen in pictures, but it wasn't bad. I took the rest of the gear out of the rucksack. All the things I wasn't going to need for the journey I rolled up in a sheet of polythene as tightly as I could. Then I put them all in the rucksack and put the rucksack on my back, tightening the straps as far as they would go. I then sat down to wait for *Meggie*.

15

The barge appeared through the mist like a boat out of 'Morte D'Arthur'. I could hear it some time before it became visible, first the turret, and then the little puffs of smoke, and finally the armoured sides of the boat itself could be seen. I retreated into the reeds. I was surprised that Cap'n Hook didn't appear at first, as he usually did. But then I saw Captain Sam's familiar face, eyepatch slipped over to one ear, hat awry. He heaved his bag of tools out, climbed on to the jetty, and plodded off to the electricity station. I waited. I knew that being in the water wasn't as dangerous as I'd always believed, but I still didn't want to stay in it a moment longer than necessary, so I was waiting for the last possible minute. I had timed the Captain's maintenance visit on two earlier occasions, and they took approximately fifteen minutes.

Forty minutes later he still hadn't reappeared. I was beginning to get worried. He was always telling me how risky his job was. One of his favourite stories was of how a power cable had once snapped, sending him ten metres in the air. If he'd been hurt – worse still, killed – my whole plan would end there. I was toying with the idea of going to look for him, when I heard footsteps at the far end of the jetty. It was him, his hands and face covered in grease. Something had obviously needed more than just maintenance. Breathing a sigh of relief, I waded into the water on the far side of the barge. I unrolled my harness in the water so as not to make any noise. I got the idea from pictures of rock climbers. Four ropes, each with a clip at the end, joined by two cross lines, one for under my knees, the other under my armpits. It was a gamble. I could sit in it all day, hanging from the water tank in the loft at home, but in moving water, in *Meggie*'s wake – that was a different matter. I attached each clip to the bottom ridge of the aft starboard porthole, braced my feet against the hull, and hoped for the best. Strapped to my arm, where I could reach it with my mouth, was my longstop, a snorkel, the only piece of equipment I'd been able to buy, after saving for a year. I hoped I wouldn't have to use it. I'd watched the wake the barge made, and I'd calculated that, even at full speed, my chin should still be out of the water. If I was wrong, I'd have to use the snorkel. If I was very wrong, I'd drown.

The clump, clump of the Captain's footsteps reached the barge, and he stepped aboard. He climbed to the turret, closed the hatch, and went below. In another few minutes, the engines coughed and spluttered into life, and we moved off.

As the speed picked up, I found myself pushed by the water on to my side. Rather than fight it and try to keep both feet against the hull, I let out some of the for'ard line, wrapped the aft line twice around my left forearm, and allowed the current to push me on to my back. The rucksack cushioned me against the hull, and was reasonably comfortable. In fact the journey was much easier than I had anticipated. The water was as still as a pond, and I was able to breathe easily. My only problem was that I could no longer feel my left arm, as the rope acted as a tourniquet. I had no idea if the Captain had other stops to make outside the Wall, or how long it would take to get back downstream to London. I hung on, and prayed.

I was lucky again. We went directly downstream. We passed an enormous building, with a huge tower belching steam or smoke, and from then on downstream the water

101

was noticeably warmer. It was also noticeably dirtier, and I was glad I didn't have to put my head under completely.

The journey seemed to go on for ever. Then, as I was beginning to think that I wouldn't make it, I heard *Meggie*'s engines slow. I looked ahead, and there was the Wall. It towered above us, dwarfing the barge. It was built in a huge arch, and an enormous portcullis descended into the water. Astride the Wall, on each side of the river, stood a watchtower. The engines almost stopped, and the Captain sounded his horn. A head appeared way above at the end of the Wall.

'Oh, it's you, Sam,' it called, 'you're back early.'

'Hello, sir. I couldn't do Greenwich. I think there's a blockage in my fuel line, so I came back to sort it out.'

I realized again how lucky I had been. I couldn't have stood being in the water for the time it would have taken the Captain to make another stop.

'Okay, Sam, in you come. How long's your fuel problem going to take?'

'Sorry, sir, it's impossible to say. At least an hour I'd guess.'

'Well, in that case I'll be off duty by the time you come back up. I'll warn the next watch that you haven't been checked in, and you can be checked in and out at the same time next time down,' said the guard, laughing.

'Thank you,' called the Captain.

I heard the deep growl of subterranean machinery starting up, and the portcullis rose, dripping, from the water. The barge moved off. I'd been listening so intently, I'd forgotten that I could be seen from the watchtower. I quickly bit the snorkel, drew it out of its strap, wriggled out of the harness, and slipped under the surface of the stinking water, grabbing one of the trailing ropes as I went. I didn't dare rise above the surface, so I had to guess the time it would take us to get out of sight. I could

102

feel *Meggie* vibrating as her speed picked up. I clung on for dear life. Everything seemed to be going all right, when suddenly, I no longer had the snorkel. One minute it was clasped between my teeth, and the next it was gone. Possibly some piece of flotsam had knocked it out, I don't know. I thrashed to the surface, spitting water. I looked back. We were only two hundred metres from the Wall, and I was still plainly visible if anyone should chance to look out. Just as I decided to swim for the bank the engine note changed again. We were heading for the bank, and we seemed to be going at an angle so that I was hidden from the Wall by the barge! I couldn't believe it. *Meggie* slowed to a halt.

'I should think you're freezing by now,' said a voice from above me. 'Fancy coming out for a cuppa?' I looked up. There was Captain Sam, leaning over, smiling at me. I stuck out my hand, and he hauled me aboard.

'Look lively now, and get below. We don't want any of them blasted nosey guards seeing you, do we?'

I scrambled into the barge, and stood there, dripping, on the deck.

'There's a rug there, behind you,' he said as he came down, 'get that round you. There's tea waiting in the pot. I'd better get going again or they'll begin to suspect something.'

Wriggling out of the rucksack was tricky as the straps were tight and wet. Eventually I freed myself, pulled the rug round me, and reached for the tea. While we moved off I shouted up to him.

'How long have you known I was there?'

'Pretty well from the start, Miss Kate. I know this old tub like she was part of my own body. I could feel a slight draw to one side. At first I thought it was just weeds on the rudder or me starboard engine on the blink again.

Then I looked over and saw you hanging on. You must be heavier than you look, my dear.'

'Cheers, Captain. I'm really grateful. I couldn't have hung on much longer.' I thought for a moment. 'Aren't you worried about getting caught?'

'I won't. Anyway, I reckons they owes me one,' he said bitterly. I paused to take another sip of tea.

'Is there really anything wrong with the fuel line?'

'So you heard that did you? No more than ever. But I had to get you in somehow, and usually they search the boat, see? I know that there guard on the early shift, and he's better than most. I thought if I got back while he was still on he'd let us through. Lazy, is that one. He couldn't be bothered with the extra paperwork involved in booking me in at the end of his shift.' Crafty old bastard, I thought. I wondered if he'd known all along that I was going to use him to get in.

I unrolled the polythene packages at the bottom of the rucksack. The clothes were creased, but dry.

'Have you got dry clothes?' called the Captain.

'Yes. I'll get changed now. Is that all right?'

'You go ahead, my dear. The towels are stowed above where you're sitting. I can't offer you a bath I'm afraid, but there's warm water in the pot, and soap in the galley. Help yourself. We've got a twenty-minute journey before we dock. I'll call out before coming down.'

I sat across from Captain Sam, the tiny table separating us. It was dark outside. We'd been moored in a little derelict dock since midday. I was drinking tea, with rum in it. I'd never drunk rum before, and I could feel my cheeks burning. The Captain didn't want to know what I was going to do. He knew I was planning to kill someone, but he didn't condemn me the way Jim did. He simply couldn't understand a world which allowed me to do it, or make it necessary. His view of the world had been out of date for over a century. That was perhaps why I liked him: he was a real old gent. He didn't put it in words, but I reckon he helped me get in because he felt that he had a debt to collect from 'Them', as he called the Snorters. New regulations had been brought in a few months before. He explained that, like any city state, London suffered from a serious risk of disease. Too many people crowded into too small an area, and all fresh water supplies brought in from outside. I'd never thought of that before, but it was obvious once you did.

Anyway, regulations had been made prohibiting the keeping of pets. Captain Sam had hidden Cap'n Hook away for some weeks, but he had got out, been trapped by a Snorter and shot on the spot. He got all tearful as he told me the story. I knew how much Cap'n Hook had meant to him. Getting me Inside was his way of evening the score. Also, I dunno . . . I guess the old codger loved me. You can tell, you know. He never tried it on, not once, and he used to look at me, pat my hand and so on, like he really cared. It used to get me embarrassed; no one had ever loved me before, you know, loved me without wanting or expecting anything in return. I didn't know what to do.

It was time to go. We had fallen silent, neither of us wanting to say goodbye. I have to admit it, I was a bit scared. The cabin was warm and friendly, and part of me wanted to stay there. He took my hand in his and squeezed it.

'I must be off, Captain,' I said.

'I know, Miss Kate. You will be careful now, won't you?'

'I'll do my best, I promise.'

'This is where you'll find me, most nights.'

'Thanks.' We stood awkwardly for a few seconds, and then I hugged him and left.

Following the directions he had given me, I made my way to the road, and headed towards the lights of the city. It was cold, and my Sunday best clothes which I was wearing were not designed for March. I thrust my hands into my jacket pockets, and felt the reassuring hardness of the gun. I hoped I wouldn't have to use it prematurely. I had no Work Permit, no papers, no address. If I was challenged, it would be all over bar the shooting, and I really didn't want to use it until I met Mr Henry Jordan.

16

I waited, as patiently as I could, in the queue for the 'Enquiries' desk in the hallway of the Ministry of Social Planning. Finding the office building had been a lot easier than I had anticipated. On almost every street corner there were glass cubicles, with telephones in them. They had directories in each, just like I was used to, but in addition to the private listings were the numbers of all the government departments and their personnel. It was impossible to get those numbers on the Outside. Jim reckoned that it was deliberate policy, to prevent non-workers from having direct access to government officials. I just looked up the 'Ministry of Social Planning' and it gave me the phone number and address.

I was prepared for heavy security, but, Jesus! the place swarmed with Snorters. The 'Enquiries' desk was near the entrance. Further into the hall was a metal barrier, two armed guards manning it. In the centre: some sort of electronic screening device, triggered by metal? also manned by armed guards. They were checking not only Work Permits, but another sort of pass also. I could see that the people with queries were being asked for their Work Permits, but were not being searched until they passed the desk and went on into the building. I'd have to play it by ear, but I still felt I had a chance.

'Next.' The woman ahead of me was called to the desk.

'Work Permit please.' She handed the card across the desk. The man behind the desk put it into a machine, and looked at the screen.

'Yes, Mrs Adams. What is your query?'

'I was asked to attend for reassessment as to family planning.'

'Ah, yes, I have it here. Second elevator on the left after the security screen, fifteenth floor, room number 1542. Got that?'

'Yes, thank you,' said Mrs Adams. She took her Permit back, and moved off to the security guards.

'Next.'

I took a deep breath and stepped forward. I smiled my prettiest smile at the man and handed him a note. The smile slipped from his face as he read. It said: '*If you look carefully over the counter, you will see a gun pointed straight at your balls. I am going to blow them off unless you do exactly as I say.*'

He peered over the desk and saw the gun. I was holding it with both hands, just as Jim had shown me, and was aiming it, as promised, at his groin.

'Yes, Miss,' he said, quite calmly, considering.

'Please put your hands on the desk where I can see them,' I said quietly. 'I don't know where the button is, but I'm sure there is one. Before you press it let me tell you this; I'm not after you or your job. You'll just have to believe me. But as you can see, I have very little to lose by killing you or all these innocent people behind me in the queue. If I see any of those guards even so much as take a step towards me, I'm going to start shooting. You will be dead before I am.'

'I understand entirely, Miss. I shall do as you say.'

'Good,' I said, keeping my body between me and the people behind me. 'Please pick up the telephone, and get Mr Jordan.' He opened his eyes wide in surprise.

'His job is – '

' – protected, yes I know; nevertheless, I want him down here. Now.'

'I'm not at all sure he's in yet.'

'Let's hope he is, for both our sakes.' He picked up the phone, and pressed some buttons.

'What's your name?' I asked.

'Miller, Miss. Peter Miller.'

'Well, Mr Miller, try to look a little happier, if you can.' He smiled, or at least tried, and said to the man behind me at the rope: 'I shan't keep you long, sir.' He turned back to me. 'Who shall – ' He was cut short by the phone being answered at the other end. 'Mr Wiles, this is Miller down on the Enquiry desk. There's a young lady here who hasn't got an appointment, but wants to speak to Mr Jordan . . .'

'Tell him,' I interrupted, 'that I have news of Marie, for the ears of Mr Jordan only.' He did so. There was a long pause. 'Yes. Yes. Thank you sir.' He hung up. 'Mr Jordan is on his way down.'

'How long will that take?' I asked.

'Two, three minutes. He'll come down in the executive lift.'

'Good. It would be better if you could look busy in the meantime.'

In fact it took ninety seconds. I recognized him immediately, lean face, intense, dark eyes, and hooked nose. He was shorter than I had imagined, only ever having seen him on the Box, or in photos. He was alone and, as far as I could see, the guards were still in their positions.

'I'll take over, thank you Miller,' he said. He turned to me with the utmost courtesy without apparently noticing the gun.

'If you'll just come this way, Miss,' he said, and led the way to a doorway that I hadn't noticed before. I put the gun in my jacket pocket, and kept it pointed at him. As he reached the door and put his hand on the handle, I touched him lightly on the shoulder, and prodded him in the back with the gun.

'If there is anyone else in that room, Henry, I shall shoot you.' He nodded without turning round, and then very slowly – presumably for my benefit – he turned the handle, opened the door, and showed me into an empty room, with a table and two chairs in it.

'It's an inspection room; you can see the hall and stairs from here.' I looked behind the door, and saw a screen that filled the entire wall. Jordan went in, and sat at the table. I closed the door behind me, took the gun out of my pocket, and pointed it at Jordan.

'Put that away! What the hell do you think you're doing?' he said, very angrily. It was not the reaction I had counted on. 'Now, what's the message?' I wasn't sure what was happening.

'There's no message, Mr Jordan. I'm here to kill someone.' Now it was Jordan's turn to look confused. Then, as he realized that I was still pointing the gun at him, his expression changed again. Fear, I could see, yes, but there was something else in his eyes too. Amusement.

'I see,' he said, still sitting at the table. 'What do you expect me to do – or are you going to kill *me*, in which case my part in the proceedings is very simple.'

'No, Mr Jordan. I hope I shan't have to kill you. I admire and respect you, even though you are responsible for my present predicament. You are going to take me into the building, get me past security, and deliver a Mr Eric Swayne to me.' He looked surprised again. 'Swayne eh? Why him?'

'He is two grades down from you, isn't he? The directory has him down as "Senior Clerk, Ministry of Social Planning". And his job is not protected.' Jordan actually smiled. Something was going on that I knew nothing about, but I had no time to find out what it was. I thought quickly, and decided to carry on. I didn't have much choice and, anyway, I'd never get this close again.

'There's no need for me to take you up. I'll get him to come down.' I thought about that. 'How?'

'If you let me call Miller over here, I'll get him to phone up.'

'Why should you want to make it easier for me?'

'I could say that it would be fun. Or I could say that to call him down involves less risk to others who might get in the way. Finally, I could say that he's no bloody good at his job anyway, and that a change would be refreshing. You can pick whichever reason you prefer.'

'Okay. Do it. But – ' I stopped him as he stood ' – just beckon Miller over here. If you utter one word . . .' I left the threat unspoken. He opened the door. Miller was already looking worriedly in our direction. Jordan beckoned. Miller left the person he was dealing with, and came across. He entered the room, and I closed the door.

'Miller. Please phone upstairs and ask Mr Eric Swayne to come down. You will find him having coffee with the typists. Do not say anything, other than I wish to speak to him urgently.' Miller nodded and left the room.

'May I sit down again, please?' asked Jordan.

'Yes.' I heard my voice tremble slightly. I wasn't sure how much more I could stand. Jordan was speaking again.

'I'd like to ask you a question while we're waiting, if I may?'

'Go on.'

'At the desk, you mentioned the name "Marie". Why was that?'

'Marie Fowler, your predecessor.'

'Of course, but why should you think I would come down here because you gave her name?'

'She's missing isn't she? Presumed kidnapped.' My breathing was getting laboured. I felt a small pool of sweat gathering at the base of my spine.

'Again, yes. I concede; had you been bearing a message

111

from kidnappers, I would have been concerned to receive it.' I looked at him. It was like he was playing chess. He was enjoying it! 'Surely, however, you didn't think I would risk her life, when, due to her . . . er . . . absence, I have had the good fortune to be promoted.'

'I knew you'd care. Personally.'

'How is that?' he asked, still smiling.

'"The Impact of Technology on Occupational Structure etc." Your book. Remember? "To my dearest Marie." You dedicated it to her.' Jordan's expression changed again, to surprise, and then to something bordering on respect. There was a knock at the door which surprised us both.

'Come in,' he called. The door opened, and in came a plump, fair-haired man. I gestured with the gun. He almost jumped out of his skin.

'Stand on the other side of the table, next to Mr Jordan,' I said. Jordan spoke to Miller, who was standing in the doorway.

'That will be all, thank you Miller.' The door closed.

'What is your name, please?' I asked the newcomer.

'Eric Swayne,' he answered.

'Are you sure?'

'Of course I am.'

I lifted the gun and shot him once, between the eyes.

17

I stood looking at the body lying crumpled in front of me. People were rushing everywhere, commands were being shouted, but I was oblivious to all of it. Somehow I no longer cared. I was conscious of someone taking the gun out of my hand and removing my rucksack, but I couldn't take my eyes off Swayne, the look of surprise on his face, and the little black hole, like a third eye, in the middle of his forehead. Demon had been wrong. It was easy to kill someone – too bloody easy – and I didn't feel a thing. For six years I had worked, schemed and planned just for this moment. I had imagined every single step, run it through my mind a hundred times, considered every possibility, except this. I had known from the start it would end in my pulling a trigger, sticking someone with a knife, or twisting a wire around someone's neck, but that was the one part I'd never thought about or imagined. Now there was a dead man in front of me; I knew I had pulled that trigger, but I didn't believe it, the link wasn't there. I felt as though I was watching a film on the Box. There was the baddie, dead on the floor, and there was the girl, smoking gun in hand.

'Miss? Miss?' I turned to the voice at my ear. It was Miller. On each side of him were guards, pointing machine guns at me. He nodded to them and they each grabbed one of my arms. I was lifted almost bodily off the floor, and was about to be taken out of the room, when Jordan stopped them. He came right up to me and, very gently, put his hand under my chin and lifted my head till our eyes met. He looked at me for a few seconds, then stepped back. I was whisked out of the room, along a corridor, down a spiral staircase, along another corridor, and down a flight of steps. There was a heavy steel door ahead of us. I was marched to it and one of the guards unlocked it.

'In you go, Miss,' he said, stepping out of the way. I paused, and looked at him. He stood implacably in front of me and hoisted his machine gun across his chest. It was not a threatening gesture, but I knew what he meant. I went into the room, and the door closed behind me.

The room was four metres square, with absolutely nothing in it. The walls were unbroken by any window, and I remembered that we were at least two levels below ground. I was too tense to sit on the floor, so I paced around the room. A few minutes later a Snorter came in with an ink pad and some paper. Without speaking he took my wrist and forced my fingers on to the pad. Then he took each finger in turn and rolled it on to the paper, leaving a neat set of fingerprints. He left without a word. An hour later there was a knock on the door and it opened. Two Snorters stood on the threshold.

'This way, Miss,' said the one who had spoken before. I stepped into the corridor, where I saw a third man in a suit. He set off, and I followed, flanked by the Snorters. I was led to a room on the same corridor. The door was opened by the man in the suit. I was sat in a chair in the middle of the room, and my arms were strapped to the chair. Facing me was a long table. The Snorters took up positions on either side of me. The man in the suit sat at the table and was joined by another bloke. They left a space at the table in the middle, directly opposite me.

'Please remain silent until the Settlement Proceedings are officially opened,' said the newcomer.

We sat in silence for another few minutes, and then the door opened behind me and the guards snapped to attention. A little geezer in glasses came into my field of vision. He sat at the middle chair and put some things down on the desk. I saw a file with a photograph of me pinned to the front. He opened a notebook, and began to read from it.

'I am obliged by Rule 3, Sub-Rule 7 of the Usurpation Order 1999, as amended, to caution you that these are Settlement Proceedings as defined by that Order, and that everything you say will be recorded and may be used against you.' He rattled it off so fast I could barely understand what he was on about, but I'd come over so tired, I wasn't really listening anyway.

'You are obliged to answer my questions. Failure to do so may result in your summary execution. Do you understand?' I nodded. I was too tired to do anything else.

'You have to answer. A nod doesn't register on the recording.'

'Yes.'

'You are Kate Mason, 34 Aldersbrook Bridge, Manor Park, E.11., Social Security number M487 2011 769E. Lives with mother, name Jean Heather Mason and . . . Sidney Penton . . . father deceased . . .'

'What! What do you mean, "deceased"?'

'Er, yes, that's right,' he said calmly, looking back a page in his notes, 'remains found Romford High Street on . . . let me see . . .'

He paused, lost in his notes. The man to his left put a hand on his arm and said something quietly to him, and he looked up at me.

'Are you all right, Miss Mason?' he said. 'Miss Mason?'

I sat there, stunned. So Mum had been right after all. He'd been done in on his way back from his bit of 'spare' up Romford. I felt numb.

'Miss Mason? Shall I continue or would you like a short adjournment? Miss Mason?'

115

'What? No . . . no . . . that'll be all right . . . you carry on, mate.'

He shrugged. 'As you wish.'

There followed an hour of questioning. Position to be taken, experience, skills, and so on. Then there was a pause while the three men conferred. One of the other two, who had not until then said anything, addressed me.

'Miss Mason, there are a couple of other matters that must be cleared up before you are allowed to leave. The first is that we must inform you that your Dole entitlement from office number . . .' he paused and referred to his papers, 'D45 is terminated forthwith. Your Medicard and Social Security fiche have been withdrawn. Are you listening, Miss Mason?' I realized that my head was beginning to drop on to my chest. I had missed his last words.

'What this means, of course, is that should you pass the Competency Board in seven days' time, you will be unable in any event to change your mind. You have committed yourself irrevocably. Do you understand?'

'Yes.' My voice was hoarse. Of course I knew. Everybody knew; once inside it was a question of survival. Do the job – or you were out, Street Scum. Back on the Outside, but with no Dole, no home, nothing.

'There's one other matter . . .' He stopped, and began fiddling with some of the console buttons in front of him. I caught an inflection in his voice that hadn't been there before. I realized that the other two men were looking hard at me, and there was an air of tension in the room. The previous comments had been fillers; he had been working up to this last question. I kept my head down and tried not to show that I had noticed anything.

'That is the question of your entry into the City. Did you have help?' I was about to answer him when he cut in. 'That is, from *Inside*,' he added with a casualness which belied his intensity. A voice answered him immediately from behind my chair.

'Come on, Mr Cheevers, that question is not relevant to these proceedings, as you very well know.' It was Jordan. I hadn't heard him enter, and I wondered how long he'd been there. 'That is a matter for internal security, which, as I'm sure you'll appreciate, is *my* concern. In any event, Miss Mason has to take up her new duties tomorrow and I would like her as fresh as possible. This really isn't the time for inconsequential chit-chat.' I could hear the smile in his voice, but there was a hard edge to it as well. Again, I had the sense of something going on which didn't really involve me.

The inquisitor paused, like he wasn't sure if he should press the point. Then he smiled, and conceded.

'Yes, of course, Mr Jordan. You are absolutely right.' He beamed at me, showing a row of sharp white teeth, like a shark's. 'Thank you, Miss Mason, I think that will be all for the present. I declare this Tribunal adjourned for seven days, to 6th April.' I had the impression that a little battle had just been fought, and Jordan had won.

The three men stood, and came round the table towards me. The guards undid the straps securing my arms. Cheevers held out his hand to me.

'Best of luck. Mr Tench here will attend to the remaining forms, and you will be taken to your accommodation. We provide a courtesy car to take you to the apartment of the deceased. I gather Swayne lived in some style,' he said with a mysterious smile, and left the room.

'The apartment of the deceased?' I asked, turning to the others.

'Yes,' said the third inquisitor. He was tall and thin, and his suit looked two sizes too large. He handed me a sheaf of papers and an envelope.

'It's all explained in there. Please make sure that you

read it. Part of your Competency Hearing will be on the contents. I must draw your attention to Obligation 14, the effect of which is that the Usurper is obliged to make the reparations listed in the Schedule, to the spouse and/or offspring of the Usurped within the required period, which effectively means twenty weeks from today's date. Obligation 25 requires you, of course, to take upon yourself all rent and/or mortgage obligations of the Usurped. You will be given time to meet any arrears that may exist. Failure to do so may be considered by the Means Committee, but eventual default will mean eviction and possible loss of your Work Card. Sign here please,' he said, holding out a clipboard and a pen. I signed.

'Please note that you are also signing for the receipt of one hundred New Sovereigns enclosed herewith. The loan is repayable out of your first month's wages if Competency is proved. If not, it is deducted from your estate.' With that he left.

I turned to Jordan. I was exhausted; on the point of collapse. I could feel my lips trembling as I spoke.

'He still didn't explain. I have to live in Swayne's apartment?' I had visions of going back to his family, the murderer of a father, a husband.

'Of course,' replied Jordan, 'where else could you go? There's a fixed number of workers, a fixed number of apartments. Surely you realized that. You take over his job, his *place*, in fact, his entire life.'

'But his family . . . I can't stay with them . . .'

'You can. You have no choice. In fact you're rather lucky. As far as I can gather, there wasn't much in the way of family at all. Come on. There's a car outside.' He took my arm.

I was escorted out into a sort of pound, surrounded on

all sides by a huge wall topped with spikes. In the middle was the flashiest transport I had ever seen.

'I'll see you tomorrow, bright and early. Don't worry,' said Jordan with a smile. 'You'll cope.'

I got into the limousine. We moved off, descending a ramp which I realized went under the Wall. We came up again into busy streets. I wanted to watch but I could barely keep my eyes open. I hadn't slept for a day and a half. In that time I'd been half drowned, threatened with guns, and interrogated. And I'd killed someone. All I wanted to do was sleep, and I had to face the wife of the man I'd just killed. I suddenly realized that I didn't have my rucksack. I sat up with a start, and then saw it next to me on the back seat of the transport. I grabbed it and went through it. No gun. I didn't have time to think any more about it, as the transport had stopped. The driver turned to me and slid back the glass partition which separated us.

'Second floor, Miss Mason, apartment 216.'

'How do I get in? Who's up there?'

'I can't help you, I'm afraid, Miss. Try ringing the doorbell.' The rear door opened automatically. I grabbed the rucksack and climbed out of the transport. The door closed and the vehicle sped silently away. I walked across the pavement and pushed the swing doors in front of me to be greeted by a person coming the other way wearing an evening gown, a fur stole, and three days' growth of beard.

'Thank you my dear,' it breathed silkily, as it wafted past me in a cloud of perfume. Unable to find a lift, I climbed a flight of stairs and found the door marked 216. I took a deep breath and rang the bell. No one answered. Eventually I tried the door. It opened. I stepped into shag-piled darkness. I reached for a light switch, found one, and saw that I was in a hallway hung with paintings, predominantly of naked men in athletic poses. Four doors opened off the hall. I weighed my choices. If there was someone in one of the rooms they would certainly have heard the bell, which meant that I had no chance of taking them by surprise. On the other hand, if I called out they would know I was a girl, and alone. I decided on stealth. As quietly as I could, I stepped to the nearest door and listened. I heard nothing. I turned the handle as slowly as I could, and opened the door a fraction. The room was in half darkness, but it was empty. I went to the next door, and opened that like the first. It was a kitchen, and also empty. I was about to close the door again when I had an idea. I went over to the far wall where, next to the window, was a rack of knives. I took the largest and crept back to the hall. Two doors left. I chose the one on the left, immediately adjoining the front door. I opened the door with my left hand, the knife in my right. This room was also in darkness, but this time the darkness was complete, but for a thin slit of light coming from the almost-drawn curtains on the far side. I felt for a light switch and found nothing. I took a half step into the room when, suddenly, a light blazed on. I looked up, and dropped the knife at the same time.

'Another migraine, Duckie? Or is this an afternoon quickie?' said a blond man from the bed. He rolled over to face me. 'Jesus Christ!' he said as he saw me. 'Who the hell are you?'

18

'I hope that's not too uncomfortable,' I said, as I stepped back to survey my handiwork. The blond man was securely bound to a kitchen stool. His ankles were tied to the legs, and his wrists tied together behind his back and then under the stool to the front legs. For good measure, I had secured another rope around his neck, and looped it around the light fitting above his head. If he struggled, and fell off the stool, he would probably hang himself.

'I'm sorry about this,' I said, and genuinely meant it. He looked so forlorn in his striped silk pyjamas and slippers. 'But I have to sleep for a few hours, and I just can't trust you.'

'What do you think I would do?'

'I don't know. But I don't know who you are, or what you're doing here – *and*,' I raised my voice as he tried to say something, 'I don't care, at least for the moment. I'll feel better in a while, and then we can work it out.' I went to the door and propped it open with my rucksack. I looked around the room and then walked back past him to the window.

'I'd best take these so you won't be tempted,' I said, as I removed the rest of the knives and put them in a drawer well out of reach.

'You can't do this,' he said.

'Oh God! You sound like an old movie. Don't you mean, "You'll never get away with it"?'

'My . . . the owner will be back any minute. He only popped out . . .' He stopped as he saw me shaking my head.

'No,' I said, firmly, but quietly. 'Mr Swayne has not "just popped out". And he won't be coming back.' He started to say something else and then hesitated. He looked at my dress, and then across to the rucksack. He slowly returned his gaze to me.

'You . . . you're . . .' he whispered. He shook his head slowly. 'Eric,' he finished. His eyebrows contracted into what I at first took for a frown, and his whole body shook with a sob. His head bowed, and the rope pulled taut, but he seemed oblivious to it.

'You've . . . killed . . . him?' he said between gasps. I went to one of the drawers and found a cloth. I lifted up his head. There were tears running down his face.

'Open your mouth.' He looked at me. I couldn't meet his eyes. 'Open your goddam mouth!' I shouted, 'or I'll cut you!' I looked round for the knife. At that second I couldn't see it but he did what he was told. I stuffed the cloth in hard until he gagged. I then left the room without looking back. There was no way I was going to be made to feel guilty for grabbing my one chance of life, even if it had meant shooting his little friend.

He was exactly where I had left him two hours before. He looked up as I entered the kitchen. His eyes were red, and his face blotchy, but he had stopped crying. I took the gag from his mouth.

'Do you want a drink?' He nodded. I found a glass and filled it with water and offered it to him. He looked at me quizzically. I put it down, took the knife, and stood before him.

'If I cut you loose, will you assure me that you won't try anything?'

'Yes.'

'Because I'll have no hesitation . . .' I held the knife up.

'I promise.' I bent down behind him and cut the rope

122

tying his wrists. His legs were still bound to the stool, and his neck was still in the noose. He rubbed his arms to get the circulation going again and I handed him the glass. He dropped it immediately, spilling water over his lap, and I caught the glass as it rolled off his legs. He lurched forward, and the noose tightened. I set the glass down and reached above his head.

'Wait a second and I'll take this off,' I said.

'I'm sorry. My fingers are still numb.' I filled the glass again, and this time he took it. He drank carefully from it, watching me over the rim of the glass.

'What's your name?' I asked from the doorway, still holding the knife.

'Graham. Graham Price.'

'I'm Kate Mason.' The conversation faltered immediately.

'How long have you lived with . . .' I said eventually.

'Two years.' Another long pause.

'Look – '

'Why – ' we both started together.

'I don't know what I'm supposed to say. I didn't know him. He was just a name . . . no . . . not even a name . . . just a job. I'm sorry. You've got no idea what it's like Outside. There's nothing . . . he was . . . it was my *only* opportunity . . .' I trailed off. 'Look!' I shouted. 'I don't owe you an explanation! I did it, right? I killed him, right?'

He stared at me and I looked down. I felt he could see straight through me.

'It's funny,' he began, quietly, 'but although you live with the threat every day and, God knows, everyone knows *someone* who's been attacked at least . . . it never touches you. You always think, "someone else" . . .'

I stared at the wet patch on his pyjamas. It had soaked through and I could see his genitals as if he wasn't wearing anything. He didn't seem to notice.

123

'One of the waiters at the restaurant didn't come in one day – we all knew why, it was on the Box – but we all pretended it hadn't happened. As though he had just gone away, abroad or something, even though we knew it wasn't possible. It was like an unspoken conspiracy. No one ever mentioned it.' He looked up at me. 'Funny, though. You always picture a man.'

'A man?'

'Some thug with muscles and a machine gun, I suppose. Not someone like you.' He paused. 'Still, a sort of poetic justice there I suppose.' I looked puzzled but he just shrugged. There was another long pause.

'How did you do it?' he asked.

'What?'

'Well, with a knife?' he said, indicating the bread knife in my hand.

'Do you really want to know?'

He shrugged again. 'I just wondered.'

'A gun. He didn't even know.' Graham nodded. 'You don't seem very upset,' I commented.

'He was . . . well, he wasn't an easy man.'

'Why live with him then?' I asked, thinking of the Prick.

'It seemed a good idea at the time. I thought I . . . I thought it would work . . .'

'And?'

'I made a mistake.'

'Why stay then?'

He looked at me strangely. 'You can't just up and move, you know. We had to wait two years before we were allocated this apartment. I don't know what it's like Outside, but Inside you live where you're told. Anyway, I hoped it would improve. It was good once, before we started living together.'

'It seems I've done you a good turn then.'

124

'How do you work that out?'

'They'll have to rehouse you now.'

'Oh yes?'

'Why not?'

'I've just told you. They can't rehouse you; there's nowhere for you to go. Surely they told you that when you . . . Usurped?'

'This is ridiculous!' I shouted, pacing up and down the room. 'I don't want some fucking pansy getting in my way!'

'I don't suppose either of us is terribly happy at the prospect,' he replied, icily, 'but the fact remains, we're stuck here, like it or not. You can stick your name on the waiting list for what they call a "Favoured Grant" by all means, but, like I said, it takes years. Otherwise, you need compelling reasons to obtain permission to change residence. And incompatibility of sexual orientation isn't enough.'

I whirled round, about to hit him. He just looked calmly at me. I turned away and sat on the floor, my back to the wall. He started undoing the ropes around his ankles.

'How do I know you won't attack me at the first opportunity?'

'Do I look the type to "attack" you?' I looked at him; he didn't.

'I don't know. Maybe.'

'Anyway, why should I? I can't do Eric's – your job, and anyway, it's illegal for Workers to Usurp for another job. It's all right for you; for us it's murder. And they hang you for it. I lived with him, yes and slept with him on occasions, but I wouldn't swing for him.'

I considered it, and I believed him. But that still left me with the problem of what to do with him.

'Can you do anything?' I asked.

'*Do* anything?'

'Yes. Could you make yourself useful around the place?'

125

'I'm not your bloody servant! We can come to some arrangement about the housework, and I don't mind doing the cooking, at least if we're in for the same meals. But apart from that, you're on your own.'

'Can you cook?' The concept of a man cooking was a new one.

'I can cook, as you put it.' He sat back on the stool, and rubbed his ankles.

'You have a Work Permit?'

'Of course. I'm the chef at "Chez Maurice".'

'Is that a restaurant? Where they serve food?'

Again he looked at me as if I was crazy. 'Yes, it's a restaurant where they serve food. Where have you been? It's known all over London, abroad as well.'

'We don't have them on the Outside. You don't understand.'

'Obviously not.'

He made to leave the kitchen. I jumped up and barred his way. 'Where are you going?' I demanded.

'I'm going to have a bath and get dressed. I'm working tonight, and I've a lot to do before I leave.' He stared at me with his head on one side, as if challenging me. I stood aside.

'Thank you.'

He turned back halfway down the corridor. 'The spare room is here,' he said, indicating the doorway to his right. 'It has its own bathroom, and the bed is already made up. I'd rather you slept there in the future, if you don't mind.' He disappeared into his room, but then his head popped out again. 'And if you will permit me, may I suggest you make use of the bath as soon as possible. You smell like a sewer.'

'It's 'cos I've been in the Thames,' I said, embarrassed.

'Pleased to hear it. I didn't like to say anything – especially while you were wielding that bread knife – but

126

I didn't relish the prospect of living with someone who dabs untreated sewage behind her ears.' He smiled briefly, for the first time since I'd met him, and closed his bedroom door.

I stared out of the kitchen window at the street lights below and, beyond the houses opposite, to the lights of the traffic. It was almost midnight, yet it was busier outside now than Ilford ever was. Despite all the extraordinary information that Graham had given me none of it had the same effect as simply looking out of the window. There, right before my eyes, was the proof that I had made it. I was Inside! I was part of the Working Class, a valuable member of the community. I had a chance to contribute, to prove myself. My mind turned to Dad. I wished he could have been there to see me. I forced myself to think about other things, the problems of living with Graham, the next day's work. I'd had my little cry while in the bath, and that was enough.

I was in a part of London called 'Bloomsbury'. Even the name somehow excited me. I had asked Graham about the area.

'Well, it used to be terribly trendy.'

'Trendy?'

'Yes, just *the* place where everyone wanted to live. Poets, artists and so on. That was two hundred years ago, of course, but it has always had that sort of reputation.' I remembered something.

'As I came in, there was a person on the stairs . . .'

'Dark, shoulder-length hair, too much make-up and cheap perfume?'

'Could be.'

'Probably Jeremy. Lovely girl,' he said drily. 'He's next door.'

'Are there many people like . . . er . . . you and Jeremy . . . in London?'

'You mean homosexuals?' he asked, with heavy emphasis on the last word. 'God, Kate, you're like something out of the Ark.'

'I'm sorry, it's just that there aren't any . . . well . . . it's just different Outside . . .'

'Forget it. To answer your question, yes, I suppose there are a few in Bloomsbury.'

'But how can he walk around like that? He wouldn't survive five minutes in Ilford.'

'This isn't Ilford. People are obviously more tolerant here. Of course, you have to be careful, even if you're straight. There are certain areas that no one goes to after dark.'

'Yes?'

'Regent's Park, for example. That's where the real freaks live, you know, the Pinkies.'

'The what?' I asked, smiling. He looked puzzled, not laughing at all.

'You really don't know, do you?' I shook my head. 'You're going to need a crash course in survival, my girl. Okay. The Pinkies.' He took a deep breath. 'All you really need to know is that they're dangerous, really dangerous. They work for the MSD, the Ministry for Spiritual Development. You'll see them on the streets I expect, or rather, you'll hear them.'

'I don't understand. It's a state department?'

'"God is State, State is God",' he intoned, holding his hands aloft and tapping his little fingers against his thumbs as though holding finger cymbals. 'You can hear them a quarter of a mile away, chanting and dancing. Yes, they're a sort of government department. Their offices are in the same building as Eric – you – work in. You'll see them there.'

'Why are they called "Pinkies"?'

'Don't ask me. Probably those awful pink robes they wear,' he said with his cynical smile. 'The Pastors, like the ones working at your office, wear – wait for it – pink three-piece suits. Or maybe because they ring those little cymbals all the time,' and he raised his hands over his head again and made the same movement with his little fingers. 'You know, as in using their "pinkies"?'

'And they're dangerous?'

'Just you believe it. Oh, they'll offer you flowers and all that, but there are some pretty unpleasant stories about them. I wouldn't go anywhere near the Park after dark. Anyway, I've got to go.'

'Go where? It's nearly midnight.'

'I told you – to work. My dear girl, some of us have to earn a living. I'm due at the Restaurant – in fact I'm already late.'

'At this hour?'

'"Chez Maurice" is one of *the* nightspots in London. Cabaret from midnight to four every night. Full à la carte menu till six in the morning.'

'What's "à la carte"?'

He shook his head. 'Eating Out is dealt with in Lesson Three.'

I smiled. I was beginning to like him. I followed him to the door.

'There's a spare set of keys in the top drawer of my chest,' he said. 'You'd better have them. Double lock, if you go out.'

'I'm not going anywhere,' I said, 'except bed.' He turned to go. 'Graham?' I called.

'Yes?'

'I'm sorry that it was Eric.'

He looked at the floor and didn't answer at first.

'Yeh,' he said. 'See you in the morning.'

19

Despite the sound of the traffic, which went on all night,
I slept pretty well. I was woken at Eight-O by Graham
knocking on the bedroom door. At first I couldn't remember where I was, and then it came flooding back: I was
Inside; Dad was dead.

'Come in,' I called. Graham came in bearing a tray.

'I was making some eggs and thought you might like
some too,' he said, and put the tray on the floor by my
side. There was a plate of scrambled eggs and the best-
smelling coffee I had ever come across. Only then did I
realize that I had forgotten to lock the bedroom door as I
had intended.

'Thanks,' I said, and sat up. He made as if to leave.
'No, hang on.' I took a mouthful of scrambled egg. It was
delicious.

'Jesus!' I said, mouth full. 'This is terrific! I've never
tasted eggs like it.' He moved to the door again.

'No, don't go. Stay and tell me more about London.'

'Wait a second . . .' he said, leaving the room. He
returned almost immediately, carrying a clean pair of
pyjamas. I'd never seen any in real life, but I knew from
the films what they were.

'Put that on,' he said, handing me the top.

'Why? Does it bother you?' I asked, looking down at
my bare chest with some surprise.

'No, it doesn't bother me. Just cover yourself up, eh?'
I shrugged, and pulled on the pyjama top.

'Now, talk to me,' I commanded.

'What do you want to know?'

'I don't know. Everything. What about where you work. Tell me about that.'

He sat on the bed while I ate, and chatted for a few minutes about the restaurant and his night's work. The club sounded great – just the sort of thing I'd expected – good food, real wine, waitresses, performers. I finished my coffee and began to get out of bed.

'I'll leave you to it,' he said, and scuttled out. Funny that: for the last God knows how long, it was all I could do to get a minute's privacy away from the Prick's wandering eyes and hands, and here I was with a poof who wasn't in the least interested, but still blushed at the sight of a pair of tits! It didn't make sense.

He knocked on the door again just as I was finishing. He looked carefully at me, and then shook his head.

'You can't possibly go out like that,' he said finally.

'Why on earth not?' I asked, offended. I was wearing my best – and only – dress.

'Well, I don't know what they wear in Ilford, but that won't do here. Unless the idea is to look conspicuous.'

'That is *not* the idea.'

'I didn't think so.'

'Well, what am I going to do then?'

'Wait there,' he said, and disappeared. I heard the front door open. Five minutes later he knocked on the bedroom door and entered with an armful of clothes.

'Where did you get – oh, Jeremy.'

'He says, for God's sake don't spill anything on them. I've brought a selection. See what you like.' I went through the dresses. I had never seen anything like them. I had a thought, and went to the rucksack and brought out the Captain's silk scarf.

'One of them's got to match this,' I said.

'Are you quite sure? The colour's not really . . .' He must have seen the look on my face, because he stopped.

'Try this one then,' he said. He handed me a tailored suit. I put it on. The skirt was perfect. The jacket was too broad, and I looked at Graham for guidance.

'Very chic. Really,' he assured, tying the belt for me so that it hung by my side. 'The nineteen thirties are very "in" this season. You know, wide shoulders and all that.'

'I know, you mean, like what's her name? With Bogart.'

'Lauren Bacall. I'm surprised you know who she is.'

'Don't ever challenge an Outsider to a movie quiz, that's all. There's nothing to do except watch the Box. We're all experts.'

'What about these?' he asked, holding up some stockings. I gasped. Ever since I was fifteen, luxury for me wasn't eating in restaurants, nor flying all over the world in jetplanes. It was silk stockings.

'Yes. I'll wear them.' I put them on, Graham showing me how the suspenders worked. I stepped back and did a twirl.

'Well?' I asked.

'Not bad,' he said quietly, and then smiled. 'It's almost enough to make a chap reconsider.'

I turned and looked in the mirror. It was quite a transformation. I wouldn't have recognized myself.

'I think we're going to have to call you Eliza.'

'Sorry?'

'As in Dolittle.'

'Do what?'

'Never mind.'

'Tell me something, Graham. Where do I work?'

'Red Lion Street. You can take the Tube if you like – Central Line to Holborn – but if the weather's nice, you can walk it in fifteen minutes.'

'What about a torch?'

'Torch?'

'To get home in the dark.'

He laughed. 'No, I should think the street lights will be perfectly adequate.'

'But I'll be coming back before Lights On.'

'Look, as it gets dark, the lights go on. It's really quite simple.'

'Oh,' I said, feeling like an idiot. I went back to the kitchen to look for a knife. Graham followed me in and watched over my shoulder while I selected a blade that Knife would have given his eye teeth for.

'You won't need it,' said Graham.

'I'll take it just the same.'

'Suit yourself.' I intended to. I wasn't going outside without a weapon, whatever everyone else did. I knew better – after all, I'd done it myself hadn't I? I knew thirty Jobbers, sitting in Ilford Library that very minute, who'd kill me as soon as spit. I was taking no chances.

'Have you thought about what you're going to do after work?'

'I haven't a clue,' I answered.

'Well, I'm on early tonight as there's a special cabaret. Private function. If you fancy coming to the Restaurant about Eight-O, I can get you in to dinner on the house.'

'On the what?'

'It's an expression. It means "paid for by the establishment".'

'Yes, okay. It's just as well. According to this,' I said, brandishing my 'Obligations', 'I don't get paid until after my Competency Test, or whatever it is. I've only got a hundred New Sovs.'

'That won't last long. It's settled then. I'll leave you instructions on how to get there for when you get home. Best of luck today.'

'Thanks.'

I walked down the stairs, through the doors, and

133

emerged, on to what I later discovered was Bedford Square, feeling more splendid than I had ever felt in my entire life. My first shock was the number of people; there must have been a hundred within my range of vision, more than I had ever seen on the streets except at a tobacco bust. And women, on their own and in twos and threes, none of them carrying weapons or looking over their shoulders. I turned right into a street as wide as Ilford High Street, and stopped almost immediately. Shops! On both sides of the road, selling books, food, furniture, and clothes as grand as the ones I was wearing. And the noise! There were transporters everywhere, cars like the one I had been taken home in the day before; and buses, big red ones, like straight out of the films. That was a real surprise, as somehow I didn't think they'd have them any more. You never saw recent pictures of Inside on the Box, even on the Nooz. Whenever they showed London, they used old film clips and library pictures. I'd always thought that the reason was that if they showed how good the Working Class really had it, there would be a mass revolt. So it was a real surprise to see those old red buses. I could just hear Demon saying how it was an anachronism. Just the sort of word he'd have picked up.

The next surprise was that there wasn't a single Snorter in sight. No harassment for the Working Class, I thought wryly.

I carried on walking and reached a major road junction. The traffic was continuous, and I was glad that I didn't need to cross the road. I followed the pavement around the corner into a road called New Oxford Street, walked a bit further, and then came to a crossroads that I *did* have to cross. I waited with everyone else on the corner, and after a minute or two, the traffic stopped and the pedestrians crossed. I ran across with them.

I paused outside the government building and looked up at the metre-high steel letters above the doors: 'Department of Social Planning'. I took a deep breath. This is it. As I approached the sliding doors they opened for me, and I stepped into the lobby. Miller was not on duty, which disappointed me, as I rather wanted to see a familiar face. I approached the Enquiry desk and told the attendant who I was. He pressed a few buttons set into the desk, looked at the screen, and handed me my Work Card.

'Seventh floor please, Miss Mason. A Miss Jennifer Stillgo will meet you at the lift.' I thanked him and walked past the security guards to the metal barriers. I stepped between the electronic portals and handed my Card to another man. He examined it, placed it into a slot in the terminal beside him and handed it back to me. I was allowed to approach the lifts. I waited with a group of people for the lift to arrive and looked at the card in my hand. That little piece of plastic, ten centimetres by five, was what I'd waited for, planned for, and finally killed for. Dad would have been proud of me. I was now a member of the Working Class.

20

All those days Jobbing had been a waste of time. I had massively over-researched Swayne's job. The work was a real joke. He just collated information from the Census for processing without needing to understand what he was doing at all. Once I had discovered which form to use in each case, and how they were marked for use by the Computer – which took about an hour – I could've done it standing on my head. I found the attitude of Swayne's late colleagues even more surprising. I'd expected a rough ride from them for having murdered their mate. Not at all. Those who didn't work directly with him seemed for the most part disinterested; the men, I suspected, relieved to be free of his wandering hands. Those who worked closest with him, the four other members of his group, were actually delighted. He had apparently been a lazy gossip, and they'd carried him. I was shown how to log on and how to input data, and any questions I had were answered with friendliness.

My biggest problem was trying to familiarize myself with the political landscape; it was a nightmare. On every floor, in every department, in every office, there was deadly internecine warfare. I'd expected people to have friends; girls going off to the canteen together, chat about their boyfriends. Not a bit of it; everyone kept to themselves, and no one trusted anyone else. People would approach you to see what you knew, and whether you were 'With them' or not. Within minutes I discovered that the Director of Family Planning and his lot were making a bid to oust the Director of Census Studies – my immediate superior; the Deputy-Director of Population Control had recently been replaced by his assistant, but was rumoured to have stage managed the whole thing so he could move sideways into Administration where, it was said, the Director was about to be sacked.

Overlaying all this was something I knew only too well. I hadn't been in the office for more than half an hour before I was propositioned by some oik from 'Printing'. I told him, as sweetly as I could, what I proposed doing to his softer parts, and he ran. No sooner had he pissed off than another bloke from my own department tried it on. I sussed it out soon enough. The men, especially the 'high flyers' in the fast stream, cultivated 'harems' of less influential women, all of whom were expected to welcome their sexual favours in return for protection against dismissal. Most, if not all, complied. I was grabbed more often than a whore's arse in those first few hours in the building and, by lunchtime, my breasts and bottom were blue with bruises. It was quite a comedown I can tell you. I'd finally got away from the Prick's amateur advances, and here I was, surrounded by professionals.

Still, I soon realized that to refuse an outright approach was to court danger; when in Rome, and all that. Besides, there was always the possibility of turning some little liaison to my advantage. With this in mind, I graciously accepted the offer to join Derek Richmond, Chief Planning Executive of the Film and Video Censorship Department, for a cup of coffee.

God, he was ugly, and from the nature of his conversation he was evidently much influenced by his daily tasks. He suggested, in his best 'Hello-little-girl-would-you-like-a-sweetie' tones, that we might 'get together' one night to view his private collection of out-takes. I nearly puked. I teased him with a postponement, and told him I'd let him know.

That was my first mistake. On returning to the office, Marcie, the Director's personal assistant, took me to one side.

'Just a word, dear, seeing as you've got "green" written all over you. I think you should know that not only is Richmond a pervert of the first order, he's also on the way out.'

'Out?' I questioned uncomfortably.

'Well and truly; the stuff Street Scum are made of, if you know what I mean. He's been caught too many times with his fingers in the film-can, so to speak. He won't get you anywhere, dear.' I blanched; what a fuck-up. 'Stick to safe options,' she said somewhat enigmatically, then returned to her desk.

Great. Four hours in and already I was associating with a loser, a passport straight back to Ilford, only this time it would be life among the Derros and Scum. I sat down to think. My new, dazzling environment had blinded me; this place was more complicated and dangerous than it looked.

The opportunity to redress the balance came the next morning. During the morning coffee break, I noticed Marcie and Don Marshall, the Director, engaged in a little tête-à-tête that was anything but businesslike. So she was more than just his typist. I hung around nearby, busying myself with rearranging those ridiculous silk stockings. Demon always got worked up over my long legs, and I was counting on Mr Marshall feeling the same. It appeared that he did. He dismissed Marcie, and loped towards me like a dog on heat. This time I was on to a dead cert. I made for the fire escape, opened the door, checked that no one was around, and then beckoned to him with a barely perceptible nod. You wanna play?

And there, with my back pressed against the doorway,

and Mr Marshall's baggy pants around his ankles, I took the matter in hand, so to speak.

Sure, he was as despicable as the rest of them, but he was the Director, and if he was a 'safe option' for Marcie, then he would do for me. I closed my mind to his pawing and panting, finished the job as quickly as I could then wiped my hands on his shirt tails.

'Plenty more where that came from, Mr Marshall,' I said, blowing him a kiss.

I returned to the office, leaving the Director of Census Studies standing on the cold, concrete landing drying his dick. Pathetic.

Half an hour later I was to discover that Hell hath no wrath like a personal assistant's scorn. A cup of cold coffee crashed on to my desk, saturating not only all the paperwork and forms, but Jeremy's fine-tailored suit. I looked up, to see a familiar figure standing over me. I was hardly surprised.

'What do you think you're playing at?' hissed Marcie. I stood up.

'Same game as you,' I said coolly, trying to brush some of the liquid off my skirt. 'You've ruined it,' I tutted, then shook my head. 'You really should be more careful.'

'My God but you learn fast,' she sneered. I stared straight back; there was no way she was going to frighten me.

'Yes,' I said, smiling sweetly, 'I do, don't I?'

Above all this, supreme and untouchable, reigned the Minister himself, Henry Jordan. I didn't see him that day, although I was told that he worked phenomenally long hours, but I found out a great deal about him. He was a favourite topic of conversation. For six years he had been Marie Fowler's lieutenant, adviser, confidant and, reputedly, lover. Since the disappearance of Ms Fowler he had become 'available', and every woman in the Department dreamed of the association which would immediately lift her out of the day-to-day skirmishes and engagements.

I met my first 'Pinkie' that day. The Ministry of Spiritual Development shared part of the building with us at Social Planning. Most Ministers guarded jealously the tokens of their position, particularly office space, but for some reason Jordan seemed unconcerned. The upper half of East Wing was given over to them. The junior officials wore flowing pink robes, and had their heads shaved. The higher ranks sported ridiculous three-piece suits in fluorescent cerise and called themselves 'Pastors'. They were to be found wandering about the corridors of East Wing chanting directives as if they were psalms.

The most extraordinary event of the day occurred during a break we took in the middle of the afternoon. A chap called Rupert, who worked in the Magazine Censorship Section across the corridor, opened the door to his office, climbed out on the window ledge and screamed at the top of his voice: 'I'm going to jump! I'm going to jump! Don't you try to stop me!' The two girls nearest him just ignored him. Three or four of the others from the adjoining offices stood in his doorway and hurled documents, requisition forms, departmental memos and insults at him and out of the window, shouting 'Go on!' and 'Jump, you miserable fucker! Do it, you arsehole!' After a few minutes they got bored and left him to it. Rupert whined for a short while, stepped back inside, closed the window and resumed work as if nothing had happened. Apparently he had done the same thing every day for the past six months. I couldn't understand how he had survived so long.

It transpired that Rupert was just the most recent in a long line of junior assistants who *had* jumped. When I started to ask questions, I was met – for the first time that day – with silence. No one wanted to talk about it.

I left work at Six-O, having accomplished twice as much in one day – according to Jennifer, who occupied the next desk to mine – as Swayne had ever done. I had two hours to kill before I had to be at the restaurant. I had planned to see some of the sights of the city, but I was exhausted. Even though the work had not been strenuous I had felt under a great deal of pressure during the day. So I decided to go to the apartment and have another bath. The power was never on long enough at home to heat up the water properly, so you never got a really hot bath. I intended to soak in piping hot water for at least an hour.

At Seven-Thirty I picked up the directions left for me by Graham on the kitchen table and took the Tube to Marble Arch. I strolled down this wide tree-lined street called Park Lane. I was wearing a black silk evening gown with no shoulders or straps, just metres of silk flaring out at the waist. Graham had left directions as to how to call a taxi, but it was a mild night, and I couldn't resist showing off on the Tube. I wasn't disappointed. People gaped as I stepped on to the platform, and there was a ripple of whispers wherever I went. If that Demon could see me now, I thought.

'Chez Maurice' was in the basement of a luxurious hotel. I was greeted at the door by a man in a dark suit and bow tie.

'Good evening. Kate Mason?'

'Yes. How did you know?'

'Graham told me to expect you. His description didn't do you justice.'

'Smooth-talking bastard,' I replied with a grin.

'Your shawl?' he said, holding out his hand.

'What about it?'

He smiled. 'Shall I put it in the cloakroom?'

'If you want,' I replied, and handed it to him.

He showed me to a corner table inside the restaurant a

141

few metres from the stage, from which I would have an excellent view, not only of the cabaret but also of the other diners. A woman in a black dress approached me and handed me a large piece of cardboard.

'Would Madam like a drink?' I knew she was talking to me, but that didn't lessen the thrill. I opened the card and found a list of words that made no sense. It wasn't in English. I hadn't anticipated this difficulty.

'May I recommend the claret,' she said, sensing my hesitation, and pointing over my shoulder at number eleven on the card.

'Er . . .'

'That's all right, Ruby, this lady's with me,' said Graham, taking a seat at the table. 'Bottle of Moët.' Turning to me he said, 'I'm glad you made it. How was work?'

'I don't know. The whole thing was strange. I think I did all right.' I couldn't concentrate on what he was saying. I didn't want to miss any part of what was going on around me.

'Graham, you simply can't imagine what this is like for me. It's like a dream. There's no such thing as restaurants outside the Wall, just plastic cups, and machines serving push-button drinks that all taste the same. Look,' I leaned towards him, 'what's claret?'

'It's a type of wine. Don't worry, you'll get used to this in no time. I'll order for you tonight. I can stay with you for a while, but I'll have to get back to the kitchen.' The champagne arrived and Ruby, the waitress, poured us each a glass.

'A votre santé,' said Graham, clinking glasses with me. I didn't know exactly what he meant, but I caught the sense.

'Cheers,' I said cautiously. 'Is that right?'

'Perfectly. Welcome to the real world.'

'Thanks. Let's hope it's not a temporary stay.'

'Don't think about that for tonight. Just have a good time.'

Graham stayed with me while I ate the first course. It was, he told me, shellfish. I couldn't pronounce the name of the dish. He was then called away to the kitchen and I was happy to divide my attention between the rest of the meal and the other diners. The entire room sparkled with jewellery. Every female wrist and bosom was decked with gems and stones, so that if you half closed your eyes it looked like moonlight on a turbulent river. All the women were in gowns like the one I wore, mainly in dark colours; black, blue and wine. The men wore dinner suits and bow ties, and they too wore jewellery, huge rings and bracelets.

Sitting on my own, I began to attract some attention. A fat middle-aged man at a table not far from mine began looking at me and trying to catch my eye. He was with a girl some years younger than he, but she was engrossed in talking to the woman opposite her. I was in the middle of my dessert when I thought he was about to get up and come over, when the lights in the room dimmed. The packed restaurant suddenly became hushed, and the fat man turned away from me to face the stage.

A man appeared on the stage and introduced the first act. A young couple entered on the stage, naked, and proceeded to screw. I watched, astonished, having forgotten the rest of my dessert. I glanced around me to see the reactions of the rest of the audience. They were all facing the stage, sipping their drinks, occasionally pointing at some move made by the performers, whispering to their companions. They acted as if it was perfectly normal! The act ended in heavy gasps from the performers and warm applause from the audience. It was followed by a pair of male gymnasts whose act was similar except they did it on a high wire. I watched in horrified fascination. I mean, apart from their balance, which was remarkable, who wanted to watch a couple of bum-bandits? I remembered that Graham had said that this was a private party, and wondered why on earth he had invited me. However, when the next act was announced I realized that this was not a cabaret staged for a private party of voyeurs; 'Les Benderos' were the resident artistes! These performers were just circus freaks, men and women with grotesquely over-sized organs, and their act entailed complicated and even more ambitious couplings with each other and themselves. To the delight of the audience, at one point a woman at a table on the far side of the room was induced, without too much persuasion, to lend her assistance to the performance.

I wondered if all the cabarets in London were on the same lines. I didn't want to appear provincial, and I'm no prude, but for me sex has never been a spectator sport. I was considering this when 'Les Benderos' finished their last 'bend', and the stage was left empty. Then came an amplified voice from off-stage.

'Ladies and gentlemen. Now comes the moment for which I'm sure we have all been waiting. Recently returned from his hugely acclaimed tour of the Continent, our next guest will need little introduction. The man whose name is on all our lips, and whose art expresses the mood of our generation, may I present to you that Master of Illusion, that Champion of the Chainsaw, the Demented Devil of Decapitation . . . The GRIM REAPER!'

The room erupted into rapturous applause and was plunged into total darkness. There was a long pause, and then a sudden flash of brilliant light and instantaneously there appeared on stage a girl in white robes floating horizontally a metre above the ground. Behind her stood a tall black figure in a cape, his features obscured by a hood. There shone a single spotlight from directly above his head. In his hands he wielded a scythe which gleamed and flashed in the spotlight. He moved his hands so that they were held as at prayer, but with the staff of the scythe between them. Then, with a deft movement of his hands and wrists only, keeping his elbows almost still, he twirled and spun the scythe, the blade describing patterns in the air. There seemed to be a continuous silver blur above his head, down by his feet, and skimming over the still form of the floating girl. He took a step back, the scythe still moving at lightning speed, and cut the air above, below and to the sides of the girl, proving that she was not suspended by any wires. Then with one final sweep, he brought the scythe up behind his shoulders, arched his back and, now using his whole body in one sinuous movement, brought the blade slicing down straight at the girl's breast. There was a sharp intake of breath in the room as the scythe stopped no more than the thickness of a dress above the girl. The watchers roared their approval.

I too applauded. The man's control was astonishing. He could have taught the Knife a thing or two! As the applause subsided, the Reaper reached down and picked something off the floor from underneath the girl. He approached the edge of the stage and held it out in his gloved hand. Only then did I realize that it was hair, locks of golden hair. I looked back at the girl, and saw that as the scythe had passed beneath her body, it had cut the hair that hung down beneath her from the back of her head. A pretty young lady from the audience stood and took the locks from the Reaper's outstretched hand, and kissed his fingers.

The Reaper returned to centre-stage and silence again

descended. Slowly, he raised his right hand and pointed dramatically into the audience.

'You!' He hissed. Everyone turned, and a lady in fur rose slowly to her feet. As if mesmerized, she walked slowly to the stage, and up the steps until she stood by his side. I realized then how tall he was as he towered above her by half a metre.

'Take her pulse!' commanded the Reaper, pointing to the floating girl. The woman did as she was told. 'Listen to her breathing,' whispered the Reaper. 'She is alive.' It was a statement.

'Yes, she is alive,' said the woman, a tremor in her voice. The Reaper turned his face away from hers, dismissing her and, as if released from a spell, the woman staggered back half a step and raised her hands to her eyes. She turned and left the stage looking bewildered.

Two assistants came on from the wings. One carried a length of black material, the other a silver basin. The Reaper turned to the first. His arms were outstretched with the material lying across them and falling down by his sides to the floor. With a slow and gentle sweep of the scythe the Reaper divided the material between the assistant's arms. I thought at first that it was a trick, as he had used insufficient force to cut anything, no matter how sharp the blade was, but then as he raised the scythe above his head again I looked harder at it. It shimmered in the light, even when he held it still. I saw for the first time that it was not a simple blade at all, but that it had a serrated edge like a chainsaw, which itself was moving the whole time, but so fast that it became a blur.

The assistant took one piece of the material and placed it on the stage under the girl's body, and spread the other over her. It hung down on both sides of the girl, not quite touching the floor. I was close enough to the stage to see the girl's profile under the black cloth. I could see the

146

cloth lift slightly each time she exhaled through parted lips, and her chest rose and fell rhythmically. She was certainly alive, although asleep, or in some sort of trance.

The second assistant placed the silver bowl on top of the material on the floor underneath the girl's head. The Reaper took up a position behind the girl so that he faced the audience and raised the scythe above his head. I expected a drum roll, but none came. The silence in the room was palpable, as if everyone in it was holding their breath. My heart was pounding. The Reaper paused for what must have been a minute, but what seemed like an eternity. I tried to see into the shadows inside his cowl. There seemed to be nothing there, just emptiness. I was suddenly filled with the certainty that this was no trick, that he was actually going to kill her. I'd had enough. I stood up, scattering glasses and cutlery with a crash on to the floor, and ran for the door. My exit seemed to go unnoticed, despite the noise. As I reached the swing doors there was a sharp whistling sound, followed immediately by a piercing shriek that lasted only a split second. It was cut off by an even more terrible sound, like that heard in lumber yards; a sudden, short screech of a saw ripping through something hard. I stood, shaking, outside the doors by the cloakroom while, inside the room, there was a few seconds of silence followed by a roar of applause.

I felt a hand on my shoulder and I whirled around, prepared to strike, but it was Graham.

'What on earth's the matter?' he asked.

'What's the matter! What's the matter? I've just witnessed two hours of perverted smut, culminating in a ritual murder, staged for the entertainment of fat, rich, fat . . .' I trailed off, unable to find words, 'and you ask me what's the matter?'

'I don't know why you're so upset. It's just a show, a bit of fun.'

'Fun? Not much fun for the girl under the sheet, was it? She's dead isn't she? It's not just a trick is it? It's real.'

'Well, . . . I don't know . . . perhaps.'

'I'm leaving. I want my shawl.' Graham looked at me for some time before answering. He took a deep breath.

'Okay. Wait here. I'll be right back; I'll come with you.'

'I don't give a damn whether you do or not. I just want my shawl!' He returned almost immediately, and I walked off ahead of him into the cool night air.

21

I left the apartment the next morning without having spoken to Graham since leaving the restaurant. I had walked home with him following a few feet behind me all the way. I had nothing to say to him. I knew he wasn't responsible for what I had witnessed – he just worked there, right? – but I found his casual acceptance of it as 'a bit of fun' just too much. Life was brutal enough in Ilford. I'd seen plenty of fights, plenty of blood. Death, if not exactly a friend, was a familiar acquaintance. On the Outside, 'Survive!' was the imperative. But that obscenity, in the plush surroundings of a London restaurant, staged for the enjoyment of an audience . . . it was, well, evil, almost insane. I couldn't believe that everyone inside the Wall was like that. I'd already decided to move out of the apartment as soon as I could find a way of doing so. If that was what Graham's tastes ran to, I'd be happier, not to say safer, somewhere else.

I tried to put it out of my mind and concentrate on work. That was made more difficult by an odd incident which occurred directly after lunch. I came back to my desk, opened the drawer to get a sheet of paper, and found myself looking at my gun. It hadn't been there when I left, an hour before, and I had no idea how it got there. Firearms were strictly prohibited inside the Wall and outside. Mine had been removed from me three days earlier, and yet here it was. I left it in the drawer, unwilling to touch it. It reminded me somehow of the events of the previous night and, in any event, I considered the possibility that it might have been a test and that I was being observed.

It was late afternoon and I was clearing my desk to leave. The air was suddenly split by the high-pitched wail of a siren. I looked at Jennifer at the adjoining desk.

'It's a security alarm,' she said calmly. 'We get them now and then. Just lock up your desk and follow me. We have to assemble in the pound.' She began closing her desk drawers and picked up her handbag. I was about to follow her, when the door burst open. A chap from the office next door shouted from the threshold.

'They've hit the main hall! Get up to the ninth floor and across the bridge to "Sanctions"!' He ran off down the corridor, leaving the door open. Jenny and the other girls in the room surged after him, fighting to get out. I was pushed to the back. I heard their feet clattering down the corridor. There was a sudden loud Crack! and the sound of falling masonry, followed by a scream, and rapid gunfire. Jenny staggered back into the room, blood cascading down her face from a gaping wound to her head. Most of her left hand was missing, but she didn't seem to notice. I was having difficulty keeping up with events. Two minutes ago I was about to finish my day's work and go home for a bath and now I was in the middle of some battle. The whole situation seemed unreal. Jenny fell back against the door, closing it as she did so. Her eyes were wide with surprise.

'They've shot them,' she said, without a trace of expression.

'Who? Who's shot them?'

'The girls,' she replied, irritated that I didn't understand. 'Suzanne and Michele.'

'*Who* shot them?'

'Outside . . . the Resistance . . .' Her legs buckled and she slid on to her bottom with a sigh, her back still against the door. I knelt down next to her and she looked into my face.

'Resistance?' I asked. She took a breath to speak, looked puzzled, as if she'd forgotten what it was she was going to say, and then rolled lightly on to her side. Something made me look up. There was the outline of a figure visible through the frosted glass of the door. I threw myself across Jenny's legs, praying that there was sufficient blood on the floor to account for me as well. A shot shattered the window, covering me with fragments of glass. I lay as still as I could. After a second there was a movement, and I heard booted feet crunching through the debris as they made their way down the corridor. I stayed where I was until I was sure I was alone, then I got up and went to the door. The corridor was filled with acrid smoke. The bodies of the other two girls were almost directly at my feet, their arms and legs at improbable angles, looking like puppets with their strings cut. Just beyond them, the corridor ended prematurely in an impenetrable tangle of rubble and steel. The other direction seemed clear.

I had to decide what to do. I could stay where I was until someone came to get me out – I couldn't believe that the Snorters wouldn't soon establish control. Whoever the 'Resistance' were, there was almost a full regiment of Snorters in the building, and only the day before I had stumbled on a complete armoury on the third floor. My alternative was to try to get downstairs alone, and out of the building. I was still hesitating by the door when my decision was made for me. Thick black smoke began to pour into the room from the air conditioning duct. I'd have to move.

I heaved Jenny's body out of the way and opened the door. The corridor was still clear. I stepped out, and then raced back into the room to my desk.

The drawer was locked, the key was in my bag, and the bag was nowhere to be seen. I searched in panic for it, and then found it by Jenny's body. I took the key out, opened the drawer, took out the gun and checked that it was still loaded. It was.

Once back in the corridor, I moved cautiously towards the stairs. I didn't dare risk the elevator, even if it was still working, in case the power was cut off while I was in it. I descended the first flight of stairs. On the landing between the floors there was a window overlooking the street. I looked down. The pavement outside was littered with people. I could make out a number of Docs in their white coats, crouching beside prone figures, several torture-wagons at angles across the road, and three or four lines of Snorters, visors down and machine guns at the ready, facing the building. But there was no sign of the people who had caused all the carnage. That meant that any that were still alive were still in the building. I thought about what Jenny had said. The Resistance. I'd never heard of any resistance group. The men who had first come into the office had said 'They' as if everyone knew who he was talking about, yet there had never been anything on the Nooz about terrorists or anything like it. 'Resistance.' It was a word out of the past, from the days of urban warfare long before I was born. My father used to speak of 'food riots' from when he was a kid, but that was long before the Wall was built. Could there be modern insurgents, fighting the State? If they were on the Inside, why on earth should they want to?

I heard the door bang from the floor below, and then voices coming up the stairwell.

'Is there anyone up there?' called a male voice. I descended the last few steps to the sixth floor as quietly as I could. I came face to face with Miller, from the front desk. His face was dirty and his hair dishevelled, but he appeared uninjured. I had not seen him since our first meeting.

'Oh, it's you, Miss,' he grinned. 'You can't go down. Most of the fourth floor is on fire. I'm trying to take these people to the ninth floor and across the bridge to Brownlow Street.' He pointed behind him and I saw about half a dozen people, a doorman, some secretaries and one of the canteen staff, looking confused and frightened.

'Is there anyone up there still?' he asked.

'I'm not sure. I don't think so. The other girls in my office have been shot, but I don't know if whoever did it went up or down.'

'They haven't come down this side of the building, as we haven't seen anyone.'

'Shot?' asked one of the secretaries, looking as if she were about to faint. 'You mean dead?'

'Very.'

'I'm not going up there!' she squealed, backing away.

'Look, Miss . . .' said Miller, turning to her.

'No. I'm not going,' she said, and started running away down the corridor away from us. Some of the others began following her. Miller looked at me helplessly.

'I doubt if you'll be able to use the North staircase,' I said. 'There's been an explosion on my floor right at the end, just before the stairs.'

'Which floor is that?' asked Miller.

'The one above here, the seventh.'

'I'd better stay with them,' he said with resignation. 'If I were you, Miss, I'd aim for the ninth.'

'Thanks.' He made off after the others, and then turned. 'I'll bet you wish you still had that gun of yours,' he called. I was too far away to see his expression. I waved in reply and went back up the stairs.

The eighth floor was a shambles. The attackers, whoever they were, had obviously been along the corridor, and everyone had fled before them. Some hadn't been quick enough. There were a few bodies, both in the corridor and in the offices opening off it. The bridge on the next floor across the street to the adjoining block was impassable. It looked as though it had been deliberately made so. A pattern was beginning to emerge. Whoever was attacking the building was aiming for a specific target. They'd cut off the Snorters and the armoury on the third floor by setting the fourth floor alight, and were making their way upwards, clearing every floor as they went. They'd also blocked the North staircase, so that any counter-attack could come from only one direction, the South staircase, the one I was on. And that meant that there was almost certainly someone waiting for me further up.

I again weighed my options. I couldn't go down as the building below me was on fire. Above me was an apparently well-organized and utterly ruthless force. They were not attractive options. I had more or less decided to stay quietly where I was, when I looked down to see smoke curling around my ankles. I ran back down the last few stairs and looked into the corridor of the eighth floor. It was full of smoke. Coughing and spluttering I ran back up to the ninth. I didn't have any choices; the smoke was coming up very fast. I'd have to keep going and hope I didn't run into trouble. I remembered from the plan of the building in Reception that there was another bridge on the twentieth floor, only used by Techs. I'd never been up there – I didn't have the security clearance – but I knew where it was.

By the time I reached the seventeenth, I was glad I had trained so hard when Jobbing. I'd passed three more bodies. Two were Snorters, in their select red Ministry uniforms. The third was a young man in battledress. He was lying in a pool of blood, clutching a machine pistol.

He had a balaclava helmet half-covering his face. He could only have been eighteen. The Snorters had obviously put up some resistance to the attackers at this point. The walls of the stairwell were pitted with bullets and, in addition to the body of the Resistance fighter, there was a trail of blood leading on, up the stairs. Just in front of the young boy was a black box with wires coming out of it. I looked at it carefully without touching it. You didn't have to be a genius to guess that it was a bomb, and that it hadn't gone off. It explained why no one was guarding this staircase; they thought it had been blocked.

Having caught my breath, I looked out cautiously down the corridor. The swing doors of the lower corridors had given way to sliding steel doors, and I could only look through the glass. These were the Techs' offices. They were a lot more plush than the ones on the lower floors, thick carpets, wood-panelled walls, old paintings. More importantly, the higher I climbed, the more extensive were the security measures. Cameras were placed so as to identify every entrant to the corridor, and special clearance was required to get through every door. I continued my journey upwards.

As I reached the step that brought me to the twentieth landing, I was greeted by the sight of a hand clutching a gun, protruding around the corner. It belonged to a man, also dressed in green battledress, lying face down in the thick red carpet. He had a bullet hole in his thigh, and another in his neck. He was dead. There was a buzzing noise, and a smell of electrical burning. I looked past the dead man and saw that his foot was right in the groove of the steel security door. The door kept trying to close, but each time found the boot in its path. I waited until it slid open for another try, and stepped into the corridor.

I got my gun out and began to move down the corridor towards the bridge. If I was lucky, I thought, the attackers might already have cleared the floor, and made their own way across the bridge. Once I was in the adjoining building, there would be several alternatives open to me; I could try to get to one of the several exits, or just sit tight out of the way of the fire until I was rescued.

I listened at the door of each office before passing it. There was nothing but the hum of computers. I reached the third door, listened, and was about to walk in front of it, when I heard something – a creak, like the sound of someone moving their weight in a chair. I pressed my ear against the wall and held my breath. There were voices coming from the office on the other side. I raised myself, centimetre by centimetre, until I could see in the window. Side on to me, on the far side of the office, was Jordan. He was sitting behind his desk, talking to someone, and pointing at them as if to emphasize what he was saying. I couldn't see who he was talking to, but I could see the barrel of a machine pistol being held by that person. It was pointing in Jordan's direction, but nonchalantly, at the floor. I craned my neck round as far as I dared, trying to see if there were any other people in the office, but without success. Again, I couldn't decide what to do. I could try and slip past and get on to the bridge. It was only ten metres away. On the other hand I could get killed in the process. Still, there was no guarantee that I'd make the bridge in any event; I might be seen as soon as I went past the door, and there were certain to be more Resistance fighters ahead. I also thought of what might happen if I succeeded in helping Jordan. I couldn't imagine that I'd fail the Competency Test at the end of the week if I saved the Minister's life. At that point I smiled to myself. The end of the week? I wouldn't have given much for my chances of making the end of the hour! I crouched there, undecided, and, again, events took

156

over. I heard whispered voices from the end of the corridor just outside the door I had come through. Resistance or Snorters? I realized that it didn't matter; whoever it was would shoot first and ask questions later. I was new to the Ministry and wouldn't be recognized and, anyway, I was crouching outside the Minister's office with a gun in my hand!

All this flashed through my mind in a fraction of a second. Whoever was approaching only had to look past the dead man as the door opened and I'd be seen. I took a deep breath and, praying that the door wasn't locked, I threw myself into the room. I rolled over once, coming to rest by the side of Jordan's desk, expecting to feel the thump of bullets as they hit me. I raised my arm immediately and fired at the man with the pistol. He spun round, fired a spray of bullets into the ceiling and down the wall, and fell backwards heavily against the bookcase behind him.

Jordan had stood up as I entered. His hand was in the desk drawer next to him. He looked at me, with an expression of what appeared to be shock, as the intruder slumped to the ground. At the same time two Ministry Snorters appeared in the doorway, their guns drawn. I saw a movement out of the corner of my eye. The man on the floor was reaching out to Jordan with his left hand, the pistol still clasped in his right.

'Jordan . . .' he gasped.

In one swift movement Jordan pulled his hand from the drawer and fired the gun he had been holding. The intruder fell dead. The two Snorters stood undecided. Jordan held up a hand to stop them from doing anything. He put his gun away and closed the drawer. He turned to me.

'You're quite handy with that thing, aren't you?' he said with a smile.

22

Jordan opened the apartment door and ushered me inside. I entered a circular room with a number of doors opening off it. As I did so, one of the other doors opened, and a small man in a black suit with tails entered.

'Good evening sir, madam.'

''Evening Marceau,' replied Jordan.

Marceau came round behind me, and I whirled to face him. Jordan laughed gently. 'It's all right, my dear. He just wants to help you with your coat.' Without a flicker of emotion, Marceau approached me again, slipped behind me, and took my coat off. I decided that it was a gesture I could get used to.

'We'll have drinks in the lounge before dining. I shall manage, thank you, Marceau.'

'Very good sir.'

'That will be all.' The little man disappeared silently. Jordan opened another of the doors off the hall. 'After you,' he said. Ahead of me, three semi-circular steps descended into an enormous room. In the centre, forming a square, were four low couches in dark green with gold piping. Above them hung four brass lights with white glass spheres suspended beneath them. I walked across the polished wooden floor and on to a rug with a large geometric design at its centre. The room looked like a greenhouse: there were plants, on china stands, in wicker baskets, and standing by the square furniture. I sat on one of the couches and put Jeremy's handbag on the hexagonal glass-topped table by my side. Jordan followed me down the steps, closing the door behind him.

'This is amazing,' I said. The room was lit by the soft glow from four statuette lamps each holding a white globe aloft.

'Drink?' asked Jordan.

'I don't know. I'm not very familiar with alcohol.'

'Okay,' he said slowly, 'let's see.' He went across to a cabinet, opened its door, and music began to play. He poured two drinks, closed the cabinet, and the music stopped. He sat down beside me, and handed a glass to me.

'Try that.'

'What is it?'

'Gin.' I sipped at it. It was foul. 'Nice,' I lied. He got up again.

'I'll put some music on.' He went to the corner and opened another cabinet.

'That's a hi-fi?' I asked in surprise.

'The cabinet's antique. See if you recognize this. It's by a lady called Billie Holliday.'

'Not a good recording, is it?' I said as the music began.

'That's hardly surprising considering its age.'

'Don't you like modern music?'

He smiled, but didn't answer. He came back to the centre of the room, this time sitting opposite me.

'Cheers,' he said, raising his glass. Then a pause. 'May I call you Kate?'

'If you want,' I replied, guardedly.

'Where do you come from, Kate?'

I didn't answer at first. 'Look, Mister Jordan –'

'Henry, please call me Henry.'

'Mister Jordan,' I repeated, 'you don't want to know where I came from. For one thing, you know already. For another, why the hell should you be interested in Manor Park? Why am I here?' He leaned back on his couch, regarding me carefully.

'You're no fool are you, Kate Mason?'

'And flattery won't get you anywhere either. So, why am I here?'

I recognized the same look of mixed respect and humour on his face as I had seen the morning I shot Swayne.

'Don't you believe I could find you attractive?' he asked with a smile.

'Yeh, I do, but there are a lot of attractive girls at the Ministry, and most of them talk proper,' I said, playing it up a bit. 'So, why me? Fancy a bit of rough?'

'You saved my life.'

'Did I?'

That silenced him for a bit. For the first time I got the impression that he wasn't sure what to do. He changed tack.

'How did you get through the Wall?'

'I'm not going to tell you. It was a question that you prevented me from answering at the Settlement Proceedings. Why should I tell you now?'

'Because your life may depend on it.' I looked him straight in the eyes. He was deadly serious.

'Put yourself in my position,' he said, standing up and pacing behind me. 'The Resistance movement is getting stronger by the month. Out of the blue, there appears a woman who has apparently been trained in the use of small arms. She comes, purporting to bear a message from the Minister herself, who has disappeared, presumed abducted by the Resistance. She uses me to enable her to shoot one of my junior staff, and usurps her way into my own department. Finally, within forty-eight hours, there is a Resistance attack on my Ministry. Who finds herself on the twentieth floor outside my office, gun in hand? And *that's* a nice point too,' he said, turning sharply to

160

me. 'How did she come to be in possession of a gun that was confiscated some days before?'

I stared at my drink and fought to control the rising tide of fear.

'Now don't tell me you're a nice little girl from Ilford.'

'Manor Park,' I corrected, stalling for time. I had to give him some answer, but what could I say that would convince him? I hadn't even known there *was* a Resistance until the day before. I'd never heard anything about it on the Nooz. Resistance to what?

'I don't understand myself how the gun got back in my desk. As for being on the twentieth floor, you can check with Miller; he saw me on my own corridor trying to get down.'

'Correction: he saw you on the sixth floor, not on your own. You chose not to go down with him, but to make your way upwards. And, as you very well know, you were the only survivor from your floor.'

'Are you suggesting that I killed the girls in my office?' He shrugged. 'You've got to believe me. I'd never fired that gun at anyone until . . . Swayne.' He looked at me in open disbelief. 'Really. A friend in Ilford taught me how to use it.'

'And how did he know?'

'I . . . I don't know. He said he learned it from a . . . book.' I realized how unlikely it sounded.

'What's his name, this theoretical master of the handgun?'

'Jim D – ' I stopped abruptly.

He came across to me and bent forward, his hands on his knees, and his face just a few centimetres from mine.

'You're going to have to tell me what I need to know, Kate, because if I'm in the least bit unsure about you, well, I wouldn't like to terminate the career of a promising young civil servant.'

Then I knew the danger that I was in. Yes, I had known that going to his apartment would be risky, but fool that I was, I was so sure that I could handle the situation – after all, wasn't he still grateful to me for saving his life? And, I admit, I had been flattered by his invitation. I reckoned that I might as well find out why he was so interested in me over dinner, as wait for the inevitable knock on the door.

'What do you want to know?' I asked, staring at the rug.

'Okay. Firstly, who taught you to use a gun?'

'Geezer called Jim Demon,' I replied. Sorry Jim, I thought. I was more worried about the second question. I didn't want to have to give Captain Sam away unless I really had no alternative. They would be bound to arrest him, and he might be my only way out of the city in one piece.

'Who helped you get in?'

'No one helped me.'

'Then how did you get over the Wall?'

'I . . . just slipped in.'

'Where?'

'Where?'

'You heard me,' he shouted. 'Which Gate did you just "slip in"?'

'Gate Six.'

'What about your Code 4 Pass?'

'I stole one.'

'Oh, that's interesting,' he smiled without humour. 'From which Outside Worker did you *steal* a Code 4 Pass?'

'From . . . from the Librarian . . .'

'Nonsense! You give yourself away! "Slipped in" indeed. Anyone who had actually come in through the

Wall would know that it's quite impossible to "slip in".
And there's no such thing as a "Code 4 Pass".'

I cursed myself. How could I have been so foolish as to
come in on the *Meggie* and not have a credible alternative
explanation ready? I'd had to think on the spot, and I'd
screwed it up.

'So. We know you didn't get in *through* the Wall, at
least not on foot. What's left? By some transport perhaps?
Not from London East, and you didn't have time to get
round to any of the other road entrances.'

He must have seen my puzzled expression, because he
smiled, more gently this time, and sat down again opposite me.

'How do I know? Because you were at 34 Aldersbrook
Bridge, Manor Park, only thirty-six hours before you shot
the unfortunate Mr Swayne. Your Social Security number
is recorded as having been used at that address to order
food from the Hyper.' I winced. I'd used the bread for
supper the day before I left, and had ordered more as
usual without thinking.

'Or are you alleging that your mother, Jean isn't it?
committed the capital offence of using your computer ID
Number?' I didn't answer. 'No, I didn't think so. They've
denied it anyway.'

'What? You've interrogated her?' The shock hit me
like a blow to the stomach.

'I? No, Kate, I haven't been outside the Wall in two
years. But someone has certainly asked her and her friend
a few questions. Come now, did you really think you
could just assassinate a government official and walk into
his job, without any questions being asked? You might be
a Resistance member.'

'I keep telling you, I've never heard of the Resistance.'

'So you say. We'll come back to that in a while. Now
where was I? Oh, yes: the road entrances. The Commer-

cial Road entrance was closed due to the mopping up of the bust from the previous night. Security there was tighter than a drum in any event. So, your nearest road entrance was over thirty-six hours away by foot, and across some pretty unpleasant territory for a girl alone. That deals with going *through* the Wall. What's left? Over it? Under it? Now, *there's* a possibility. Or is parachuting one of your many talents?' There was a long pause. 'Well?' I still didn't answer. 'Over or under, Kate?'

'Under,' I said softly.

'That's better. Now then, tunnel, sewers, the Tube?' I didn't dare bluff again. I knew nothing about the sewers, let alone tunnels.

'None of them. The river.'

He paused to consider that for a minute, and then shook his head. 'No, it couldn't be done. Those portcullises are almost never opened these days. There's no river traffic except . . .' He turned aside, and frowned, as if trying to remember something. Then he got up quickly and walked over to a bookcase. The book he took out was some kind of map. Gradually the frown lifted, to be replaced with a knowing grin.

'Well, I'll be damned,' he said softly, more to himself than to me. 'I thought the old bugger died years ago.' He put the book away, crossed the room, and disappeared through an arch. A light went on, and I could see a study with a bank of terminals on a desk. He punched a few keys, and waited a second. I couldn't see what came up on the screen from where I was sitting. He pressed a few more keys and gave a satisfied grunt. He snapped the machine off, and approached me, holding out his hand.

'Shall we eat?' he asked.

'Pardon?'

'You did accept my dinner invitation, didn't you?'

'Yes, but . . .'

'Well, come on then. It's through there,' said Jordan, pointing to a doorway to his right.

'What were all these questions for then?'

'You've told me what I wanted to know. Tomorrow I shall order that a certain Captain Samuel Crocker be arrested and shot. Shall we go in? Why, whatever is the matter? You don't know Captain Crocker do you?'

'No . . .'

'Well then, I'm hungry – '

'But – '

'But what? Either the name Crocker means nothing to you, in which case I'd like to eat, or you *do* know him. If that's the case, you'd better tell me. I'd hate to order the execution of a friend of yours.'

I was beaten. 'I know him,' I admitted.

'Are you sure?'

'Of course I'm sure, you bastard! What do you want of me?'

'Let's try the name of that barge he runs.'

'The *Meggie*,' I answered. 'I hitched a lift on the side of the barge. He didn't know I was there.' I felt tears stinging my eyes.

He came towards me, and held me gently by the shoulders. I turned my head away from him, but he took my chin in his hand and gently forced me to look at him. I saw in his eyes something I did not expect: kindness, and, yes, relief.

'Don't worry, my dear. I wouldn't hurt old Crocker or that rusty old tub of his for the world. He's an old renegade, but he's not Resistance, nor anything else for that matter. He's strictly a one-man show. But I had to find out who you were.'

I looked hard at him, trying to decide if he was telling the truth.

'You thought I was part of the Resistance?'

165

He brushed a tear from my cheek. 'That was one possibility, although I didn't think it likely after yesterday; you had the chance to shoot me or a Resistance officer, and I'm still here.'

'What other possibility was there?' I said between sobs.

'Let's not worry about that. There's a lot of political in-fighting that you don't understand as yet. Either way, neither the Resistance nor my political opponents would need to get into the city with Sam Crocker as an escort. Now, I don't know about you, but interrogations make me hungry. Please may we eat?' he pleaded.

I nodded. 'Is there anywhere I can . . . ?'

'Yes, of course. First on the left in the hall.' I made to move away from him, but he caught my hand. I turned back to him, and he looked at me for a long moment, raised my hand, and touched it lightly with his lips.

'I'm sorry that was necessary. Will you forgive me?'

'Maybe.'

23

I looked down at Jordan's sleeping form, and decided that I hadn't quite forgiven him. His hand lay across the pillow, well manicured nails, long fingers, a fine covering of light hair. I remembered those fingers on my skin hours before, their tender expertise. The hands of an artist. And the hands of an executioner – my executioner perhaps.

I don't know why I went to bed with him. It was not as if he had not given me a choice. If anything I had invited it. Maybe because I was lonely. Maybe because I told myself that I'd just survived the most stressful days of my life. Maybe because I wanted a measure of control in a situation where I'd felt completely impotent. Or maybe because, as Mum would have said, I was a slut. Don't ask me. The only thing I was certain of was that I had not done it for the Great Man's favour. My intuition told me that to have 'come on' like any of the other girls at the Ministry would have earned his transient interest, and then his contempt. So I had told him that I wanted to go to bed, that he could come with me if he liked, but that if he did, he wasn't to assume that it would ever happen again. He had said that that was understood, and that he'd like very much to go to bed with me. That was that.

Another reason occurred to me for my being in his bed. More than once since I had arrived in London I had had the feeling that I was missing something, that something was going on that I didn't understand, and I had a lot of questions. I hadn't planned it, but perhaps unconsciously I had realized that by getting him into bed I might get him to talk more freely. I cast my mind back to the conversation.

'Henry?'

'Mmmm,' he had said, obviously not listening.

'I have a question. Will you please surface and talk to me?'

'Well?'

'Who are the Resistance? Henry?'

'Later,' he said, and returned to what engrossed him.

'But I want to know who was shooting at me yesterday. What are they resisting?' I pulled gently at his hair, and he sat up reluctantly.

'You get some malcontents in any society who don't know when they've got it made.'

'Reformers, protesters maybe. But not commandos who attack government buildings and kill innocent secretaries.'

'They're just unprincipled guerillas who can't face up to the fact that this is the way society is. Biting the hand that feeds it.'

'Bullshit, Henry, and you know it! That might be good enough for some of the occupants of this side of the bed, but it won't wash with me. We've not forgotten "The Impact of Technology on Occupational Structure" etcetera, have we? What happened to the bright young man who wrote: "Security measures to separate the Haves from the Have-Nots will be," what was it? "vital"?'

He looked stunned. 'Where did you – '

'Ilford Public Library. We're not all cretins on the Outside you know, despite the "vitamins" you bastards pump into the food.'

He smiled grimly. 'I thought I'd removed every copy years ago.'

'Well you missed one.'

'I shan't underestimate you again.'

'Stop changing the subject. You predicted this. They're Outsiders, the Have-Nots, right?'

'That book was written thirty years ago. It was bound to contain some errors, miscalculations. The Resistance is not the Have-Nots on the Outside. Of course there are Outsiders who get in, but the Resistance is largely made up of Working Class people, Insiders.'

'But what do they want? Aren't they happy?'

'They're obviously not happy, or they wouldn't keep blowing up my staff, among others. As for what they want, who knows?'

'So they just go around blowing things up without any apparent reason?' Jordan shrugged. 'I don't believe you, Henry. You can't tell me that you haven't thought about what's wrong with your brainchild.'

'"Brainchild"? We'll come back to that one. But, yes, I've thought about it. There's a theory that it's a policy to force decentralization – disrupt London enough, and you create a need for provincial resources. The Outside economy, outside the Great Cities, will be regenerated. I'm not impressed with that. Many of their targets seem picked totally at random; how can cutting the power lines to most of Surrey, which is what they did last month, stimulate anything except candle production?'

'Okay, then what do you think?'

'I honestly don't know. If I were forced to guess, I'd put my money on nothing more complicated than the personal ambition of some of my political opponents within the Technocratic Party.'

'You mean part of the government?'

'That's certainly a possibility.'

I thought about that for a moment. 'Do you think that Marie Fowler has been kidnapped?' A look of what I took to be pain passed across his face.

'No. I think the Resistance killed her.'

'Why?'

'I can't give you a precise reason, but she was popular with all factions of the Working Class and the Party. She was the "acceptable face of technology", and she was a danger to the Resistance.'

'At the time I kept wondering why they were so intent on reaching the top floor. If they were after you – Marie Fowler's replacement – that would explain it.' Again I stopped to assimilate this new information. Jordan's hands started moving again.

'There must be someone working for the Resistance inside the Ministry,' he said. 'I only moved my office to the twentieth floor the day before yesterday, and the new security drill was due to start there today. The attack was timed perfectly, and executed with intimate knowledge of the layout of the building.'

'Do you know who it is, the spy?'

'Let's just say I have some candidates that I am looking into.'

'Ha! And I was at the top of the short-list!'

He grinned at me. 'You were. But, on the assumption that no spy could have eyelashes as beautiful as yours, I'm left with only one other suspect.'

'Who's that?' I asked, ignoring the comment.

'He's an assistant-secretary in the MSD, the Ministry of Spiritual Development, called McCready. I've heard that he's been caught once or twice breaking into computer files that don't concern him.'

'What are you going to do about him?' I asked.

'Just watch and wait. After yesterday's attack failed, I should think that they'll try something again soon.'

'Failed? They killed twenty-three people and disabled dozens more! What you mean, you arrogant bastard, is that they didn't get you!'

'Sorry,' he grinned. 'Criticism accepted. In any event, I

170

think they'll try again. And McCready's the man to watch.'

'I'll keep my eyes open.'

'You be careful, Kate. He's a dangerous man. On two occasions in the past three years his rivals for promotion have been the targets of Usurpation attempts. One survived, the other didn't. It may just be coincidence, but I doubt it.'

'I'll be all right,' I said, laughing. 'I've got my trusty revolver.'

'I don't know what I'm going to do with you,' he said, and then proceeded to prove himself wrong.

24

The next couple of days were hectic. Although Swayne's job was easy enough, I had a great deal of research to do for the Competency Hearing. In addition to learning the detailed 'Obligations' which I was now under as a successful Usurper, I had to be prepared to answer questions on the social and political obligations attached to membership of the Working Class. I had been completely unaware of this side of Usurpation. Now I realized that the city needed to screen potential workers to make sure they would fit without disruption into a closed and over-populated society. Usurpers were by definition violent killers, fitted for survival Outside. Most, like Jim's friend Freddo, were completely unsuitable for Working Class society.

Working at home was impossible. Graham's night life meant that he was clattering around the place when I got back from work, and by the time he left for work I was too exhausted to study. So on the last night before the Hearing I decided to stay at the Ministry late, and catch up on some reading.

I was using one of the terminals in the Library Section on the eighth floor to go through an 'Acclimatization Programme' prepared for Usurpers into the Civil Service. The eighth floor was not divided into small offices like my own, the seventh. The whole floor was open-plan. At one end was a maze of racks and shelves, and at the other were individual desks, each with its terminal and lamp for private study. I had been working intently for over an hour, unaware of the time, when I looked up. Only two other desks were occupied and had their lamps on. One was the Librarian's, and at the other sat a Pinkie in his distinctive bright suit. His head was bent over his desk as he wrote. There was a small sheaf of paper on the floor by his feet filled with his handwriting. Every now and then he would stop, key a few instructions, and then hunch over the desk as he resumed writing. At first I thought nothing of it, and returned to my work. Only after a while did I realize that there was something odd about what he was doing. I was used to sitting in a Library, and taking notes from books, but Inside no one did that. All the information that you could possibly need was in the computers, and to take away a reference in hard copy all you had to do was punch one button, and the printer produced it for you in seconds. Why would anyone bother to write such voluminous notes? Unless . . . The computer made a record of everything printed out. The advantage of taking a note by hand was that no one would know what had been researched. That meant that the Pinkie was up to something. And I was prepared to bet that I knew his name.

I got up from the terminal and approached him.

'Excuse me?' I said. His hand shot to the keyboard and hit some keys, and his screen went blank.

'Yes?' he said, standing up and casually pulling a clean sheet of paper over the one he had been writing on.

'I wonder if you could help me. I've just taken over a job in Social Planning, and I'm not familiar with the codes on this terminal,' I said, pointing behind me to where I had been sitting. 'Could you show me how to get out of this programme?'

He didn't reply at first but looked carefully at me.

'You're the girl who shot the terrorist in the Minister's office, aren't you?'

'Yes. I'm Kate Mason,' I replied, a little surprised that he knew who I was. I held out my hand.

'Bill McCready,' he said, taking my hand and shaking it.

'Fortunate you were there, isn't it?'

'Yes,' I replied noncommittally.

'And with a gun too.'

'I suppose so.'

'It's all round the Ministry, as you can guess,' he said. 'You're certainly proving yourself more versatile than your predecessor. It's even been suggested that there's a personal involvement with the Minister himself.' He was smiling with his mouth, but his eyes looked hard and dangerous. 'Terrible place for gossip this,' he concluded. I decided to counter-attack.

'Writing a book?' I said, pointing to his notes, and casually touching the top page.

'No,' he replied very firmly, all traces of a smile gone. He picked up the notes and put them under his arm.

'Anyway, what's the problem?' he asked, walking to my desk. 'You want to end the programme?'

'Yes.'

'Just hit the "Exit" key,' he said as he pressed it. McCready looked at me suspiciously. 'Surely you must have known that?'

'Have you ever been to Ilford? I suppose not. Well, Ilford Public Library does not boast a working terminal, and as I'm sure you know, the Social's terminals are built for use by morons. They don't have functions like these.' Which was, of course, nearly all bullshit, but then he wasn't to know, was he?

'How interesting. You must have many quaint stories about Outside.'

'Many.'

'As you've finished, I'll walk to the lift with you. I've got to get back to the East Wing.'

I collected my things and we left the Library. He called the elevator, and we waited in silence. When it arrived he gestured that I should take it.

'After you. I'm going up to the bridge on the ninth. I'll take the next one.'

'Thank you. Goodnight.' I got in, and the doors closed. I had wanted to follow him, but the bastard had out-manoeuvred me. I couldn't think of any plausible reason for going to the East Wing. I knew that he would be watching the indicator to see where I went. I couldn't hesitate any longer, so I pressed the button for 'Ground'. I cursed myself for being so easily beaten. The elevator stopped, and I got out. I looked back up at the indicator. Two of the four elevators were at the tenth, where they returned when not in use. The last was on the ninth. I turned to leave, and then hesitated. I don't know what it was, but I just had a hunch that although the elevator was on the ninth, McCready wasn't.

I stepped back into the elevator. On the way up I opened my bag, took out my gun and checked it. I got out at the sixth, and crept up the stairs to the seventh, my floor. I stopped outside the swing doors and peered through the window. The corridor beyond was dark and deserted. Dotted along it were piles of rubble from the Resistance attack still awaiting clearance. No McCready; I'd been wrong. I was about to return to the elevator when, suddenly, a light went on in the first office to the right. My office. I put my bag on the floor, then opened the swing door just enough to allow me to slip in, and, keeping close to the wall of the corridor, tiptoed towards the rectangle of light spilling out into the corridor. I peered round the frame of the open door. McCready had his back to me, and was leaning over my desk. He had one of the drawers open, and was going through the contents.

'What the hell do you think you're doing, McCready?'

He whirled round, and at the same time as I registered that there was a gun in his hand, there was a sharp explosion just above my head, and bits of plaster fell on me. I dived to my left out of the doorway, landing badly on my side and dropping my gun. I could hear him colliding with desks in his hurry to get to the door and I knew I had to move fast. I scrambled to my feet. I couldn't see my gun! I wasted two precious seconds finding it in the shadows. I lunged for it and turned back to face the doorway just in time to see McCready appear. I fired. The window of the next office – the only one to survive the explosion of the previous week – smashed, but McCready leapt back into the room. I raced off down the corridor and dived through an open door. The corridor was tipped into almost complete darkness as McCready turned off the light in my office. The only light came from the stairways through the swing doors at either end and a faint blue glow from the monitors on the desks around me.

I felt my way back to the door, and stood with my back to the wall, the gun held in both hands in front of me. I tried to still my laboured breathing and listen. All I could hear was the pounding of blood in my ears. I imagined McCready standing exactly as I was, each of us waiting for the other to move into the corridor. I looked at the desk immediately to my left. A telephone. I could call Security. No: he'd hear the phone. I didn't think he'd seen which room I had gone into, whereas I knew where he was. That gave me an advantage which I didn't want to give away. The seconds ticked by. I could wait as long as he could. Then, I heard the swing doors at his end of the corridor open and close. Could he have gone? I stayed

176

where I was: it could be a trick. Then I heard the soft pad of light, careful footsteps approaching. It *was* a trick! I waited. I wanted him near enough not to miss. I imagined him passing the second door, the third. I took a deep breath, and swung round the door jamb, arms out to fire. It wasn't him. It was someone else, a man. A man who I recognized immediately, even in the half-light: Jim Demon.

'Kate?' he called softly. 'Is that you?'

Almost as Jim spoke, McCready stepped into the corridor from my office and levelled his gun at me. Jim was directly in the line of fire between us. He took another step towards me, unaware of McCready's presence.

'Kate – ' he repeated, holding out his hand.

'GET AWAY!' I screamed, and dived to my right as I fired.

Part Three

25

I kept losing sight of the Knife as he threaded his way through the crowds ahead of me. Every now and then he would pause, tapping his foot in irritation, and let me catch up.

'For Chrissake, Demon! Will you keep up?' he hissed on the last occasion.

'But – '

'No buts! I want to get as far away from *that*,' he said, pointing back at the Wall, 'as possible.'

I could understand why. It was a very intimidating structure, its blank grey surface floodlit along its length, extending a good fifteen or twenty metres above the street, dominating everything. I could see maybe ten Snorters too, parading around the top of the Wall, and if there's one thing I'm only too happy to get away from, it's Snorters. Trouble was, I was having difficulty taking in a quarter of what I was seeing. Anyway, I followed the Knife as he resumed his nipping and dodging along the pavement.

I don't know what hit me the hardest, but I think it was the colours that I found so unexpected. The pictures I had seen of London were generally black and white, and of course Ilford was yellowy grey everywhere. But here, even though it was dark, there was every colour of the rainbow! There were trees by the side of the roads with green leaves, billboards of green, purple and white – real white, not grey – and those big red buses right out of the movies. The people on the streets, men and women, wore clothes of yellow, pink, brown. Even the buildings were bright – no rusting steel skeletons, but marble and shiny chrome. I swear, the place even *smelt* cleaner, although you'll probably tell me that that wasn't possible, being only a few hundred metres from the Wall. But that's how it felt, right?

The buildings themselves ran in one continuous stretch on both sides of the road. That too was different, I can tell you; in Ilford the few remaining structures stuck up like the last rotting teeth in a Derro's gums. Then there was the noise: cars speeding up and down the road and the hundreds (honest, there were hundreds of them) of pedestrians on the pavements. It was a miracle that half of them weren't mown down every day. Middle of the bleeding night, and so much going on! And on top of the battering my senses were getting, was the pure and simple joy of being alive and Inside. Hardly surprising I felt fucking terrific!

The Knife pushed on at his swift pace. He had insisted that we 'get there' as soon as possible. Where 'there' was had not yet been explained, but I knew better than to push him for answers. In all this time Knife didn't look at the map once, so I assumed he had either memorized it already, or had been to this part of London before. Either that or he had a sort of sixth sense and could intuit where he was going, and by that stage I wouldn't have put anything past him, not a thing.

Then, suddenly, we rounded a corner, and there was this building, lit up sharp and bright against the night sky. The Cathedral. Now I must have seen pictures of St Paul's when I was a kid, but if so they hadn't sunk in at all, because the size of this domed wonder made my head reel. It also got me sort of choked, and I could not in truth tell you why. To think, this building never had a purpose; nothing was made by it, stored in it, sold from it, yet people spent fortunes and dedicated years just to

182

have it there, because, I suppose, they believed in something bigger and more enduring than themselves. Perhaps that's why I felt choked; let's face it: people don't believe in very much at all any more, do they? Still, they must have felt something for the place, because I could see that the doors were still open even though it was after midnight, and every now and then someone would go in or come out.

I begged the Knife to find a corner somewhere so that I could stand and stare at the magnificent structure just for a moment. He had relaxed somewhat by then, and seemed in pretty good humour. Every now and then he'd say 'Well, Demon, what d'ya think?' and lean back as if he was showing me a piece of art he'd just finished.

It was just after we crossed this enormous road bridge that I noticed the shops for the first time. They were all closed, but you could see what they were selling through the windows. Not just one or two shops mind, but dozens, each stocked with different items, just like in the old photo of Ilford High Street. There was one that sold nothing but chocolate in all different shapes and sizes. Even Knife lingered by that one.

We must have walked for nearly an hour when we reached a huge intersection. Knife pulled me into a small alley, took out the map and looked at it. We were standing directly under a street lamp, and as we stared intently at the map, I became aware of another presence.

'Excuse me?'

We both looked up swiftly and saw this very tall geezer standing right in front of us. He was wearing a long overcoat and a funny-shaped hat, and he carried a small square bag and a stick.

'Excuse me?' he said again.

Out of the corner of my eye I saw the Knife reach very slowly inside his jacket, and I felt the panic rise in me. In

Ilford, nobody, but nobody, approaches you in an alley at night unless they are looking for trouble. I watched the man's hands, particularly the one holding the stick, and felt sweat on my forehead. My heart was pounding heavily and my breathing was suddenly tight. I looked at the Knife. His expression was the same as always, except perhaps for his eyes, but you could tell that his whole body was tensed up, the way he gets when he's about to hit someone. I thought, This is it, and I looked down the alley to make sure that there was no one else about and that our exit was clear.

'I'm sorry to trouble you, but do you happen to know where Theobalds Road is? I seem to have become rather lost.'

The man spoke with a strange accent, and the thought flashed through my mind, He's foreign! The Knife removed his hand from his jacket. It was empty. He scratched his head for a moment, and then spoke, but not in a voice I had ever heard him use before.

'Certainly. Just turn right over there,' and he pointed back down the alley in the direction from which we'd come, 'and then right again at the top. You can't miss it.' He spoke in an accent every bit as foreign to him as the gent's accent was to me. It was perfect Working Class to the last syllable!

'Thank you so much,' said the gent, who doffed his hat, and walked off. We didn't say a word to each other, but just walked back to the intersection, crossed over, and continued swiftly away. Some ten minutes later, Knife spoke.

'Now, will you get it through your fucking head that this isn't a sodding tourist trip! Do the slightest thing to draw attention to yourself, and you could kill us both!' He spoke furiously, through clenched teeth. I realized he was right. I was like a fish out of water, and there I'd been a few minutes earlier treating the place like it was a playground. No wonder he had been so anxious about getting out of the open.

'I'm sorry,' I said, meaning it. 'It's just that everything is so . . .'

'I don't give a damn!' he said, spitting the words at me. 'You gotta understand, Demon, you can't mess about till you know the ropes. It's only good luck that saved us back there.'

'What do you mean?'

'Look, people who use maps are unfamiliar with a place, right? The Working Class know London like it was part of them; they've lived in the same few square Ks all their lives. You get out a map, and you're saying "I don't belong here". That geezer must have been foreign, a visitor or something, otherwise we'd have been rumbled.'

He stalked off, leaving me to digest that in silence. I moved swiftly up behind him, and that's where I stayed for the rest of the journey.

We walked for another twenty minutes. There could be no doubt that we were in the West End by then. Knife led me through some interesting back streets full of all manner of cafés and restaurants, just like those Kate had talked about, all apparently open despite the late hour. Going in any of them was obviously out of the question, but I found myself looking through each window as we passed to see if Kate was inside, eating the Working Class food which had been served to her, drinking champagne, and planning her trip to the South Pacific.

We ended up in a side street round the back of all the restaurants. Knife looked around cautiously before pulling me into a doorway and up three flights of stairs. I hadn't a clue what was going on, and I wished Knife would be a bit more forthcoming with his information; it was late and I was by now exhausted. We found ourselves standing on the third-floor landing in front of a door marked 3C. It was not the sort of place I wanted to hang around. There was a grubby piece of card pinned next to the door which read 'Victoria French'. The Knife knocked on the door twice, then once, then twice again.

'This where one of your friends lives?' I whispered, no longer able to control my curiosity. Knife nodded and smiled. The door opened a fraction, then closed again, then opened fully to reveal this absolutely stunning looking blonde wearing the most exotic underwear I had ever seen. Then, to cap it all, she threw her arms round the Knife, kissed him powerfully and deeply on the mouth, sighed heavily, and then stood back to look at him.

'Nigel!' she exclaimed at last. 'Where have you been?' I knew then that when it came down to brass tacks, smart as I thought I was, I didn't really know anything, did I?

26

'Linda, this is Jim Demon, an old mate of mine.'

I saw her cast a wary glance at Knife.

'He's all right. Demon, meet Linda.'

'Delighted,' I said, looking at her and meaning it.

'Linda will be looking after you for the next couple of days, Demon, so you behave yourself.' Linda stepped forward and held out her hand.

'Pleased to meet you, Jim,' she said. I took her hand.

'Linda?' I asked, confused. 'Not Victoria?'

She smiled, and looked at Knife again. 'No. That's a . . . a work name.'

'Oh!' I said, catching on, and feeling like a right idiot. 'I didn't realize there would be a demand for . . . that, Inside.'

'Don't be daft, Demon,' replied Knife. 'There's a demand for *that* everywhere. And very useful it can be too.'

'Eh?'

'Don't worry, old son,' he said, patting my cheek. 'Everything will be explained in due course. You just relax. You're safe as houses here. Now,' he said, going into the living room as if he owned the place, 'how about a drink?'

Linda closed the door behind me, and ushered me in after the Knife. I sat on a soft sofa, and suddenly realized just how tired I felt.

'A couple of gin and tonics, love,' said Knife, and Linda smiled again and left the room. Tired as I was, I couldn't help noticing that she had just about the best pair of legs I'd ever seen on a woman. Mind you, they were set off by a pair of stockings and black suspenders which it would have been impossible not to notice, if you get my drift. Knife sat down next to me, lit up a J, inhaled deeply and sank back into the luxurious softness. Disorientated though I was, one thing was nagging me more than anything else, so I thought I'd ask.

'Nigel?' I tried. Knife gave me a very sharp look and then scowled.

'Cut it out, Demon,' he said seriously, noticing the look of suppressed amusement on my face.

'I don't believe it. Is that really your name? Your real name? I mean, I knew you must have had a real name, but . . .'

'Say one word about this Outside, and I swear it'll be your last.'

'Okay, okay!' I said with a grin. 'Not a word . . . Nigel.'

'Easy, Demon!' threatened Knife, making a grab for my throat.

'Sorry, sorry!' I cried, backing away. We sat in silence for a few seconds, enjoying the J.

'Listen, Knife. What's going on? I mean where are we? How do you know Linda? And what do you mean "look after me"?'

He didn't have an opportunity to answer before Linda reappeared. She had put on a white towelling dressing gown which reached the floor, her blonde hair falling evenly around her shoulders. She still looked terrific, but it was just as well I couldn't see any more of her, as there was no way I would have been able to concentrate on anything with her sitting around half-naked. She had a glass in each hand, and gave one to each of us.

'Hungry, either of you?' she asked.

'Starving,' replied Knife.

'You, Jim?'

'Eh? Oh, yes, I could eat something.' She disappeared

again, and Knife followed her. I sat on the couch, sipping the drink. They were gone only a few minutes, but I felt myself starting to drift off. I was only half there when Linda came back in with a tray.

'I think that can wait till morning,' she said firmly, putting the tray down. 'I think it's time for bed.' I didn't argue. I still had a hundred questions, but I wasn't sure I'd have understood the answers at that moment. She got a pillow out of another room, and threw a blanket over me. Knife picked up the tray, and they left the room.

'Sleep well, old son,' he called. I think I was asleep before the door closed.

'Coffee?'

'Huh?' For a second I forgot I wasn't at home in bed. Then the curtains were thrown back and I recognized the small room with its three doors, the light brown carpet and the heavy furniture. Linda stood over me with a cup in her hand.

'Yeh, thanks,' I mumbled, struggling to sit up. My head was fuzzy and my throat felt like someone had poured sawdust in my mouth while I was asleep.

'Sleep okay?' asked Linda, handing me the cup.

'Fine. But I feel a bit rough . . .'

'Combination of exhaustion, cannabis and gin, I should think.'

'Could be right.'

I propped myself up more securely on one elbow and took a sip of the coffee. It was hot and dark and bitter. You could almost taste it before it reached your lips. I'd never tasted coffee like it before, and to tell the truth, if Linda hadn't told me it *was* coffee, I'm not sure I would have recognized it. Linda perched on the edge of the sofa and smiled. She had quite a pretty face, something I hadn't noticed the previous night. To be honest, I'd not

189

got that far north. She was also dressed a bit more conventionally, blue jeans and a red pullover. I took another mouthful of the steaming brew and felt it hit my stomach and spread its warmth through me like a drug.

'You slept for nine hours – it's gone Ten-O. How about breakfast?'

'I think I'll leave eating until I've decided if my stomach's on my side or not.'

'Okay,' she smiled.

'Where's the Knife?'

'What knife?' asked Linda, looking as if I'd just asked her where the pet elephant was.

'Nigel?'

'Oh, Nigel. He's gone. He left a couple of hours ago.'

I suddenly felt very nervous. 'Where's he gone?' I sat up with a start, and felt immediately dizzy. I wondered if the coffee really was fixed.

'It's okay, Jim, don't panic; you're in safe hands. Nigel left instructions that I was to look after you until he returned. He said you weren't to worry, and that he'd get in touch as soon as he could.'

'But where is he? I mean, he can't just wander round up West! Someone might take him for a Usur – ' I stopped short and stared at my hand. It was shaking. Linda started to laugh, although I couldn't see for the life of me what was funny. She leaned over and took the cup from my hand.

'You haven't ever had real coffee before, have you, Jim?' she said, still giggling.

'What? Well, I thought I had.'

'Don't worry, you're not being poisoned.' She put her hand on my arm and grinned, then left the room. I shook my head in disbelief, and then stood up. I felt a bit wobbly, but managed to get to my trousers with the blanket wrapped round me just as Linda returned holding a glass. I sat down again, feeling foolish. She didn't seem to notice.

'Try this. It's orange juice.'

'Thanks.' I tried to put aside my suspicions that this too might be tampered with, and took a big gulp. It tasted great.

'I'm sorry. I don't really think there's anything wrong with what you're giving me. It's just that you tend to trust your taste buds, and when they let you down . . .'

'They haven't let you down. In fact they're doing too well. They're used to counterfeit flavours, and are noticing the difference between them and the real thing. This is obviously your first time.'

'Huh?'

'Your first time Inside.'

'Yeh,' I answered. I have to admit, I was thinking less about the conversation than the fact that I still didn't have my trousers on, and I was feeling more than a bit vulnerable. She must have read my mind, as she stood up.

'I'm just going to tidy up next door. Why don't you get dressed? The bathroom's through there,' she said, pointing to a door behind me.

'You don't know where Knife's gone then?' I called from the bathroom.

'Oh, I've got a pretty good idea. But for the next couple of days you're my guest, so don't concern yourself about "the Knife" or whatever you call him. He's got business to attend to.' She came and continued speaking through the bathroom door. 'I'm sorry to say that you're going to have to stay here for the meantime. It's really too risky to go out unless you have no choice. So you might as well relax and take it easy. You're going to be pretty busy when Nigel gets back.'

'Busy?' She didn't answer, whether because she didn't

hear me or because she didn't want to answer I couldn't say. I opened the door. 'What do you mean busy?'

'Nigel has asked me to leave all the explanations to him. He'll be back soon, honestly.'

'The only thing I want to be busy with is finding someone, and I can't see why I can't get on with it. Why would it be so risky to go out? You know your way around the city. Couldn't you give me directions?'

'Of course I could, but I don't mean the risks of getting lost or of looking like a stranger like last night. I'm not sure you understand what it's like Inside, Jim. There are spot security checks every day. I'm asked for my papers at least once a week.'

'What for?'

'I don't really know. I used to think it was to check for Usurpers, but I doubt that now. In the last couple of years Workers have had to carry all sorts of passes, security clearances and so on. They're even talking about security passes to get into public buildings like museums.'

'What possible justification could there be for that?' I asked, incredulous.

'They *say* because of the Resistance. They've started attacking government buildings. My guess is that the Resistance came along just at the right time so as to give them an excuse to tighten up even more.'

'Just hang on a minute,' I said in exasperation. 'Every time you answer one question, you raise two more. Who or what are the Resistance?'

Now it was her turn to look incredulous. 'You mean you don't know? Where have you been living, Jim?'

'Ilford.' She looked blank. 'Jesus Christ, don't you lot ever wonder what's outside the Wall? You really mean you've never heard of it?' She shook her head apologetically. 'Well, it's about fifteen Ks east of here, although by the sound of it, it might as well be fifteen thousand.

And in Ilford we've never heard of a Resistance. At least I haven't, and to the best of my recollection I've never heard anyone else mention it either.'

I pulled my shirt on and took her by the hand.

'I understand what the Knife told you about answering my questions,' I said as I led her into the kitchen, 'so I'll keep off any questions relating to him, but you had better fill in some background for me.'

27

I suppose the least I could say was that by the end of that day, I was no longer half as confused as I had been at the beginning of it. Depressed, yes, disillusioned, yes, and miserable, but not confused. Do you know that film, *The Wizard of Oz*? It's one of Dad's favourites; he knows all the songs and half the lines off by heart. Thing is, I used to go on at him because he always missed the point. He never understood that the land at the end of the rainbow wasn't the paradise it was cracked up to be, or that the Wizard was an old fraud. I once tried to explain it to him, that no one was going to wave a magic wand and change everything; if you didn't like the way things were, you had to put up with it or change it yourself. You could Usurp. And all the time it was me that hadn't understood it. Even if you *did* Usurp, nothing was any different. Inside still wasn't Paradise, and the Wizard was still a fraud. Perhaps the old man wasn't so daft after all; he'd given up, stopped fighting, gone AW. It was me, and people like me, who'd been blind in believing that over the rainbow everything would be better.

Linda's life sounded just as miserable as mine, perhaps worse. Sure, she could go to posh restaurants, buy nice clothes, go to the theatre. But every day someone demanded to see her Work Permit. Every day new security measures were introduced, limiting her freedom to move within the city, and the Ceepee, the City Police, were given greater powers of entering and searching people's homes. At least the Snorters Outside were readily identifiable in their leather riot gear. Inside, the

194

Ceepee wore no uniforms. They mingled with the Workers, arresting them without warning, breeding suspicion and distrust throughout the city. Every month a few hundred had their Work Permits revoked and were cast out of the city destitute. The Nooz announced daily the names of the victims of the latest Ministerial 'purge'. They were the lucky ones, the ones that didn't simply disappear.

'Why haven't I heard anything about this?' I asked.

'Don't you see the Nooz Outside?'

'Of course we do,' I replied.

'Well, you must have heard about Marie Fowler's disappearance.'

'Yes. They said that they thought she had committed suicide. After a while they reckoned it was a kidnapping. Then a bit later they said it was "mysterious". Not a word was said about civil unrest!'

'I expect she was too important just to forget about.' Linda paused for a while. 'But Jim, why should they bother to censor the news you get Outside? It makes no sense.'

'I don't know. I want to think about that one. But what about the Resistance?'

'I can't tell you very much. All I know is that a few Technocrats are assassinated every month, and things get blown up, and the Nooz says that the Resistance have claimed responsibility.'

'What do they want?' I asked.

'I don't know. Change?'

'They're Insiders aren't they? Members of the Working Class? They've all got passports, so why don't they leave? Fly off somewhere.'

Linda laughed, but without mirth. 'You're joking! Is that what they tell you – that you can "fly off" somewhere? Jim, I can't leave England any more than you can. Sure, I have a passport, but there aren't any exit visas.'

'But the Act, the Security of Employment Act says you can apply for a – '

'Apply, Jim; it says you can apply. It does not say a visa will be granted.'

'But what about Expo?'

'What's "Expo"?' she asked.

'It's a competition. The winner's entitled to an Exit . . .' I trailed off as she shook her head. 'You've never heard of it?' She continued to shake her head. 'Jesus Christ!'

'Have you ever met anyone who's won it?' she asked.

'That's a joke we have Outside. You never meet an Expo winner 'cos he's already pissed off. I always said it was a con, but somehow I still believed in it. I wanted to believe in it.'

So that was it. Meet Jim Demon, Mug. You know, you don't meet many Usurpers do you, that is, not real ones. Oh yes, there's always a Library full of supposed Jobbers, but how many of them actually did it? Actually handed in their Library cards for good and disappeared? I always wondered how many of them were there just to relieve the boredom, get away from the AWs at home, keep warm. Some of them had been Jobbing for years. Being a Jobber gave you some status around Ilford. It showed the world that you had the bottle to put your life on the line. For the first time I wondered how many of them had been conned like me. Maybe they'd known all along. I was the only one stupid enough to have been taken in. Me and Freddo. And of course Kate the idealist.

I thought about her then. Even if she survived, what had she gained? Stuck for good in some mind-numbing job, but at the same time terrified of losing her Work Permit; constantly looking over her shoulder, waiting for the man who is going to take her job and her life. Possessing her treasured passport, but with her coral island completely unattainable. No way forward, and no way back. Had she been fooled into pursuing a false dream, only to forsake one nightmare for another?

You know, maybe my mum and dad were right after all. They're content. Just watch the quiz games on the Box and dream of winning Expo. Don't let anything else bother you. As long as you don't win, you can't be disappointed.

28

As you might imagine, the next couple of days were pretty depressing. I liked Linda a lot; she had an easy personality, and sharing cramped living accommodation with someone who looked the way she did was no hardship, but we were both aware that she was effectively my gaoler until the Knife returned. She tried to distract me with stories about some of her clients and life inside the Wall, but after a while the conversation flagged. All I wanted to do was get out of the flat and start looking for Kate. I had this feeling that she might need me.

By the afternoon of the third day I was pacing the floor like a caged tiger and feeling about as benign. Linda was in the kitchen clearing up from lunch, and had put on the Box to distract me. I turned the volume right down. I wasn't interested. I had spent the whole of the day before watching every programme – not one of which did I recognize – in the hope of picking up clues about Working Class life. One thing I did notice, and that was that my clothes looked as though they were out of some Histo-drama. On the night we got in I had noticed the bright colours the Working Class liked to wear, but I hadn't seen that the styles were completely different too. No wonder Knife was worried about us being spotted. Anyway, I had spoken to Linda about it, and she had shown me into her bedroom, and thrown open her wardrobe doors. Now, I may not have mentioned this before, but in my reading at the Library I got really quite keen on the Bard, you know, Shakespeare. It wasn't something I spoke of much; spouting the soliloquy from *Hamlet* doesn't do as much for your street credibility in Ilford as you might imagine. Anyway, as I was saying, Linda showed me her clothes, and I swear, it looked like a theatrical wardrobe. There was a clown's outfit, all sorts of leather gear, an angel's get-up (complete with wings!), a cowboy costume and other stuff. She said that some of her clients 'liked to pretend' when giving it the prod. Among this lot were a couple of men's suits, one in her size, and one that fitted me like it had been made for me. Apparently that one had belonged to a particular client who had left in a bit of a rush. I said that he must have been in a bloody hurry to have left stark bollock naked, but she wouldn't give me any more details, which was a pity. I swopped my clothes for that suit. Linda was well pleased, saying that she could use my stuff when clients wanted to pretend they were slumming it. Charming.

For the hundredth time I asked Linda where Knife was, and for the hundredth time she told me that she didn't know. I had got to the point of believing her, but I was sure that she knew more than she would tell me.

'He's always disappearing for days on end and then turning up as if he'd just popped out for five minutes,' she said. I believed that all right; he did just the same Outside. All the same, I'd had enough.

'I've had it!' I cried.

'What?' she called from the kitchen.

I went into the hallway and found my jacket. Linda came out, wiping her hands on a towel.

'What did you say?' she asked.

'I'm going out.' She looked at me hard.

'Look, Jim, I know it's difficult, but please be patient. I'm sure Nigel will be back soon.'

'Don't worry. I'm just going out for a walk. I'll be back in a bit.'

'Don't worry? You don't know the city, you idiot! You'll get yourself killed!'

I eased past her and opened the door.

'I may not know the city, Linda, but I'm not helpless. I'm an Outsider, remember? It's not exactly a picnic living in Ilford.'

'But what do you think you can do?'

'I'm not going to *do* anything. I just need to get out for a while.'

'Wait there!' she commanded. She reappeared a few seconds later with her coat.

'What are you doing?' I asked.

'What does it look like? I promised Nigel I wouldn't let you out of my sight.'

'It's really not necessary – '

'Then humour me!' she snapped. She locked the door and pushed past me. 'Well; shall we go?'

We walked down the narrow wooden staircase to the street, and Linda indicated that we should turn left. She took my arm.

'Just in case they are looking for you and Nigel. They'll be less likely to notice a couple,' she said, without looking at me. We turned left on to a busy road, and continued in silence for about ten minutes. I began to sense that her anger was dissipating. She held my arm with less force, and walked a little more slowly.

'I'm sorry, Linda,' I said. 'I simply had to get out. We'll have a short walk, and then head back to the flat.'

She sighed. 'It's okay, but you must promise to do exactly as I say if there are any problems.'

'Agreed, but it won't be necessary. We're just two hard-working members of the Working Class enjoying an afternoon stroll.' Which was in fact just what we looked like. There were a lot of people about, none of them appearing to hurry, and we blended in without difficulty.

After about fifteen minutes we turned left down a wide street with theatres on both sides, and eventually came to a big plaza with enormous statues of lions and a column which Linda said had been built by a chap called Nelson. I must say I recalled his name from Second Ed., but I couldn't remember in what context. It was nice to see some of his architecture.

The plaza was full of pigeons, squabbling and strutting in droves, and even landing on people's heads and arms. It was then that my attention was drawn to a little group by one of the lions. There was a young chap in a white and blue suit, and with him there was a girl. They were talking to two older men. I was about forty metres away, but even from that distance I could see that something was wrong. The chap looked very tense, and the girl's expression was one of fear. I could only see their backs, but everything about the two older men smelt of 'Snorter'. I squeezed Linda's arm and nodded in the direction of the group. She made to move away, but I held her back. One of the two older men had grabbed hold of the girl. The young chap was just standing there, his arms hanging helplessly by his sides. The girl was struggling fiercely, thrashing her arms about. It was at this point that something very strange occurred. From across the other side of the plaza there came a line of people dressed in flowing pink robes. They moved in single file, and every few steps they did a little skip, as if dancing, so that the whole line rose and fell in a wave. They carried musical instruments, cymbals, triangles and tambourines, and seemed to be singing or chanting, although, because of the distance, I couldn't quite hear. Their leader seemed to change course abruptly, and headed straight for the scene by the lion. Within seconds the two groups met. The two Snorters were pushed apart by a pink wave of chanting dancers. They began shouting, waving their arms, and giving commands, but no one took a blind bit of notice. In the mêlée the girl seemed to become detached from the Snorters and slipped away.

'It's time we moved,' said Linda urgently. She was right. As we turned away, a number of men who I had not seen before began to converge swiftly on the spot. We turned to go back the way we had come, when I saw a line of men approaching us. They were herding together everyone in their path, and I saw people reaching into pockets and getting documents out.

'Quickly!' shouted Linda, and pulled me off to the left. She ran straight into the road, gripping my sleeve and dragging me with her. Now, as you may remember, there's little or no traffic in Ilford. Linda ran straight into the path of at least a dozen vehicles each doing forty Ks, and I don't mind telling you that if I had been given a chance to object, she would never have got me off the pavement. As it was, there was a squeal of tyres from all sides, and a blare of horns, but we made it across. I followed as Linda sprinted up a flight of steps, through some swing doors, and into the packed lobby of a building. I looked back. I wasn't sure that anyone had seen our dash across the road, but even if they had, there were now at least a hundred people separating us from any pursuers.

'Where the hell are we?' I asked.

'The National. It's an art gallery.'

I expect you will find this hard to believe given the circumstances, but my heart leapt with excitement when Linda said that. There are museums on the Outside but you'd have to be pretty desperate to spend time in any of the ones I've seen. Every piece of art or sculpture that you ever read about or saw on the Box was Inside, so I'd never actually seen any real art.

'Can we look around?' I asked.

Linda looked over the heads of the throng. 'If the Ceepees saw people running in, I doubt that they'd expect them to come straight out again. So we might get away with walking out immediately. On the other hand, if they saw our clothes, we might be recognized. I don't know, Jim. What do you think?'

'Stay.'

'Okay.'

The next hour was stupendous. The place was full of paintings, some of them hundreds of years old. Most of them had been done by foreigners, which I thought strange. Why should they be in an English art gallery? I wandered around in a daze, not really knowing what I was looking at, but having a great time. Linda said that many of the best ones had been sold off to pay off some national debt or other, but there were enough to satisfy me. Apparently there had once been two galleries, with the newer stuff in the other place, but as so much had been sold, they had put the lot in this one gallery. One of the rooms contained what they called 'Modern' artists, although most of them had been dead for the best part of a century. It was in this room that I found this amazing picture.

It wasn't a painting as much as a bunch of big coloured shapes stuck on a white background. It was absolutely huge too. So big, so colourful, that's the way it hit me first off, before I realized what it was. I wrote down the name of the artist so that I wouldn't forget – Matisse. He was the bloke that thought up the idea, although Linda, who strangely enough seemed to know something about him, said that he had been too old and sick to make it himself. So he had just directed some of his fans (Matisse being a pretty popular sort of bloke) to stick the bits of paper where he said. It was called, and I must get this right, 'L'Escargot', which Linda said meant 'The Snail'. It struck me as a pretty silly name at first, until I realized that that was exactly what it was. It was a picture of a snail! When I realized that I was even more taken with it, and I stood looking at it for ages.

Now I can't explain exactly why this was, but somehow Mister Matisse and his snail put me in mind of the City, and Henry Jordan. I had learned a lot in the last few days, but I was having difficulty putting it all into order. Like L'Escargot, close up it looked like a lot of meaningless blocks, each coloured so brightly you could be blinded to the whole. The closer you got, the more difficult it was to see any sense in it. Most people would probably take one look at L'Escargot and give up, move on. But if you looked carefully enough, if you looked at the whole thing, then it began to make sense. Mister Jordan hadn't built the Wall; he hadn't created the Haves and the Have-Nots, but he'd been the one with the idea; other people had put it together under his direction. In some ways his society was just like L'Escargot; after all, what was it? Just a slimy, ugly slug with a fancy name and a pretty exterior.

Linda was nagging me to move on, and within a few minutes we were moving swiftly through the dark streets to her flat. We had no trouble on the return journey, but I'm not sure I'd have noticed anyway. My mind was full of coloured images, among which a black and white photo of Henry Jordan kept coming up. Oh yes, there was something else. That hum deep in my head. It was still there and, if anything, a bit louder.

29

The Knife turned up that night shortly after we got back. There was the same knock at the door, two-one-two, and I opened the door. There he was, looking for all the world like he'd been in a collision with a very large block of concrete.

'Jeesus, Knife! What the hell happened to you?'

His face was all bruised and it looked like his ear had been half torn off. His right eye was multicoloured and completely closed. He pushed past me and walked over to Linda, gave her a big kiss (wincing a little on contact with her lips) and then headed for the kitchen without saying a word.

'Knife?' I called out after him. 'Knife, what happened?'

'Eh?' he said, returning from the kitchen with a drink in his hand. 'What you going on about, Demon?'

'Your face!'

'You trying to be funny?' he replied, and took a large gulp from his glass.

'Have you looked at yourself in the mirror?' I asked. Linda shook her head and tutted with about the most complete lack of concern imaginable.

'Don't drip blood on the carpet, Nigel,' she said, and sat down again.

'As a matter of fact, Demon, no, I haven't,' said Knife, ignoring Linda. He disappeared into the bathroom for a moment, reappearing with a big grin on his face. 'I see what you mean. Bit messy I suppose. Don't worry yourself, mate, it's nothing.'

'But a bit conspicuous don't you think, Nigel?' chided Linda softly. Knife grunted and sat down next to her.

'Suppose so,' he acknowledged. 'Anyway, how've you two been then? My girl been looking after you, has she?'

'Linda's been great. I've been learning a great deal – '

'I'll bet you have,' interrupted the Knife with that lascivious gap-toothed grin of his. He ran his hand right up along Linda's thigh and then grabbed her. She giggled and pushed him away.

'You bloody pervert!' she said, obviously not upset. 'For heaven's sake, go and clean yourself up, or poor Jim will think you're going to bleed to death. Just look at the mess you're making on the sofa!'

'Sorry, babe . . . it's just a bit of blood; it'll wash out. Now then,' he said as he went to the bathroom, 'what have you been doing to my mate over there? You ain't been practising on him with any of that disgusting equipment you keep under the bed. Has she Jim? Has she shown you her "Continental Collection"?'

'Cut it out, Nigel,' she replied, looking quite embarrassed.

I thought it was time to change the subject. 'Where have you been then?'

'We can talk about that later,' replied Knife dismissively. 'Right now I'm starving. What's for dinner?' he asked, turning to Linda.

'Let's not talk about it later!' I shouted. 'I want to know what's going on!'

'Easy, boy. We'll talk about it later, okay?' said Knife. Now normally I recognize and respect that hard edge to Knife's voice, but I was just about at the end of my tether, so I ignored the danger signals.

'No, it's not okay! You know why I came in, and you just fucking disappear leaving me sitting on my arse! Then

206

you saunter in after three days as if nothing's happened. You owe me an explanation!' I cried.

'I don't owe you nothing, Demon. I've had a hard day training, I've got me face a bit squashed, and I'm hungry. So I'm going to eat. Right?' He approached me as he spoke, stopping right in front of me. His voice was even softer this time, but I was still too angry to notice.

'Fine. And before you do, you can tell my why you bothered to help me get in at all, if all I was going to do was sit around in a fucking brothel.' I was sorry for Linda that I'd said it quite that way, but I could see her grinning good-naturedly.

There was an uneasy silence for a few seconds, during which Knife and I stared at each other. Linda stood very still on the other side of the room. Now as you know, I'm not exactly the tough type. I mean, anyone on the Outside has got to know how to look after themselves, right? Losers don't survive long, and I'm big enough to make some people want to see how tough they are. But I don't look for trouble. Knife, on the other hand, does. I've seen him fighting for real, and he's an animal – fast, strong and totally pitiless. There are few things in this world that I'm frightened of as I've told you before; closed-in spaces and wild dogs, is what I always say. But there is something that frightens me even more. The Knife. Nothing scares me like the Knife, even though he's my best friend. So this was new ground for me. At this point I usually backed down for the sake of my health, that is, when his nose was three centimetres away from mine, and he was still and quiet. This time I wasn't going to do it, even if I *was* shitting myself.

'Well? Well? Are you going to answer me or not?' I asked, trying to keep the tremor out of my voice.

There was a long pause. I probably only waited for half a minute for his answer, but it felt like an hour. Eventually Knife stuck out his lower lip, and sort of shrugged.

'Okay, Demon. What do you want to know?'

30

Against the backdrop of blue-black sky and faint stars I saw the shape of a tower rising from between naked trees. I shivered. It was very cold, and it had been a long walk from Linda's flat. We had stumbled across the parkland in the dim moonlight barely passing a word between us, the Knife insisting that we keep all conversation to a minimum. Twice in the last two or three minutes he had grabbed my arm, and we had halted, while he appeared to listen. On one occasion he had given a hoot like that of an owl, and there had come an answering hoot from off to our left.

As we came out of the trees I saw another structure ahead of us, to the left of the tower; a dome. It was gold, and glowed eerily, reflecting every fraction of light from its surroundings. I began to feel even more nervous than when Knife had told me about the place, and I wasn't sure I wanted to carry on. I chose that moment to express my worries to Knife.

'Look Demon, you're the one that wants all the answers. You've come this far, and I sure as hell ain't taking you back. So unless you want to start wandering around the Park in the hope of finding your way back to Linda's, I suggest you fucking well get your shit together, okay?' I didn't reply.

We climbed over some railings and moved swiftly into the lee of the building where it was even darker. Knife approached the door and performed his now familiar knock, and the door opened immediately. I followed him inside. No sooner had I heard the door close behind me, when a thick muscular forearm appeared out of the darkness and caught me under the chin. My knees were struck from behind me and I was forced to the floor. It happened so quickly that I didn't have a chance to shout out, and with my face pressed into cold hard stone there was no way I could make a sound. It had been a trap! There was a grip like a vice around my throat, and I felt my head swimming. I began to drift away, when I heard Knife's voice.

'It's okay, boys, he's with me.'

I felt myself being lifted bodily from the floor and set back on my feet. I was subjected to a couple of perfunctory blows on the back, whether designed to dust me down or to break my ribs I'm not sure, and then the forms of my two attackers merged into the darkness. I spat blood from my mouth, and tried to breathe normally again. I began to realize that my surroundings were not completely dark. As my eyes grew accustomed to the light I saw that I was in a circular room, possibly eighty metres across. I was inside the dome!

'This way,' said the Knife. I followed his silhouette. 'Okay. Just stop there a minute,' he said softly. Then he bowed towards the room. I was just about to make some crack, when I saw past him into the middle of the room. In the half-light I could make out the forms of dozens of still bodies, all in an identical pose, each one as still as a statue. There must have been a hundred people there, but you could have heard a pin drop. I looked up. Suspended from the ceiling were a number of large glass bulbs giving a soft orange glow to the strange tableau. Each of the 'statues' was wearing a pink suit, with baggy arms and a belt around the waist, and they were all barefoot. In front of them, standing just as still, was a man in a black robe with the bottom gathered up and tucked in his belt so that I could see his bare legs. I stared around me at the extraordinary circular room, and for the first time realized what the building was.

'It's a mosque!' I exclaimed. 'Knife? Isn't it?'

'Yeh. Well, it used to be a mosque.'

'What's a mosque doing in London?' I asked, totally baffled. The mystery of why the building was there at all temporarily overwhelmed the question of what was going on inside it. I mean, why should there be a mosque in England?

'Beats me,' said Knife offhandedly. 'Anyway, it ain't a mosque now. It's "The Centre". It's where we do all our training. Those,' he pointed at the motionless figures, 'are the trainees.'

'Don't tell me you were beaten up by a load of frigging ballet dancers in pink suits,' I said sceptically.

'I wouldn't mock if I were you, Demon. Any one of them could approach you from behind on almost any terrain, and kill you with a single silent blow. They're also all trained to use firearms and at least half of them are pretty handy with explosives.'

'Here,' I said, remembering the incident at the plaza the day before, 'are these the same people who go around the streets in pink robes with musical instruments?'

Knife smiled as if at a private joke. 'Could be, old son, could be.'

'But they're just religious fanatics according to Linda.'

'Well, what better place for us than in a mosque?' he said.

'Us? You mean you're one of them? You and religion? You've got to be joking!' I exclaimed, in complete disbelief. Knife was perfectly serious as he answered.

'And why not? I'm not religious the way the geezers who used to pray here were, but . . . Look, let's not discuss it here. We're disturbing them.' He slipped off his shoes, beckoned to me to follow, and padded across the marble floor, around the circumference of the room. I followed suit. Knife disappeared through a door on the far side. I took one last look at the 'trainees'. They were moving in perfect unison, their left arms pointed straight out from their bodies with clenched fists, and their right forearms held across their faces, as if shielding their eyes. They all skipped to the right, their bare feet slapping on the marble, and kicked their left legs in a wide sweep at head height. I shook my head, and pushed open the door through which the Knife had gone.

I found myself in a small anteroom lined with books. There was a table, a few chairs arranged in lines, a couple of Consoles, and a blackboard. The Knife had changed into a black robe like that of the man facing the trainees. Again I fought the impulse to make a joke.

'Sit down, Demon,' he said, indicating a chair facing him. I did so.

'I don't pretend to understand what you've got yourself involved in, Knife, and far be it from me to tell you you're off your chump. If you want to ponce about in pink robes and practise high kicks, best of luck. But what's it got to do with me? As far as I'm concerned, I came Inside for one reason, and one reason only – to find Kate. And that's all I want to do.'

'Can't you see, Demon, that this is far more important than one loopy girl?'

'Not to me it isn't.'

'But you've seen what it's like Inside. It's all a con! Those poor bastards on the Outside are being used, and they don't know it. We can *do* something, Jim – '

'Not me, mate.'

'But you've got brains, Demon. You must have worked it out by now – '

'No, Knife! I don't want anything to do with it.'

'But you're the one who's always going on about what a pile of shit life is! You didn't know the half of it! It's not a case of the Haves and the Have-Nots as your Kate used to put it. We're all in the same shit. It just *smells* different Inside, that's all.'

Now I've got to tell you that, believe it or not, this was the most articulate thing I'd ever heard the Knife say. During the last few weeks I'd had to adjust to a lot of things about the Knife that I'd never imagined. But his being a philosopher was just one too many. There comes a time when impatience outweighs curiosity, and for me, that time had just arrived.

'If you and your terrorist ballet-dancing friends want to go round assassinating people and blowing things up, that's fine by me. I personally don't believe in it. I'm here to find Kate, and nothing more. And you said you'd help me – '

'Correction: I said I'd help you across the Wall, which I have duly done. I even risked one of the few secure routes we have. I've even kept you safe and sound since we arrived. So if you're going to mouth off, let's at least get the facts straight.'

'What do you want, Knife? Thanks? Okay: thanks a lot. Now, if you don't mind, I'll be off, doing what I intended to do from the start.'

'Finding Kate?' He started shouting. 'For a smart geezer, Demon, you ain't half a fuckwit sometimes. Don't you understand? Wherever she is, if she's not already six feet under, and whatever she's doing, she's one of *them* now. Demon, she's a Worker! And you, you're nothing but a threat. You're an Outsider, boy; you're a wanted man here. Your only way to stay alive is to kill someone for their job. As far as Kate is concerned, you're the enemy now.'

'But I'm not a Usurper!' I shouted. 'She knows that!'

'Does she? What's she going to think when she sees you? "My love has found me"?' He affected a high-pitched voice for that last bit, and I swear, I came within an ace of throwing myself across the table that separated us, and killing him with a single blow, silent or otherwise. He continued with his attack. 'There's only one thing she can think: he's after my job. You try telling her you're only here for love when she's levelling a gun at your head!' He leaned across the table and stabbed me in the chest with his finger as he spoke. 'She's gone, Demon. Don't you understand? She's gone!'

'But we were . . .' I withdrew from the words 'in love'. I knew what his reaction would be. Saying them, to him, in that place, devalued them. They didn't belong there.

'In love?' he sneered derisively.

I pulled my hand back to hit him. His right hand shot up from where it had been prodding my chest and slapped me hard, disdainfully, before I could land my blow.

'The moment you come within a hundred metres of her, Demon, you're dead meat.'

'You don't understand, Knife. You just don't understand.'

He sat down again with a heavy sigh and leaned back against the wall, shaking his head.

'Jeez, Demon, I really thought you had it up here,' he said, tapping his head.

'Don't you worry, Knife. I know there are risks, but I'll be careful, very careful.'

'Yeh,' he said flatly. 'That's just what Freddo said.'

31

It was four days since we had broken into the city, and six since Kate had left me lying in her bed, and here I was, cooling my heels again, no nearer to finding her. I had had to spend the night at the Centre; Knife refused to guide me back to Linda's, and the others effectively ignored me. I knew that I wouldn't be able to find the way, and even *I* recognized that it would be suicide to wander around a strange and reputedly dangerous part of the city alone and after dark.

Some of the trainees disappeared later that night, whether to go on some mission or just to go home I don't know. The rest settled down to sleep. I say 'settled down', but in fact they did precisely the opposite. At one end of the building was a line of columns, and towards the end of the evening one of the pink-suited girls strung between them what looked like a line of fishing nets. I thought they were some sort of safety device until later on I looked out, and I saw that a number of them had people in them! The nets expanded and gave way so that a person could lie down. I was told that I could take any one to sleep in, so up I climbed. It was a bit tricky getting in, but having managed that, it was wonderfully comfortable. The net was flexible and gave to accommodate the shape of my body. I lay there looking up at the dome above me, swinging slightly, and taking stock of my situation. Some of the others around me talked quietly for a while, but eventually I was left alone with my thoughts.

Knife was right about one thing; he hadn't promised to help me find Kate. I should have realized we were at cross-purposes when he agreed to get me in. His attitude from the start was that it was a waste of time worrying about her, so I should have asked myself why he had agreed to help. Still, even if I had thought about it, my being a potential recruit for some private army would not have immediately come to mind. Can you believe it eh? My mate the Knife, an Ilford hoodlum who likes to show off by slicing people up, was a leading light in a movement designed to Change the World. Life, as they say, is full of surprises.

As you may be aware, I thought the whole idea of armed revolution pretty daft. Not that I was exactly happy with the world as it was, especially now I understood a bit more about it. It was like Usurping, see? The odds were so much against you that it wasn't worth it. I'm not saying I had any better ideas; it was just that the idea that even a few hundred well-trained men could defeat the whole Technocratic machine seemed idealistic, not to say fucking ridiculous. The Resistance were fighting with their bare fists (or feet, to judge from what I'd seen of their training), and weapons that had been obsolete for over a hundred years. One squad of Snorters equipped with their high-velocity projectiles and blast guns would wipe out the entire Resistance movement in two minutes.

One thing I will say for them though, and that was there was a palpable air of purpose at the Centre. That was something I'd never experienced before. The greatest cause of misery on the Outside, what hangs in the air like smog over Ilford and, I bet, every other place too, is boredom. No one ever has anything to do. It's like one of them progressive diseases; it spreads insidiously, first attacking your brain, then your soul and finally your body. That's what almost everyone dies of, at least those that die of natural causes. My dad reckons that a hundred years ago most people lived till they were eighty or ninety!

216

Even allowing for the old geezer's funny memory, I'd be prepared to bet they lived beyond fifty-five or sixty, which is as old as anyone I've ever heard of. With the exception of the Jobbers in the Library, nobody actually *does* anything. You know, I've only ever met one or two people who could actually tell you what day of the week it was. There's nothing different about the days, so what's the point remembering their names? The old folk go senile or AW or both. The young ones smoke Js and wipe out what few active brain cells they have with lethal vodka.

This place though was different. People laughed, talked all the time (at least when their instructor allowed them), and they all looked bright, active. None of them had that grey, zapped expression you see everywhere on the Outside. I wondered if it was the training they did, or just the fact that they were doing *something*. Personally, I don't think that anyone in Ilford could give a flying fuck about changing the world, but if it wasn't presented to them like that, but just as a way of spending some time, using up the endless hours that drifted from one dull day to the next, well, who knows?

That was my last thought before drifting off into sleep. I could just see the old man in a pink robe doing high kicks and discussing politics. That would be the day.

I awoke late, feeling refreshed and cheerful. Now I knew that I would have to find Kate on my own, I too felt less useless, more purposeful. I clambered out of my bed to find that most of the trainees had already departed. I couldn't find Knife, but one of the young men who remained told me that there was coffee in the anteroom. I wandered in and poured myself a cup, taking care to sip it slowly so as to prevent myself from keeling over like the last time. I turned on one of the Consoles, and I watched the Nooz at Eleven while I waited for Knife. He turned up after a few minutes in his street clothes. He was obviously agitated.

'Is it on yet?' he asked.

'Is what on?'

He swung the Console round to face him and turned up the volume. 'The attack on the Ministry of External Affairs! They didn't mention it at all last night, but we heard that there was to be a press release by midday.'

'What attack? A Resistance attack? By you?'

He didn't answer, but I didn't have to wait long for the information. The announcer received a piece of paper from out of shot, and began to make what he called a 'Stop-Press Announcement'.

'News has just come in from the Ministry of External Affairs that there has been a bomb attack on the building. At approximately Five-O this morning – '

'Five-O! It was at Three-O, the lying bastards!' shouted Knife at the Console.

' – without prior warning there was an explosion at the Ministry in Whitehall. It was followed immediately by an assault by between a dozen and twenty armed men – '

'What?!'

'Early reports indicate that casualties have been heavy. We are receiving reports of thirty wounded and two killed. Four are still missing, and firemen are presently searching the rubble – '

'There was no assault! One bomb, that was all!'

The announcer continued. 'One of the dead men was Mr James Hogarth-Spiers, the Under-Secretary – '

'I don't believe this . . .' said Knife, looking astounded.

'. . . found shot in the head. It is thought that the bomb was simply a diversion while the real purpose of the attack was the assassination of Mr Hogarth-Spiers, whose appointment only six months ago was seen as a concession to the hard-line – '

Knife punched the Console and switched it off. He slumped into the seat on the other side of the table, and glared at me.

'It's been fixed! Now I know why those bastards delayed the announcement. We didn't kill that bloke. That building was completely deserted when we left it, and none of us were anywhere near the bloody place when the bomb went off. *And* we gave them a thirty-minute warning!'

'You've got to give it to them, whoever did shoot him must be pretty well-organized,' I offered. Knife looked at me enquiringly. 'Well, your attack was at Three-O. Within two hours they found the bloke they wanted, shot him, got his body to the scene, and generally added to the destruction to make it look good.'

Knife looked grim. 'Believe me, Demon, I don't care if they kill each other – all the fewer for us to worry about. But this time I was given information – ' He looked up from the table suddenly and stopped. He looked regretfully at me, and then shook his head.

'Have you thought any more about what I said?' he asked.

'Some,' I answered.

'And?'

'I'm going to look for Kate. You may be right – I don't think you are – but if you are, I'll go back to Ilford.'

'Have you thought it through, Demon? Just say I'm wrong, and she's still alive and receives you with open arms; then what are you going to do? You can't stay here unless you kill someone, which you say you're not prepared to do. She can't leave the city now.'

'I know,' I admitted. 'I'll have to play that one by ear. At the moment I just want to find her – to know she's still alive. If she is, I expect she'll want to talk to me at least.'

'I think you're bloody mad.'

'So you've said.'

'Well,' he said, getting up, 'I've got to go. How you gonna go about this?'

'I want to have a think about that.'

'Keep off the streets this morning, eh? The Ceepee will be out in force. You can stay here for today, but keep low, and get one of the others to give you a robe. We're a religious group, right?' He left, and then stuck his head back round the door. 'Oh, by the way, Demon. Don't go back to Linda's until tonight. Her place is being used for something,' he said mysteriously and departed. It appeared that I was really on my own from now on.

I sat for a while finishing my coffee, and then got up and looked around at the shelves of books around me. I was surprised to find so many. The only reason that the Library at Ilford had so many books was because they'd accumulated over the years and no one had put them on to the computer. Inside, they had operators trained simply to do that – at least two of the Jobbers at Ilford were training for that very job – so I'd assumed that manuscripts were pretty rare. It didn't take me long to realize why these particular books were not available on the computer. They were almost all banned. There were books by people I'd heard of, Marx, Engels, Galbraith, and Bentham, and by others whose names meant nothing to me, like Durkheim. Don't get me wrong, I hadn't read any of them; you couldn't get them at all on the Outside. But if, like me, you spend most of your waking hours in a Library, and, like me, you're keen on history, you can't help bumping into their names every now and then. And every time I read one of their names and was faced with an empty shelf when I looked for what they'd written, my curiosity was raised further. Human nature isn't it?

There was enough stuff here to keep me busy for a

couple of years. I took a few volumes at random off the shelf, put them on the table and sat down. I picked up the first volume. Now, I don't know if it's ever happened to you, but every now and then, life takes one of those odd turns. I mean, no matter how much you plan and think about things, some decisions are just taken out of your hands. At those times I almost wonder if those Christians and so on who believed in a god and all that stuff knew something that I don't. I was holding a book called *The Impact of Technology on Occupational Structure in Post-Industrial Society* by, you guessed it, Henry Jordan. I felt in my pocket and brought out the sleeve that I had taken from the Library. I couldn't really tell you why I had carried it with me since leaving Ilford, any more than I could explain why I pinched it in the first place. It was as if something had clicked in the back of my mind, but I couldn't bring it forward so as to put my finger on it. I turned over the folded piece of paper and looked at his photo, the narrow eyes, that arrogant look. Then, suddenly, like a camera shutter clicking, a series of pictures flicked through my mind. The photo was replaced by a picture of Kate, looking up from her work at the Library, her frown of concentration melting into that lovely smile. Click! That picture was gone, and I saw Jordan again, this time talking, but without sound, on the Box, the night before Kate left. Click! A picture of Kate again, angry, sullen and, yes, something I hadn't noticed before, frightened, as she turned the Box off. Jordan – Kate – Jordan – Kate. I don't know why I'd been so dense! It was like a light had been switched on in my head, illuminating something that had been there for some time. I reckoned then that I knew where Kate was – at least if she was still alive.

32

I left the Centre at around Three-O, without seeing Knife again. The Centre's books included detailed maps of the city, and I had spent over an hour drawing and re-drawing both the route I was to take and the roads around it until I was sure I knew the entire area. If I was forced off the direct route by up to two hundred metres I reckoned that I would still be able to get there. I was going to a place called Holborn. I calculated that it would only take an hour, and, although I would have preferred to move in darkness, I had to leave enough time to make sure that my hunch had been right, and get to Linda's in daylight if not.

I crossed the park without seeing another person. That part of the journey didn't worry me: I was used to crossing the Waste when I had to. It was a different story when I got to the street. It was swarming with people. Outside, a crowd on the street means trouble. You cross over, right? I tried to tell myself that this time it was to my advantage, that I would look less conspicuous, but I was still pretty nervous.

It was just after Four-O, and the light was just beginning to fade, when I arrived outside the Ministry at Red Lion Street. I took a deep breath, and climbed the stairs. The doors opened, and I stepped into an enormous entrance hall. Away to my left was an 'Enquiries' desk, in front of which was a lengthy queue. A metal security screen spanned the hall, broken in the middle by a metal archway through which all entrants passed after showing documents to the guards. I could sense my breathing quicken, but I forced myself not to think of my fear but to concentrate. I looked around the hall to see if there was anything that might help me, give me a clue as to where Kate might be, but I couldn't see anything. More haste less speed as the old lady would've said.

'May I help you, sir?'

My heart leapt and I whirled round. There was a guard in front of me, broad and tall, almost as tall as me. On his face there rested a bland smile, and on his machine pistol there rested his hand. I did my best to smile.

'Yes indeed,' I said as slowly as I could, imitating Linda's accent as well as I could, and sounding a right prat I can tell you. 'I need a single piece of information, but to be honest, I haven't time to queue at the desk there. Perhaps you can help me?'

'I'm sorry, sir, but you'll have to – '

'A friend of mine has just been transferred to the Ministry, but I don't know which floor she's working on.' I hesitated, wondering if I should give Kate's name. If she *was* working there it might convince him that I was genuine. On the other hand, if she had been gunned down in that building only a few days before, her name was unlikely to open any doors – at least none that I wanted to enter. I decided against it. The guard eyed me suspiciously for a moment, then pointed to the wall to my right.

'You'll find a listing in the directory over there,' he said, not moving.

'Thank you so much for your help,' I replied, and walked immediately to where he was pointing, feeling his eyes on my back all the way. There was a small console with only a basic keyboard. Jesus! I'd never seen one like it, and I hadn't a clue how it should be operated. For all I knew, every Working Class child of five played with these! Was it indexed by Department? Order of seniority?

Alphabetically? I knew I'd only have time to try once. If the guard saw me having difficulty . . . I typed in 'Mason'. There was an agonizing pause of a few seconds, and then the screen showed: 'Please insert first name/names.' Okay, so far so good. Feverishly I typed in; 'Kate', and waited. Another pause, longer this time. 'There is no listing under that name.' Oh God, is she dead? Have I guessed wrong? I racked my brains. Did she have a middle name? Then, like an electric shock, I had an idea. I typed in 'Mason' again, and then added 'Katherine'. It wasn't her name – her full name was in fact Kate – but she always said that she liked Katherine; maybe, if she was starting a new life . . . Yes! There it was! 'Mason, Katherine; Social Planning; Room 702 – Ext. 78665.' I actually smiled with relief, and looked up. The guard had not moved from his spot, and was still staring straight at me. My panic rose again and I exited from the programme.

I waved to the guard, and walked as calmly as I could to the door. His impassive face turned to watch me, but he made no move to follow. The doors opened again, and I felt the cold spring air hit my sweating forehead. I stepped lightly down the steps and out of sight.

I looked at my watch. Four-Twenty-Five. I turned right and right again, and found myself at the rear of the building. I needed to know how many exits and entrances were in use. There was what looked like a goods entrance at the rear, but people were being turned away by two security guards and given directions to the front. There was a large sign saying that due to the present security problems, all traffic was to use the main entrance. Thanks Knife, I thought.

I spent the next three-quarters of an hour walking as inconspicuously as I could up and down the main road outside the Ministry, looking for a vantage point to observe the main entrance. As luck would have it, it started to rain, so I took shelter in the entrance to a passageway almost directly opposite, tried to look as though I was waiting for it to stop, and hoped that no one would speak to me.

By Six-O the first Workers started to appear, walking down the steps and away. The trickle became a steady flow. By Seven-Thirty hundreds had come out, and most of the lights on the upper floors had been extinguished, but there was still no sign of Kate. The rain had stopped, and I couldn't remain where I was without attracting attention to myself. There was a gap of almost ten minutes during which no one left the building. I decided to call it a day. Either she hadn't been at work that day or . . . I suddenly realized I'd been an idiot! The rear door might be closed to people *going in*, but that didn't mean that people couldn't *leave*. I cursed myself. I could have missed her! Ignoring the traffic, I ran across the road and round to the back. The security men had gone and the forecourt was in darkness, which suggested that the door was not in use. I was about to run back to the front entrance when I heard the sound of metal on metal and mechanical whirring, and the heavy steel door began to open. I moved back against the wall and ducked down behind an enormous rubbish trolley. The door opened fully, and two men in overalls came out, carrying a plastic bin between them. They grunted and panted as they lifted the bin to shoulder height and tipped it into the trolley behind which I crouched.

'Doing anything tonight?' one of them asked the other.

'I thought we might pick up a Chinese and get an early night,' replied the other. Pick up a Chinese? I filed that away so as to ask Knife.

'Listen, mate. Do you mind if I slip off now? I'm going to miss my bus otherwise.'

'No, you go ahead. I'll take this back up.'

'Cheers.' I heard the sound of buckles being undone. 'Sling my overalls in the locker, would you?'

'Yup.'

'See you tomorrow,' said one.

''Bye,' called the other. I heard footsteps moving off towards the main road. I stayed crouched where I was. The remaining man carried his load inside. The door remained open! Even though I wasn't sure Kate was still inside, I couldn't afford to miss the opportunity. I stood up swiftly and slipped inside the entrance. The doorway led to a small landing. In front of me were swing doors beyond which was a corridor, and to my left was a staircase leading up to the higher floors and down to the basement. There was no one in the corridor, which meant that unless the remaining cleaner had actually forgotten altogether to close the rear door, which I doubted, he was coming back, either from above me or below me. I chose the corridor. I pushed open the swing doors and took a few steps when I heard a noise on the stairs coming up from the basement. I turned to see a bloke in overalls mounting the last steps. He had another set of overalls slung over his shoulder. He hadn't seen me yet, but I knew I wouldn't have made it to the far end of the corridor. I retraced my steps and returned to the door.

I pushed the swing doors open hard so that they banged back against the walls. He looked round, startled.

'What do you think you're playing at, leaving the door open like that,' I shouted. 'My God, man, don't you realize that anyone could just wander in off the streets?' His face turned quite white. 'What on earth do you think these security procedures are for?'

'I'm terribly sorry, sir . . . I . . . it was only a moment . . . I'm sure no one . . . that is . . . there was no one outside . . .'

226

'Don't make excuses, man! Just make sure it doesn't happen again,' I called as I started up the stairs. 'Consider yourself very lucky that I don't report you!'

'Yes, sir. Thank you, sir,' said the poor man as I disappeared from sight.

Well, Jim, I thought to myself, you might as well run with your luck while it holds. I climbed to the seventh floor. At each level there were swing doors leading off down the corridor. I looked through the window. The seventh floor was in darkness. She wasn't there. I decided to go down the corridor anyway. I could descend the stairs at the far end, and would avoid meeting the cleaner again. As to getting out of the building, well, I'd work that one out when I had to. I stepped silently into the corridor. I could see the outline of what looked like conical piles of rubbish dotted along the corridor. I had taken only a few steps when something crunched under my feet. Broken glass, and lots of it. The hairs on my neck suddenly stood up, and I shivered; something was wrong.

I continued towards the end of the corridor, pausing before I passed each doorway. I was now halfway along, where it was darkest, heading towards the light on the far staircase. A door opened off to my left, and I could see a faint blue light emanating from that room. I was about three paces away from the doorway when a figure swung out into the corridor, its hands held in front of its chest. It was Kate!

'Kate,' I said softly, 'is that you?' Her pose looked very familiar, distinctive, but at that second I couldn't work out what it meant. I couldn't see her face. Her hands seemed to waver for a second but then resumed their position. Then I realized: she was pointing a gun at me. You may think it odd, but I smiled to myself. Could she really think I would harm her?

'Kate,' I repeated.

'GET AWAY!' she screamed, and shot straight at me. It wasn't a warning shot; it wasn't to frighten me. It was aimed directly at me.

As the gun exploded I threw myself down and towards her. The bullet missed me, and my forward motion swept her legs from under her. I rolled over once and stood up. Kate was in the process of rising, on her knees, with her gun still clasped in her hand. She looked away from me, back down the corridor, as if looking for help, and then turned back to me. I didn't hesitate. I dived at the swing doors, and out into the stairwell. I raced down the stairs. I had to get off the staircase! The clatter of my running down the concrete stairs was certain to attract attention. I reached the landing on the fourth floor and looked through the window into the corridor. It was dark and apparently deserted. I pushed open the doors and sped along the corridor as quietly as I could. As I ran at the far doors, they opened, and a woman entered. I collided heavily with her, knocking her to the ground, but I stayed up, and ran on.

I reached the ground floor and the inside of the steel door through which I had entered. It was shut. I looked at the push-button control panel beside the door and punched it in frustration. Given time I could have worked out or over-ridden the combination, but time was one thing I didn't have. Assuming Kate had contacted Security from the seventh floor, I could expect company within seconds. I decided to try the main entrance. Perhaps I could bluff my way out. I turned to go back the other way, when I heard an electronic 'beeping' as if someone was playing a music game on the First Ed. console. I spun round. It was coming from the door control. Someone had keyed the code to open the door! The door began to open inwards. I threw myself flat against the wall and

228

waited for whoever was coming in. The door opened to its fullest extent. Silence. I looked through the crack. No one! I didn't stop to consider why or how the door had opened for me, I just ran out and into the night.

33

I have only a dim recollection of the events of the following half an hour. I remember running like crazy through the streets, not caring where I went. I remember noise, traffic, lights, people's staring faces. Tears stung my eyes, blurring my vision. I know I knocked flat a number of innocent Workers in my feverish flight. I wasn't thinking, and I didn't know what I was running from. All I knew was that I hurt. Looking back, it was a miracle that I wasn't picked up, but at the time I couldn't have cared less.

I don't know how long it was after leaving the Ministry, but when I became aware of what I was doing, I found myself crouched like a ball in the dark, by the service entrance of some hotel. There was a green sign flashing above my head, and I could hear music coming from inside. Someone was leaning over me. I thought desperately for some story, and tried to wipe the tears from my face.

'Is he okay?' said a voice.

'Drunk, I think,' came a reply. I took my lead from that, and staggered up, swaying.

'Hello,' I said to the world in general, pretending not to focus on the two men beside me.

'Definitely drunk,' concluded the first. 'Where have you got to go, fella?'

I didn't want to give the address, but I hadn't a clue where I was, so I did need directions. I racked my brains for the name of a main street near to Linda's flat. 'St Martin's Lane,' I slurred, triumphantly.

'No problem,' said the second man, who proceeded to tell me the route. The first man interrupted.

'He's in no condition to remember all that. Have you got any money?' he asked, addressing me.

'No more money, no more money,' I sang, 'All gone.'

'Come on, Pete, let's get him round the front.'

They each took an arm, and helped walk me to the main road. I did not recognize it.

'Taxi!' called one of them. A taxi drew up.

'He needs to get to St Martin's Lane. He's a bit drunk, but I don't think he'll throw up.'

The cabbie looked hard at me, and I did my best to look like a drunk who wouldn't throw up.

'All right,' said the cabbie after a while, 'put him in.' They manoeuvred me inside, and shut the door.

'This should cover it,' said the first man, handing some money to the cabbie.

'Okay, that'll do. Cheers,' said the cabbie, switching on his meter.

The cab pulled away from the kerb, and the two men waved good-humouredly to me. I waved back.

Now I don't know why it was, maybe because of the kindness the two chaps showed to a stranger, but at that moment I simply broke down. The tears came, and wouldn't stop. The cabbie looked at me once or twice in his mirror, but said nothing.

As soon as I recognized St Martin's Lane, I jumped out of the taxi. I doubled back once to make sure the cabbie wouldn't have known where I was going, and then walked up the alley to Linda's flat. I climbed the stairs, and was about to ring the bell, when I remembered Knife's distinctive knock. I copied it, two-one-two, and waited. The door opened almost immediately. Linda peered through the gap, hiding most of herself behind the door. She

231

looked at my face – I guess I must have looked quite a sight – and whispered.

'Go up one floor and wait on the landing.' The door closed again. I walked up and waited. It was dark, and the place smelt damp and close. A minute or so later, Linda's door opened, there was some whispered conversation, and then footsteps receded away down the stairs. I waited a few seconds.

'Jim?' called Linda. I descended to her door.

'I'm sorry . . . Knife said you'd be busy . . . but . . .' I didn't want to cry, especially in front of Linda, but the tears welled up again. She opened the door wide and took me in her arms.

'Oh, Jim! Come here my dear,' she said, and cradled my head in her warm embrace.

There wasn't very much that Linda could say. She gave me a drink and listened sympathetically while I told her what had happened. The one thing that did interest her was the fact that the door seemed to have been opened for me. She wondered if Kate could have seen the rear yard from the seventh floor. I said I wasn't sure. Linda thought it possible that having scared me off, Kate didn't actually want to kill me, and so she had opened the door to let me out. I thought about that. Kate must have seen that I was unarmed; she must have realized that I wasn't trying to kill *her*, so maybe Linda was right. It didn't really matter. Either way, Knife had been right. Kate saw me as the enemy, a threat. Anything that there had been between us was over, at least in her eyes. I would have to learn to see it the same way. I apologized again for having barged in.

'Oh, that's all right. You didn't interrupt much. He was about to leave anyway.'

'How did you get rid of him?'

'I told him I'd had a tip-off that the Ceepee were doing a routine vice sweep through the area. He was only too happy to leave. Anyway, don't worry about that. What are you going to do now?'

'I don't know. Go home I suppose. That is, if Knife will help me back out.'

At that second there was the coded knock on the door, and Knife barged straight in. He looked straight at me.

'I thought if you were still alive I'd find you here. Thank God you're okay!' I'd rarely seen Knife so agitated. After the last couple of days I was quite surprised he was so concerned.

'I'm okay, but how do you know where I've been?'

'I should think the whole of London knows where you've been tonight, old son. What on earth happened?'

'I don't understand. I went to look for Kate, that's all. She shot at me – as you said she would – and I ran for it. That's it.'

'That's it?' he cried. He strode across the room to the Box and turned it on. He then paused, and turned it off again. He came to sit beside me.

'Jim, this is very important, so don't bullshit me. Are you seriously saying that that is all that happened?'

'Yes. That is all that happened. Why?'

Knife looked up at Linda, and then at me. He bit his lip.

'I don't know how to put this, mate,' he said, and then paused, looking at the carpet. 'Kate's dead.'

34

The same bloke that announced the sports results, the one who read the weather at the end of the Nooz, was giving a Nooz-Flash on the Box. He gave it with the same sober expression that he had used the night before to announce that the New Sov had fallen and that exports were down, but tonight he was saying that my Kate was dead.

'. . . now take you over to the scene where I understand that Mr Jordan is available to be interviewed.' The image changed, and I saw the familiar steps of the Ministry building. Standing in front of them, his face white with the glare of the TV lights, was Henry Jordan. A number of microphones were being pushed towards him. He was talking, but at first there was no sound. Then:

' – came into the Ministry late to pick up some papers. I heard shots and I went on to the seventh floor to find Mr McCready lying there.'

'Was he shot?' came a voice from out of camera.

'He was, but he was still alive. I understand however that he died before reaching hospital. It is a great tragedy. Mr McCready was one of the best men in the department – he was due to be promoted next month.'

'Minister! Minister!' shouted another voice. 'We understand that another employee was involved. Could she have been a Resistance "plant"?'

'The other person involved was a Miss Katherine Mason. She had joined the department only a few days before, by Usurpation. I needn't remind you gentlemen that many of our best employees have come from Outside, so that in itself does not mean that she was a terrorist – I prefer not to glamorize these thugs by calling them "Resistance". It is too early to say one way or the other, but the evidence presently available suggests that she was not.'

'Can you tell us what happened to her, please Minister?'

'It was she who shot Mr McCready. McCready himself managed to tell me so before he died. While I was by him, the Mason woman took a shot at me, perhaps because I had seen her. I regret that I was forced to shoot her in self-defence.'

At that moment the doors behind Jordan opened, and two Docs appeared carrying a stretcher. They came down the stairs, and the camera shot changed, although Jordan's voice continued. I watched the scene, numb. There was no blanket over Kate's body. She lay, face down on the stretcher, her lovely hair spilling over the end. Her forearm had fallen off the stretcher, and blood was plainly visible dripping from her hand. Jordan was still speaking.

'. . . Can only assume that there was some sort of private dispute between them – '

'But is it usual for Ministers to carry their own firearms?'

'Since the latest round of attacks on government buildings and officers, it has been decided that all potential targets should have bodyguards and carry weapons if advised.'

Knife turned the Box off. 'What happened?' he asked softly.

I shook my head. 'Nothing like that. She was alive when I left her.'

'Was there anyone else involved?'

'No. No one.' Linda came and sat next to me, her hand

235

on my arm. Funny, but I sort of expected to cry. I would almost have felt better if I could have cried, you know? Maybe because Knife was there – it was different when I was alone with Linda, I could let go – or maybe because I'd done as much crying as I had in me, I don't know, but there were no tears. I felt hollow, as if a cold wind were blowing straight through my guts, and I felt anger, ice-cold anger.

'Is it possible that you missed something?' asked Knife.

'No! I've told you.'

'Well, it's not the first time the Techs have used events as a cover for their own activities, but . . . there's something not right about this . . . I can't understand it . . .'

'There's nothing to understand!' I exploded. 'Jordan shot her. It's simple!'

'But why should he?' asked Knife.

'Does there have to be a reason? The man's a user! Look at the way he uses Outsiders as fodder! He plays us along, tells us "It's all here, all you have to do is work for it", knowing that hundreds every week fall for it and are killed for their pains!'

'Hang on a bit, Demon. I know you're upset and all that, but there's something not right about all this – '

'Oh, you've noticed that have you?'

'*My* information is that Jordan was nowhere near – '

'*Your* information? That's just fine! It was spot on last night wasn't it? Your lot didn't kill the under-secretary for whatever it was, but he still ended up dead!'

'All I'm saying is – '

'I don't care a fuck what you're saying, Knife! Kate's dead; the man who shot her was there on the Box calmly admitting it. That's enough for me!'

Knife stood up and began pacing about the room. He seemed to reach a decision. 'Linda?' he called. 'Linda, can Jim stay here for a few hours?'

236

'Sure. I won't be doing anything else tonight.'

Knife turned to me. 'Please, Demon, will you do as I ask? Just stay here and don't do anything till I get back. There's more to this than you realize, and I'm not just talking about Kate's death. I want to try and find out a bit more.'

Linda answered. 'He'll be all right Nigel; I'll look after him. But, please, no three-day disappearances this time.'

'Okay. Will you be all right, Jimbo?' I didn't answer. 'Okay,' he repeated. He kissed Linda briefly and departed.

35

Looking back on it, I guess most people would say I went crazy for a while. It was a bit like being in a dream; everything makes sense while you're asleep, but all the links evaporate when you wake up. When I 'woke up' two days after Kate shot at me, I realized that I'd been acting pretty strange. It's not that I don't remember what I did; I can recall with vivid clarity exactly what happened. But it's as though it wasn't me, like I stood above it all, just an observer.

Whether you put it down to morals, or just the futility of it, I wasn't a believer in violence, right? But something changed in me when I saw Kate's body on the Box. I'm not pretending that I sat down and thought it all through, like I have now. All I know is, the minute I saw Jordan saying that he had shot Kate (with 'regret'; remember his 'regret'?) I knew that I would kill him. That was why I couldn't answer Knife when he asked if I'd stay put. I knew I wouldn't, and I didn't want to lie. Funny eh? There I was, planning to murder someone, and I didn't want to lie to my friend.

I slept in Linda's bed that night. She had turned in shortly after Knife had gone again. I sat up, staring out the window, wrapped in the blanket she had lent me. I don't know how long I stayed there, but after a long while I became conscious that I wasn't alone. I turned round. Linda was standing in the bedroom doorway in her nightgown, looking at me.

'Come to bed, Jim,' she said softly.

'Can't sleep. You go back. I'll be fine.'

She came over to me and took me by the hand. 'Come on,' she said, pulling me gently. I went into her room and got into bed with her. The bed was big and soft and comfortable, and she felt so good that I began to relax. She held me in her arms, and at some time before daybreak, with the smell of her hair in my nostrils, I fell into a troubled sleep. I dreamed I was being chased along a narrow dark tunnel, a sewer perhaps, but that I couldn't run fast enough. Every footstep echoed and thudded in my head, so loud I couldn't think. Above it all, there was this music, twangy, repetitive music.

I woke up the next morning feeling exhausted, with the same tune still going through my head. I knew what it was too. It came from a really old film that I'd seen a dozen times on the Box, called *The Third Man*. I couldn't work out why I should have dreamed of that music.

Linda had already gone out by the time I awoke. There was a note saying that she'd gone shopping, and that she'd be back after lunch. I slipped out of the flat and walked to the phone booth on the corner. I didn't want the call being traced to her console. I keyed the number of the Ministry.

'Mr Jordan's private secretary please.'

'Who's speaking please?'

'My name's Jim Dobson. I'm the assistant editor of current affairs on "Nooz Round-Up",' I answered.

'Hold the line please.' There was a series of clicks, a short pause, and then a man's voice.

'Webber,' it announced.

'Good morning, Mr Webber. I'm one of the "Nooz Round-Up" team who interviewed the Minister last night. He agreed to give me an appointment for a follow-up this afternoon.'

'I have no record of such an appointment.'

'Well, he told me to phone to confirm, but that he would be free after Four-O.'

'He's not in yet, so I haven't had a chance to speak to him, but as far as I know, he has a very full schedule today, and that doesn't include press interviews.'

'I'm sure if you speak to him he will remember. Can you tell me what time he will be in, and perhaps I could call back?'

'Try after midday, Mr . . . ?'

'Thanks very much.' I broke the connection. I couldn't be sure, but there was a reasonable chance of Jordan being at the building after Twelve-O. Now all I had to do was get in, find him without being challenged, get him alone, and kill him. Ha! The crazy thing was that, at the time, it seemed easy. I saw the whole thing with absolute clarity. I was going to get in and kill Henry Jordan. Nothing else mattered. I wasn't even concerned about getting out afterwards.

I returned to the flat. I spent the rest of the morning racking my brains for a way of getting myself into the Ministry. Security would be even tighter than before after last night. By One-O I still hadn't come up with anything, and I was worried that Linda would get back soon. I knew she wouldn't let me go, even if I didn't tell her what I proposed to do. I decided to leave, and see what happened. I needed a weapon, preferably a gun in view of the fact that Jordan was carrying one. I searched the flat from top to bottom in the hope that Knife might have left one of his illicit weapons there, but without luck. It was probably just as well; other than that one afternoon with Kate, I'd had no experience with guns, whereas I'd had to use a knife often enough. I went into the kitchen. There were a number of knives there, and I found a short-handled one with a wickedly sharp blade, which I took

240

from the drawer. I left a note for Linda, telling her not to expect me back till nightfall, and left.

I walked to Holborn. I went to the main entrance of the Ministry to see if there were any new security measures in operation, but everything looked as it had on the previous occasion. I didn't enter the building, but walked round to the rear entrance. It was closed, and the automatic barrier into the yard was down, preventing vehicles from getting in. I settled down in a doorway opposite to wait. I knew that just standing there in broad daylight would be dangerous, but I couldn't see any alternative. I had no definite plan, but it occurred to me that if the same cleaner happened to come out, I might be able to talk my way in.

36

Okay, so it was a dumb idea. I worked that out after I'd been standing there for an hour, my fingers and toes deadened by the cold. During that time, I'd hummed or whistled that fucking 'Third Man' tune thirty times, I'd been approached by three different women all of whom seemed to think I needed to be shown a 'Good Time' (I mean, I was having one already, right?), and no one had gone anywhere near that door, let alone gone in or come out of it. I was, as you can imagine, pretty pissed off.

That film music though; that was the strange part. Do you ever get that feeling that you *know* you've forgotten something, but you can't remember what it was? Something flits about like a moth in the back of your mind, but when you try to pin it down, it slips away. That's what I felt; that tune was trying to tell me something. I tried to think if I'd heard it on the Box recently. I didn't think so. Had Linda been singing it? No. I tried to remember the film itself but it wouldn't come to mind. I hummed the tune again. I remembered that in the film it was played on a strange instrument, unlike anything I'd ever heard before, whereas in my mind I heard it differently, as though it was played on . . . Yes! As though it was on the music module of the First Ed. programme. I used it as a kid to learn music scales; when you press the Console keys, the machine makes electronic notes. Then I had it! I'd heard notes like that as the door was opening the night before. But so what? I was so cold, I couldn't concentrate. Think! Electronic locks do not, as a rule, play film scores. Okay; maybe I damaged the control panel when I

242

punched it. But if it still beeped when a number was keyed, then all I had to do was to press the keys that reproduced the same tune, and . . .

I raced over to the door. I sang the first notes of 'The Third Man' to myself, and frantically punched 1-2-3-2-3-2-3. The panel beeped, but the door didn't budge. The notes were too low! I tried again: 7-8-9-8-9-8-9. Nothing. I wondered abstractly how long it would take the security computer to alert someone to my tampering. I tried 6-7-8-7-8-7-8. Still nothing. Then 5-6-7-6-7-6-7. Got it! The door began to open. I slipped in as soon as the gap was wide enough, and hit the 'Lock' button. The door reversed direction and closed with a clang. I was in.

My next problem was to find Jordan. The corridor beyond the swing doors was full of people coming and going, and I had about as much chance of getting past them unnoticed to the elevators as an ostrich playing the harmonica. As I hesitated, the swing doors from the floor above me banged open. I had no alternative but to descend to the basement. I reached the foot of the stairs. There were two doors before me, one marked 'Fire Escape', the other unmarked. I chose the latter. I eased the door open a fraction. It was dark inside, so I slipped in and pulled the door almost fully closed behind me. I waited for the footsteps to recede, closed the door properly, and felt for a light switch. Strange eh? I'd only been Inside for a few days, and already I took for granted the fact that they had power throughout the day.

I found myself in a small room with lockers in it, the walls covered with pornographic photographs. The obligatory Console was on a table in the centre of the room. In the corner was, of all things, a vending machine! So Kate wasn't entirely right; Insiders also drank stuff that tasted second-hand. The room looked like some sort of rest room for the cleaning staff. I opened the lockers. In the second I found a set of overalls. I put them on over my own clothes. There was nothing in the room that gave me any clue as to the layout of the building. I stepped outside, and pushed at the door marked 'Fire Escape'. I was in the corner of an ill-lit cavernous area which smelt of fuel. The security pound. All the top brass arrived and departed in bullet-proof personnel carriers and this was where they entered the building itself. To my left was an ancient service elevator with manual gates. If it still worked it just might go to all the floors. Fine; I still didn't know which one to go to. On the other hand I might be able to hide myself in the pound until Jordan went home. I was considering my options when I heard a noise at the far side of the pound. There was an attendant pottering about with a tool box in his hand. I stepped back into the shadows, hoping that he hadn't seen me.

'Is that you, Arnie?' I'd been seen. To get back out through the door meant stepping further out of the shadows. I waited where I was.

'Hey you! Who's there? Step out so I can see you.'

I heard a click, and the lights above me suddenly flickered into life. Within a second, the entire pound was awash with brilliant light. I shielded my eyes, and walked as nonchalantly as possible in the direction of the voice.

'It's not Arnie,' I said. 'My name's Bill. I started today.'

'Oh yeh?' replied the voice, obviously suspicious. 'Well just stay there now, while I go and check . . .' I heard him drop the tool box with a clatter and begin to edge away from me as he spoke. I reckoned he was still about thirty metres distant from me. My eyes were still getting used to the glare, but I heard his footsteps quicken.

'Hang on a sec,' I said, also walking faster, 'I've got my pass here, if you want to – '

'No!' he shouted. 'You just stay where you are while I – ' he broke into a run. I had to reach him before he could get to an alarm. I sprinted after him. I could see by now that he was heading for a glass cubicle at the entrance to the pound. I was gaining on him, but he was only twenty paces away from it . . . ten . . . five . . . he scrambled up the wooden steps and into the cubicle. He reached the phone and lifted the handset. I reached up the steps and grabbed him by the ankle, and heaved with all my might. He came tumbling down the steps, dropping the phone on the way.

'Help! Help!' he squealed. I had to shut him up quickly. I punched him once to the stomach and once to the side of the head. He lay still. I raced up the steps and picked up the phone. There was a woman at the other end.

'Hello? Hello?'

'Hello,' I said, quickly. 'Sorry about that. Arnie fell down the steps and knocked the phone off the hook.' I thanked the stars that there was no visual link on this extension.

'Do you need first aid?'

'No, he's fine,' I said desperately.

'Well, I'll send down a Medic anyway.'

'That really won't be – ' I started, but they'd gone. I threw down the handset, and ran down to the attendant. He was alive, but out cold. I slapped him round the face twice. No response. So much for the films. I picked him up and put him over my shoulder. The entire contents of his pockets fell on to the floor. I swore and kicked what I could out of sight under the cubicle. Then I ran as quickly as my load permitted across the pound and retraced my steps to the rest room. I put the man down on the floor, threw open the door of the nearest locker, and dragged him to it. I managed to bundle him inside and shut the door. I whirled round in time to see the door open. A woman in a green suit came in. It's all go being an assassin, eh?

'Hi,' she said. 'I'm duty Medic today. I gather someone's fallen and hurt themselves or something.'

'Yes,' I answered, wiping the sweat from my forehead.
'He's just out there,' I said, indicating the door she had
just come through.

'Oh, where?' she asked, turning towards the door. I
leapt forward and grabbed her from behind, one arm
round her chest, the other round her face.

'I can snap your neck in a split second if you struggle,'
I warned, wondering if either of us believed it. 'Just stay
calm, and you'll be fine. I need to know which floor the
Minister's on. Do you understand?' She didn't respond.
'Do you understand?' I hissed, exerting more pressure on
her face. She nodded. 'I'm going to allow you to speak in
a second. All I want from you is the number of his floor.
I shall be leaving you tied up down here. If you lie to me
I shall come back and kill you,' I threatened, 'just as I
have killed Arnie,' I added for good measure.

'Right. Which floor?' I loosened the hand round her
mouth. She said nothing. I replaced my hand.

'Look,' I said calmly, 'are you married, got a boyfriend?
Children perhaps? You've got to decide: is it really worth
it? I mean, Jordan may be a nice guy, but is he nice
enough to die for? 'Cos I swear to you, unless you give
me the floor number, you're going to die, here and now,
on the floor of this room. If you tell me which floor, you'll
be out of here in an hour, and you can tell them you
refused to say anything. You may even be a heroine.
Now, which is it to be?'

I thought it was a pretty effective speech. Don't ask me
why I didn't ask for the actual room number, only the
floor. I removed my hand from her mouth to allow her to
answer.

'Twentieth floor,' she gasped.

'Thank you,' I said. 'Very sensible.'

I reached into my pocket with my free hand and drew

246

out my knife. I spun her round so that she was facing me, and put the knife under her nose.

'We're almost there,' I said, 'so let's not be silly now, eh? I'm sorry, but I've got to tie you up.'

I reached over to the door of the first locker and pulled it open. In its top compartment was a reel of flex. Without taking my eyes from her I reached over and grabbed it.

'Sit on the floor, please,' I instructed her. She did as she was told. I bound her wrists behind her, and tied them to the table leg. I then passed the same wire over her shoulder and bound her ankles. I needed something to gag her, but nothing came immediately to hand. I looked at her clothing, wondering what I could remove without her screaming rape. She was wearing a scarf round her neck, so I took that off her, and, as gently as I could, stuffed it in her mouth. Didn't want to hurt her now, did I? I surveyed the room quickly, and went to the door. For an amateur I reckoned I was doing pretty well. Shows you how wrong you can be. I had been in a position to make myself completely safe, by Usurping, *twice* in the last five minutes, and it hadn't even crossed my mind!

From where the girl sat she could hear but not see me. I flicked off the light, and, leaving the door slightly open, started up the stairs to the ground floor, making enough noise for her to hear my footsteps. I then crept back down and slipped into the pound. With a little luck, if rescued, she would say that I went up the stairs, or used the main elevator.

The pound was deserted. I ran over to the service elevator and opened both gates. There was a panel of old-fashioned buttons numbered 'B2' to '20'. I stepped into the elevator and a light went on above my head. I didn't know if there would be a window at each floor, but I couldn't take the risk that I would be seen as I went by. I stepped back out and smashed the bulb with the hilt of

247

the knife. I was about to get back in again when a thought crossed my mind. I turned and ran back across the pound to the steps of the cubicle and felt underneath. I was sure I had seen . . . Got it! I opened an oil-covered wallet. There was a security pass inside. 'Edward Bricker – SP No. 46139E' stared at me from a glassy-eyed photo. There was no way anyone was ever going to think I was Mr Edward Bricker, but it might come in handy. I ran back to the elevator. Just as I closed the gates, the phone in the cubicle started ringing. Things were beginning to hot up. I pressed the button marked '20' and the elevator clanked into life.

I crouched on the floor in the corner, the knife in my hand. There were windows. As the elevator passed each floor, a rectangle of light appeared at the top of the gates, widened, travelled down to the floor, and was cut off. I counted each as it passed. The elevator slowed before the twenty-first, and rumbled to a halt. As it did so I opened the gates and stepped out.

I had counted on there being swing doors at the entrance to the corridor as on the lower floors. I was instead faced with sliding steel doors, cameras, and an armed guard standing by a security screen. There was someone else waiting to enter the corridor, a tall thin man whose suit was a size too big for him. I remember thinking that he looked rather like a stick insect I had once seen on one of Mum's favourite nature programmes on the Box. He and the guard were chatting away. Although neither of them had paid me any attention, they must have seen me, as I was only three or four metres away from them. The guard handed a card back to the chap, pressed a couple of buttons, and the steel door slid back. I leapt forward while the door was still open, and bundled Stick Insect out of the way.

'For Chrissake, mate, let me through!' I said, flashing

Mr Bricker's card at them. 'The Minister's just rung to say that water's pouring through his ceiling!'

'Just a sec, who are – '

'Pete Robinson. Started today!' I called back as I sailed through. 'Don't just stand there; get on to the electricians – there could be a fire any minute.' He hesitated, one hand on his gun, the other on the phone. I stopped, five metres away from him, and spread my arms wide. 'Look, mate, it's up to you. The Minister's probably up to his ankles in water by now, but if you want to play silly buggers, fine. It's your job. Now either search me or whatever you want to do, or show me the Minister's office and let me get on with it.'

He looked at Stick Insect, who shrugged. 'Third door on the left,' he called, and he picked up the phone.

I turned and strode off down the corridor. I got to the second door and reached into my pocket for the knife. There was a shout behind me.

'Hey! Where are your tools?' He ran at me and grabbed my arm, spinning me round. I brought my knee up hard in his groin, and he doubled over. As his head went down I hit him with as much force as I could on the nose. There was an audible snap of cartilage, and he went down. I distinctly remember being glad that I hadn't had to use the knife. I looked back and saw that Stick Insect had the phone in his hand and was twittering about which buttons to press. I turned to Jordan's office and threw the door open. The room was empty. I leapt towards the next door and cannoned straight into a chap coming out of it and he went down too. I looked in the room. No Jordan. I made it to the next one. A number of staring faces, none of them Jordan's. Lights started to flash and I was aware of a siren too, but I ran on to the next room. Empty. Then a room to my right. There he was! He had been talking on the phone and was just hanging up as I crossed the threshold. I closed the door behind me.

'Jordan. I've got you, you bastard!' I said. He looked at me, puzzled, and then saw the knife in my hand. He looked up again. It was funny, but he didn't seem scared.

'I'm going to kill you,' I said, as calmly as I could.

'Are you?' he asked, as if I'd said I was going to make a sandwich. Why wasn't he frightened? He was supposed to be frightened!

'You'd better get on with it then,' he said, completely unconcerned. 'Although I expect you already realize that you can't possibly escape,' and he pointed towards the corridor where all hell had let loose. Over the sirens I could hear footsteps running towards us. I took a step towards him so that the point of the knife was centimetres from his breast.

'I mean it, Jordan!'

'Do you?' He stared me straight in the eye. Suddenly I wasn't really sure. The look in his face seemed to say 'It doesn't really matter, you know.' I knew that look. I'd seen it every morning in the mirror when I bothered to shave. I thought about it, and I knew in my heart that he was right. Nothing mattered. Kate was dead. Nothing I did would bring her back. All my life I'd said that killing was too high a price for a job, and here I was, about to kill someone, for what? Revenge? Killing Jordan wasn't going to make me happy. It didn't matter. All this went through my mind in a split second, and as it did, the fury disappeared. I can't explain it; one minute I was crazy and out of control, and the next I was me again.

I shrugged, and smiled, and lowered the knife just as the door burst open. I just had time to turn before I was flung forward by a body of people. They seemed to be in ordinary clothes, suits and so on, and I remember thinking that that was lucky; had the Snorters arrived first I would have been blown to pieces. But my attackers didn't seem to be armed. Hands grabbed at my clothes, and I made an attempt to shake them off. They were getting more numerous and were beginning to pull me down. I swept the knife around in the air and for a second I was free to move again. Out of the corner of my eye I saw Jordan. He smiled at me, as if to say he understood my problem.

'Jordan,' I said. I felt a heavy blow on the back of my head and simultaneously my legs were knocked away from under me. I hit the ground hard and lost the knife. Blows were raining on me from all angles, but I still managed to crawl a bit further.

'Jordan,' I said for the third time, before finally losing consciousness. The last thing I remember was that familiar hum in the back of my head. It was now so high-pitched that it ceased to be a note – it was just a presence, lodged somewhere in my brain.

37

I was at home in bed. The old lady was banging on the ceiling with her broom and shouting up the stairwell.

'Jim!' she shrieked. 'Wake up, Jim! It's Gina on the phone!' I turned over, but I didn't want to open my eyes. I was in the middle of a dream, about something important, something I had to do.

'Jim!' called Mum again. Bang, bang, bang came the thuds, and I felt the dream fade away. I turned over and forced my eyes open. The thudding continued. My bedroom was unusually dark. I sat up sharply, and wished I hadn't. The pounding in my head told me I'd been abusing the rest of my body badly the night before. Then I realized that I wasn't in my bedroom. Where the hell . . . ? Then I remembered: the Ministry, Jordan, hands grabbing at me. My first thought was, Christ, I didn't do it after all that. My second thought was, Why am I still alive? I carefully explored the back of my head. There was a lump the size of an egg.

I felt around me with my hands. I was sitting on some soft spongy substance which extended around me for as far as I could reach. And it was dark. Completely dark, without a glimmer of light anywhere. I opened and closed my eyes in quick succession, and it didn't make the slightest difference. My first thought was that I was closed in. I felt my chest tighten immediately. My breath came in short gasps, and it was suddenly hot. Then I remembered the rain of blows on my head and back and had a second thought. It wasn't just dark; I was blind! Now you're not going to believe this, but for a second or two, I actually felt relieved.

I knelt, and widened the area of my search. I reached a junction with a wall. That too was covered in soft dimpled material. I removed one of my shoes and left it at the junction and followed the angle along. After only a couple of metres the wall turned a right-angle. Three more angles, and I found my shoe. I was in a small square room with padded walls. I stood up slowly and felt up the wall with my hands. I couldn't find the top. I decided to go round the walls again and see if I could feel where the door was. Nothing. I could feel no crack, join or irregularity in the dimples. The panic began to rise again, and I forced myself to think.

'Come on, Jim, let's work it out,' I said out loud. 'If you didn't get in through the wall, how could they have put you in? Obviously, through the floor or through the ceiling.'

I felt for the wall and moved into a corner. I began to crawl up and down the cell in what I hoped were straight lines until I felt the far wall against my shoulder. Again, the floor seemed unbroken.

I stood up, and, keeping one hand against the wall, jumped up with my other arm stretched upwards. Crack! My knuckles smacked a hard surface above me. Funnily enough, the pain helped focus my attention, and the fear receded a bit further. I stood on tiptoe and stretched upwards slowly. The tips of my fingers scraped along something cold and smooth with a sharp raised edge. It felt shiny, like glass. I moved a metre towards the middle of the room and repeated the action. I felt the same smooth surface, and then, at the end of the sweep, something else. I had to do it again before I realized that the 'something else' was a cable. It led away to my right across the ceiling. I followed it towards the far corner and

253

encountered something hard with lots of corners. As I ran my fingers gently across it and moved underneath I saw a tiny pinpoint of red light coming from the side of the thing. Then I knew what it was: a camera!

I crouched under it, thinking, my fear forgotten. I stood, slipped out of my jacket and shirt, and threw the shirt up over the camera. I then groped around for the shoe I had left in the far corner. I gave up on it, and took the other one off. If something didn't happen soon, I would run out of clothes. I put the jacket over my head, positioned myself in the centre of the room under the trap door, gripped my shoe by the toe, and swung the heel upwards with all my might. Before the blow landed, a voice came out of the black from all sides.

'Put it down,' it said wearily, 'you'll only hurt yourself.' I checked the swing and came out from under the jacket. Soft yellow light grew in the cell, emanating from what I could now see was a window above me. I retrieved all my clothes and put them on, smiling to myself. For the first time in my life I had beaten my fear of enclosed spaces. What's more, I had won that round. I knew that I now faced torture, imprisonment and, sooner or later (probably sooner), death. The funny thing was, I felt fine. The anger and despair had gone, to be replaced with a certain clarity. I felt washed clean.

There was a dull thud, and the wall behind me swung entirely away on hinges. Beyond was a corridor and two armed men in black and grey battledress. I'd never thought about the phrase 'corridors of power' before, but just take a look at the inside of any government building, and you'll see where it comes from. I've never seen so many identical corridors! A 'click' came from the sound system in the cell and the same voice said:

'Take him to the interrogation block. I'll be there in a moment.'

The guards motioned for me to come out, and I was marched through some doors, up a flight of stairs, through a steel door that opened as we approached it and into a small room.

'Sit down,' said one of the guards, pointing at a chair in the middle of the room, its back to the door. I sat in it, and the other guard strapped my hands to its arms. They both stood behind me, flanking the door.

I heard footsteps approaching and the guards snapped to attention.

'That will be all,' said a voice. Now it wasn't amplified, I recognized the voice as Jordan's. I heard the guards leave and the door close. Jordan came round to face me. He looked at me with some interest, as if trying to remember if he'd seen me before, and then pulled up a chair and sat down opposite me. I felt totally calm. In fact I'd never felt as clear-headed as I did at that moment. We were like two chess players, facing each other across an invisible board with invisible pieces. Sure, he was bound to win, had to didn't he? But I'd give him a run for his money. He moved first.

'You tried to kill me.' His voice was soft and clear, like one of those geezers on the late night God Spots on the Box. Like he just wanted to understand, and then everything would be all right.

'Quite right, Henry, so I did.' That surprised him, me using his first name. He shook his head slightly.

'Your insolence is wasted on me,' he said with some impatience. 'You do realize that my job is protected?'

'Ha! If I'd wanted to Usurp, *Mister* Jordan, I could have done so twice while in this very building.' He stared intently at me, more interested in my manner than my answer.

'Indeed. Then why try to kill me?'

'You wouldn't believe me if I told you.' I smiled.

'Try me.'

'Okay. Revenge.' He started, and leaned forward slightly. He *did* believe me, and this puzzled me. How could he have known who I was or of my connection with Kate? It occurred to me that I'd already been interrogated while drugged, but my sense of time told me that I hadn't been in that cell very long. You hear stories about truth drugs and so on, but I felt fine apart from the bump on my head. Surely I would have felt sleepy or something? In any event, if he already knew who I was, why was he asking all these questions? There was a long pause.

'McCready,' he said suddenly, his eyes fixed on mine, as if trying to catch me out. He looked like a bird, with his beak-like nose and those bright, shiny eyes.

'"One of the best men in the Department",' I quoted Jordan's own words straight back to him. He nodded slowly at that, and then he sat back in his seat.

'I knew it,' he said softly. 'I knew there was more than one of you.' Now I was getting confused. What did he mean 'more than one of you'? Usurpers? It must have been obvious that I wasn't a Usurper. He was smiling like a Cheshire Cat now. What was he so happy about? For the first time it occurred to me that we were not talking about the same thing. I decided to counter-attack.

'Did you really think that anyone would believe that little charade you staged?' I asked. It was his turn to look puzzled. 'Come on; don't be coy. You know what I mean. That pantomime at the Ministry last night.'

He shrugged slightly and shook his head as if it was of no importance. 'It was the best I could do in the circumstances. Mr McCready was rather quicker than I had anticipated.'

'McCready?' I asked, genuinely baffled.

He smiled, and shook his head gently, as if to say 'Nice try'.

'I'm not fooling, Henry. I don't know what you mean.'

256

'Now who's being coy? I've been on to your friend Bill for months. Where else do you think he got the Minister's name? I was just sorry he couldn't be of any more use.' He looked really smug, whereas now I was completely lost.

'I haven't the foggiest idea what you're rattling on about,' I said truthfully.

'"Rattling on about"?' he repeated.

'Oh, yeh. Sorry, Henry, you lot up West don't talk like that do you? What I mean is: I do not follow your drift. No comprendez. Don't understand.' He stared at me and slowly the smile fell from his face.

'What's your name?' he asked.

'Jim.'

'Where are you from? Which Ministry?'

'I'm not from any Ministry. I'm from Ilford.'

'Ilford?' He said it like it was from another planet, as if I'd said 'Mozambique' or 'Jupiter'.

'Yes mate, Ilford.'

'Who are you?' he shouted, standing up. 'Why did you try to kill me?'

'I've already told you. My name's Jim, Jim Demon. And I want to kill you because you killed Kate Mason.'

He almost screamed. 'What? Kate Mason? What the hell do you know about Kate Mason?' He didn't allow me to answer. 'I don't believe you!' He swept his arm back, and struck me across the face with the back of his hand. The blow itself didn't have that much force, but it was so unexpected, and the conversation that went before it so incomprehensible, that it really shook me. He stormed to the door and shouted some orders that I couldn't make out. The door closed.

I waited for half an hour. Then I heard the door open again. Someone stepped quietly into the room and closed the door behind them.

'You okay, Demon?' said a familiar voice. It was the Knife. His black hair was all on end and his eyes were bloodshot. He looked as though he hadn't slept since I last saw him.

'Jesus Christ! What are you doing here? How did you get in? They didn't capture you too, did they?'

'One thing at a time, old son. Let's get you untied,' he said, unstrapping my arms.

'Knife, for God's sake get out! He'll be back any minute!'

'I daresay he will,' he said, without apparent concern. He freed my right arm and went to work on the left. He then moved to the door, and peered out. He pulled his head back in, closed the door, and leaned against it.

'Look, Demon, before you go any further, there's something you should know. Or rather someone you should meet.' He opened the door again, wide this time. Then the whole world stood on its head and turned itself inside out. There, wearing a grey battledress like the ones worn by the guards, was Kate, smiling at me from the threshold.

Part Four

38

'Look, Kate, I'm tied up at the moment. Can't it wait?'

'No, Henry, it can't. For one thing, I might bleed to death.'

'What?'

'Just get your arse down here, Henry, okay?' The line went dead. I dropped the phone, and slid to the ground. I was beginning to feel lightheaded. Blood was still oozing out of my blouse cuff, but I was afraid to investigate further. I knew something was wrong with my shoulder; my arm was hanging at an unnatural angle, elbow pointing forward almost. Funny . . . not as painful as I'd imagined it would be . . . I heard the swing doors open at the far end of the corridor, and then Jordan's voice.

'Wait here!' he commanded. 'No one to pass! Waterson, come with me!'

Feeling really groggy now . . . footsteps running towards me . . . 'Take the far door!' shouted Jordan . . . I think I called 'In here . . .' but I don't know if I just thought it . . . room tilting . . . must mean I've fallen over . . . hands on me . . . tearing blouse . . . poor Jeremy . . . clothes ruined . . .

It was the movement of the transport that woke me. I was conscious first of the smell of leather . . . soft leather seats.

'How are you feeling?' It was Henry, next to me, chauffeur in front.

'Lousy. How long was I out?'

'Not long.'

'We going on a picnic?'

'Yes.'

'Invited a Doc?'

'He made the sandwiches. He's waiting for us.'

'Why doesn't it hurt, Henry?'

'You've been given a shot of something. You could be run over by a tank and not feel a thing.'

'I wondered. Nice ambulance.'

'Only the best for the Minister and his friends.'

'Are we still friends, Henry? I keep shooting your staff.'

'Yes, we're still friends. I've been meaning to stream-line the department for some time.'

'He shot first, you know . . . McCready . . . making notes . . .'

'Hush, Katy, we'll talk later.'

'. . . pages of notes . . . going through my desk . . .'

'Quiet now.'

'Feeling sleepy again . . . Is he dead . . . McCready?'

'Yes.'

'Sorry . . .'

I had a dislocated shoulder. The bullet went in one side and out the other. No broken bones, but lots of blood and damaged muscle. I felt a lot better as soon as the shoulder was put back in, but the Doc said I would be sore for some weeks. After that, lots of physio.

Jordan had taken me to what he called 'The Annex', a part of the Department on the other side of the city – wouldn't tell me exactly where. Come to that, no one spoke to me at all except the Doc. I woke up early the next morning – I guess about Six-O – they'd taken my watch. I rang the bell by the side of the bed. A Snorter put his head round the door. I recognized him – one of Jordan's favourites.

'Hello, Miss. How are you?'

'Okay. When can I get up? What's going on?'

'Mr Jordan will be down to see you shortly. He's asked me to request you to stay there for the moment.'

'"Request me"?'

'Yes, Miss. I think Mr Jordan wants a word with you before anyone else does. He said he thought you'd understand.'

'Yeah, fair enough. You couldn't get me some water could you?'

'Sorry. I'm on strict orders not to move from this spot.'

'Well, if someone else comes along – '

'I'll see what I can do.'

In fact Jordan turned up half an hour later with breakfast on a tray. That made two mornings running – I was getting spoilt.

'Good morning,' I said. 'God, you look terrible.'

He grimaced. 'Your little shooting party's cost me a night's sleep,' he said wryly.

'Where are we?' I asked.

'At the Annex.'

'Yes, but – '

'Hang on a second, Kate. I'll answer your questions in a minute, but I've got some for you first.' He sat on the side of the bed. 'We've put out a story, but I need to know the details from you. What happened?'

I told him about seeing McCready in the Library, his taking notes, finding him searching my desk, and the shooting. Jordan asked a few questions, but didn't mention Demon, so I decided to leave him out of it. I mean, I wasn't barmy about the bloke, and he did almost get me killed, but I saw no reason to set the Ceepee on him. I couldn't see him Usurping, not after all that pious chat he'd given me, so it looked as though the bloody twit had come in looking for *me*! Poor sod. I was quite flattered really. The least I could do was open the goods door for him, and hope he had the sense to keep running. Jordan asked me once if there had been anyone else around, and I said no. He seemed satisfied.

'You said you put out a story. What did you say?'

'I said that it appeared that it was a personal matter between the two of you, you and McCready.'

'Why on earth do that? Why not tell the truth? You must have McCready's notes; all you have to do is show them to prove that he was plotting something.'

'It's more complicated than that.'

'How come?'

'I can't let it be known that McCready was trying to kill me – as he certainly was – once he had the evidence he was looking for.'

'Why not?'

'The reason he was trying to kill me was because he believed I was the head of the Resistance.'

'So?'

'I *am* the head of the Resistance.'

I stared at him. He was serious. I tried to digest the information.

'You? The author of "The Impact of Technology and so on"? The inventor of the Working Class? Sorry, Henry, but I don't get it.'

'Ever heard of Frankenstein's monster?'

'Don't give me that! You created a monster and are trying to destroy it?' I snorted.

'You can deride it if you want, Kate, but that's about the size of it.'

'But . . . but . . . I don't get it. You're at the top! You're the Big White Chief! You can do whatever you want, go wherever you please. You're the winner. Why do you want to change *that*?'

'What about all the losers? Don't tell me you enjoyed life in Ilford, or wherever it was?'

'Of course not! That's why I Usurped.' I stopped to

think for a bit. I was having difficulty adjusting to Henry Jordan, man of social conscience. Then something occurred to me.

'If you're so concerned, why not just knock down the Wall?'

'Don't be silly, Kate. There'd be mayhem, and you know it. In any event, most of the Techs like things the way they are.'

'Too bloody right! I'm with them. I've lived Outside – if you can call it living – for twenty-odd years, in a hell you personally created.' I was getting really angry, stabbing at him with my finger as I shouted. 'Now I've risked my fucking neck to get Inside I intend making up for lost time.'

He got up from the bed and went to the window.

'What is it, Henry? What haven't you told me?'

He turned to face me. 'You may have to be a bit patient.'

'Why? The Doc says I'll be up and about in a couple of days.'

'It's not that. Officially, you're dead.'

'What?' This was a joke, right?

'We had to announce that you were killed. You no longer exist.'

'Why?' I shouted, astonished. 'You had no bloody reason – !'

'We had *every* bloody reason! You killed McCready, remember? I know that sort of thing isn't quite so important Outside the Wall, but Inside it's called murder! What's more, you did it in a public building at a time when there were dozens of other people about. That's not the sort of thing you can just ignore, you know.'

'Wait a minute! It's *not* called murder when it's in self-defence, and you know it! What you're really saying is that telling the truth would mean blowing your cover!'

'I won't pretend that that wasn't one of the considerations,' he said smoothly. 'Much as I care about you, what I'm doing is important, and I don't propose letting anything interfere with it!'

'So what am I supposed to do?'

'Don't worry, you won't have to go back Outside. For the moment you'll have to lie low. As soon as we can arrange it we'll organize another identity for you.'

'When will that be?'

'I don't know, Kate. I can't promise anything. We have to wait for a computer identity to become available.'

'Come again?'

'Look: the Techs know to the last person who is and who is not Inside the city. You can't just get false papers – you need a new identity for the computer, and that may take a while. That was what McCready had stumbled on to. Every time a suitable person dies, a Resistance member is able – '

'Stop! Just stop there! What you're saying is that I've got to wait for someone to die! Is that it?'

'Well, not necessarily, but that is one of the – '

'You bastard! You fucking bastard!' I lunged at him, but he skipped out of reach. 'I've gone through all this – years of being pawed – waiting, scheming, plotting – I get half-drowned, shot at – God knows what – to get away from the life YOU sentenced me to – and I finally make it – and save your miserable life TWICE – and you say "Sorry, Kate you'll have to WAIT"? You *owe* me, you bastard! You *personally*!' He approached me with his arms open. 'Get away from me! Don't you lay a finger on me!'

He shrugged. 'I'll come back later when you've calmed down a bit.'

'Calmed down? Calmed down? You'd better not come back at all if you value your balls!'

'I'm really sorry you're taking this attitude, Kate. I had

266

thought you might consider lending us a hand in the Resistance. You've got skills that we – '

'GET OUT! GET OUT!!'

He got out.

Almost immediately the door had closed, it opened again. I reached for the breakfast things to throw them at him, but it wasn't Jordan.

'Hello, Kate.' It was Demon's mate, the Knife. 'How's tricks?' he said with a broad grin.

'I don't know what you're doing here, but you can fuck off too!'

'Charming. Boss man asked me to say hello. Thought I might be able to cheer you up.'

'Oh, Jesus, don't tell me you're in on this too.'

''Fraid so.'

'I don't think I can take any more.'

39

By nightfall I was bored out of my mind, and still furious. At lunchtime a Snorter had come in bearing a cup of tea and what he claimed was scrambled egg. Both were still on the floor where he had left them. Other than that, no one else had entered the room since the Knife had left. Apart from anything else, I was starving, so I rang the bell. After a while a Snorter came in. It wasn't the same one as before, but I knew his face. Another of Jordan's 'specials'.

'I'm getting up,' I announced.

'No you're not,' he answered without humour. 'My orders are to keep you in here.'

'Oh, yeh? Is that what Henry said?'

'Those are my orders,' he said finally, and made to leave the room.

'Just come back here a minute,' I said, and he paused. 'Just go and check that with Henry, will you? I think you'll find that you've misunderstood.'

'I understood very well – '

'Look, arsehole! You're going the right way to losing your Work Permit! You may be able to keep me here for the moment, but later on tonight, when you go off duty, I'll be with Henry, right? Get my drift? A few words in his ear at the right moment, and what do you think your job's gonna be worth? If you're sure those are your orders, fine, it's your neck. But if I was you, I'd get Henry down here and check.'

He left without any sign of having been persuaded. Twenty minutes later the door opened. It was the Knife.

'I gather you're making a nuisance of yourself.'

'I just want to get up.'

'How do you feel?'

'Not as bad as you look,' I replied. He really looked dreadful, as if he hadn't slept for a week.

'Seriously.'

'Pissed off, bored, hungry and sore, in that order.'

'I've spoken to the Doc. He says you can get up for a short while if you insist, but you'll probably be sorry.'

'Yeh, yeh,' I said impatiently. 'Where are my clothes?'

'Haven't the foggiest. Probably in the incinerator, judging from the state of them when you were brought in.'

'Well what am I supposed to wear?'

'Try these,' answered Knife, bringing out a bundle from behind his back. It was a large grey one-piece battledress like the ones worn by the Snorters. 'It's probably a bit big, but you'll be able to keep your arm in the sling inside. Do you need a hand?'

I took them from him. 'I don't know. Let's find out,' I said, wriggling out of the hospital overall.

'I meant from a nurse,' said Knife.

'I'm not embarrassed if you're not.'

'I'm not concerned about seeing your body, darling,' he said sarcastically. 'I just don't want you bleeding all over me.'

'Fine. I'll bear it in mind. Just hold it up would you?'

He helped me get into it. I wasn't going to admit it after making such a fuss, but the effort of just that left me feeling weak and dizzy.

'Now, where to?' I asked.

'I don't know; you're the one who wanted to go walkies.' He was obviously irritated to have to look after me. He looked worried, as though there was something far more important on his mind.

'What's there to see in this place?'

'Not much; anyway, it's all off limits until you get security clearance, but – ' he saw me scowling at him ' – we can walk over to the refectory if you like. I'll fill you in on the way.' He took my arm. "Cos I fancy you,' he explained, 'not 'cos you need any support.' I didn't complain.

We walked slowly down the corridor. Almost everyone was in uniform, mainly pink and grey, Pinkies and Snorters. We had only got a few metres when there was a clatter of feet behind us.

'Sir!' came a shout. Knife whirled round as two men in pink robes raced up to us. They looked warily at me, and Knife drew them to one side. There was a hurried whispered conversation at the end of which Knife gave them some orders and they walked off. Knife took my arm again. For the first time since I had seen him he had a broad smile.

'Fancy paying a little visit before you eat?'

'What?'

'Got a surprise for you,' he said mysteriously.

We carried on down the corridor to a lift at the far end. We waited with a few others for it to arrive, and travelled up a number of floors. The lift doors opened and we stepped out. There was a steel door in front of us and a console mounted into the wall by its side. Knife pressed some buttons on the console, and spoke a codeword into the microphone, and the gate slid open. I realized we were in a cell block. Knife led me down to a door on the right. There was a Snorter sitting on a chair outside. He stood to attention when he saw Knife. I began to realize that Knife must have been quite a big shot in the Resistance. He spoke quietly to the Snorter, who shrugged, and walked off to the far end of the passage and disappeared inside another door.

'Wait here a second,' said Knife. He slipped inside,

270

closing the door behind him. About two minutes passed, and the door opened again. Knife stuck out his head and winked. Then he disappeared for a few seconds, and the door opened wide. There was Demon, staring wide-eyed at me.

'I don't suppose you two need any introductions,' said Knife.

'Hello, Jim,' I said cheerfully. 'How's tricks?'

He looked from my face to my hands and then back up.

'No,' I assured him, 'no gun this time.' He turned to Knife.

'What . . . where . . . I don't understand; she's dead! Isn't she?'

'It would appear not,' said Knife. The look on Demon's face was absolutely priceless. He kept looking from me to Knife and back again, eyes and mouth wide open.

'But I saw it . . . on the Box . . . you were dead, shot . . .' Before I could do anything, he lunged at me. At first I thought he was going at me, but his arms went round me and he pulled me to him in a hug.

'Oh, Kate! Thank God you're alive!'

'Yeh,' I said, looking over his shoulder at Knife, and trying to disentangle myself from him with one arm. 'I'll second that. Look, Demon, let go eh? You're hurting my arm.'

'What?' He stepped back, still holding me, and saw my empty right sleeve for the first time.

'Are you all right?'

'Just about. No thanks to you though. You almost got me killed.' He stopped for a second, wondering what I was talking about.

'Last night?' I prompted.

'But you shot at me!' he shouted.

'No I didn't, you pillock! I was shooting at someone else! You just got in the way.' He frowned, and looked round at Knife for confirmation. Knife nodded, a bit reluctantly.

'Then . . . then it's all right . . . between . . . us?' he said, pulling me towards him again.

'Ah, well, let's not be too hasty eh? Did you say something about eating, Knife?' I said, turning away.

'Yeh, I think that's a good idea. We can carry this on downstairs. Henry – '

'Henry? Henry Jordan?' Demon cut in. 'Where is he? Are we safe? Will someone please tell me what's going on?' he cried.

'Don't panic, Demon, it'll all be explained,' said Knife. 'We can't hang around here all day. Let's go down to the refectory and get something to eat while we talk. I should think you're starving, eh?' he said, slapping Demon heartily on the back.

'No . . . I mean, yes. Look,' said Jim, turning to Knife, 'will you please just tell me this: am I safe here, or do I have to fight my way out?'

'You are perfectly safe. You are in absolutely no danger,' answered Knife with a smile, 'except possibly from the refectory food.'

We sat at a small table in a corner where it was a bit quieter. I could sense that Demon wanted to talk to me alone. I occupied myself with ordering a meal and avoided his questioning looks. He obviously decided to leave it for the moment, as he started firing questions at Knife. I didn't say much; just listened. Most of it was new information for me too. Demon wolfed down his food as if he hadn't eaten for days, asking questions between mouthfuls.

'Where are we? We're not at the Ministry are we?'

'No,' answered Knife, 'you're at a place called "The Annex". It's used by the Resistance. It is in fact an annex of the Ministry, but staffed by those people Jordan himself picks.'

'How does Jordan fit in?'

'He runs it.' Demon almost choked at that.

'What?' he said, when he'd finished coughing.

'He's the guvnor, the boss,' said Knife. Demon looked at me quizzically. I shrugged.

'Took me a bit by surprise,' I commented.

'He formed it with Marie Fowler,' Knife continued, a little more informatively. 'About five years ago, at least in its original form.'

'By why? I mean, why should he? I thought this shit-heap,' Demon waved his hand in the air to indicate more than just his immediate surroundings, 'was all his idea.'

I answered. 'Henry's apparently had a change of heart since "The Impact of Technology".' I heard the note of cynicism in my own voice. Demon looked sharply at me and then frowned, as if trying to remember something. Then he snapped out of it and began asking questions again.

'Okay. Now, where were we? Yes: how did I get here?'

I shrugged. Knife didn't seem to know either. 'I can only guess that Jordan was so surprised to find himself the target of a lunatic assassin, one who evaded his entire security screen more or less barehanded, that he wanted the pleasure of interrogating you personally. I'll tell you one thing, Demon: you were bloody lucky. If you'd been handed over to the usual bunch of security sadists, there wouldn't be much of you left by now.'

Jim again looked puzzled. 'I wondered why he didn't ask me anything about the Resistance,' he said as if musing to himself.

'Well, he obviously knew you weren't Resistance, didn't he?' said Knife.

'I suppose so,' replied Jim slowly, although he didn't

273

sound convinced. 'You still haven't told me how I got here. Are we far from the Ministry?'

'About three Ks, to the east,' replied Knife.

'How would transport be arranged?' Jim asked.

'How do I know?' asked Knife in exasperation. 'What does it matter? You're here, aren't you? I expect he had one of his personal guard bring you down. He's got a few men at Holborn who take orders direct from him and no one else, even though they're part of the Resistance. I didn't know what had happened to you until a few minutes ago when I was told you were here. I've been bloody worried about you, old son. You're developing a nasty habit of wandering off on your own.'

Knife turned to me. 'I guess you didn't mention to Henry that Jim had been in the Ministry during the gunfight at OK Corral?'

I shrugged. 'Couldn't see any percentage in it,' I joked, looking at Demon. He wasn't paying attention. Knife nodded.

'Apart from Jordan, who else controls the Resistance?' asked Demon.

'There's a Head of Operations who actually runs the Resistance.'

I turned to Knife. 'That person wouldn't by any chance be . . .' Knife smiled, and tried, but failed miserably, to look modest.

'It would,' he confirmed. 'At least insofar as Outside Operations are concerned. There's a geezer called Paul Rossi who deals with Inside the Wall. You'll meet him soon enough. That's how I knew something was wrong with what Henry said on the Box last night, but at the time I didn't know what was going on. That's also why I asked you to stay put until I sorted it out,' he chided Jim. 'You didn't know what you were playing with.'

'But if Jordan's the head of the thing he's trying to

destroy, why doesn't he simply change the Ministry's policy?' asked Jim.

'I've worked that one out,' I answered. 'I'll tell you, Jim, it's every bit as dangerous in here as in Ilford. You wouldn't believe it. There are constant plots and counter-plots even inside the government; alliances every which way. Everyone's got a knife or two sticking out of their shoulder blades. Last month Henry almost bought it himself. His hold on power isn't guaranteed. As far as the other Ministries are concerned, the Technocratic Revolution gave them power, money, everything. They don't want a change. If Henry came out and declared himself, he'd be finished.'

'And probably dead,' added Knife.

'Is the whole Ministry on Jordan's side?' I asked. 'Are they all Resistance?'

'Not at all,' answered Knife. 'We use the Spiritual Development lot as a sort of front. They do most of the recruiting. Basically, you can trust anyone wearing the pink uniforms, but it would be better if you stick close to me for the present until you learn the ropes.'

'Not you too! I don't want to learn any bloody ropes! I don't want to be part of a private army. This girl just wants to get out there and start having a good time.'

'Yeh, well, that may not be possible, Kate. Anyway, I've got work to do. I'll be back in a while. If I don't get back, Jim, either wait here, or go into the briefing and I'll see you afterwards. As for you,' he said to me, 'you should be in bed.'

'Briefing?' asked Jim.

'Yeh. That's why it's so busy in here. Henry's holding an informal briefing on recent events. He doesn't often appear at the Annex, and many of the new recruits haven't met him or heard him speak. It's something of an event. You should listen, Jim. He's quite a speaker. Maybe he can explain it better than me.'

I looked around the room. Almost every table was filled, and I could sense an air of excitement, anticipation.

Knife strode off, weaving his way between the tables, greeting people as he passed. As he got to the door three Pinkies came in, and he stopped for a moment to speak quietly to them. I saw him indicate in our direction, and the Pinkies looked over to us. They finished their conversation, Knife slapped one of them on the back, and slipped out.

There was an uncomfortable silence between us.

'Aren't you interested in how I got on?' I asked.

'Sure. Tell me.'

So I told him about everything that had happened to me since we parted, about Captain Crocker, Graham, my first days Inside the Wall and the attack on the Ministry. Jim seemed uninterested, and sat playing with the remains of his meal. He perked up when I got to the incident with McCready.

'So you weren't shooting at me?'

'No. Like I said you just turned up at the wrong moment.'

'But what was McCready doing there in the first place?'

'I don't know. Henry reckons that he was spying for one of the other Ministries, and had discovered that he was involved with the Resistance.'

'If that's so, why didn't he just get rid of him?'

'I think he was killing two birds with the same stone. He wasn't sure about *me*. I too had turned up at the wrong time. He suspected that one of the other Ministries had Marie Fowler assassinated, and I come along and use her name to get in and kill one of his staff. He wasn't sure whose side I was on, so he tested me out. He told me that McCready was a member of the Resistance, and waited

276

to see what I'd do. I didn't know it, but Henry had me watched from then on. He was told that both McCready and I were in the building last night, so he came back in to see what happened. What Henry did not count on was the fact that McCready suspected *me* because . . .'

'Because what?'

'Well, I'd been seen . . . Henry and I . . . well there was gossip . . .' I stammered. 'Look: I was screwing him, right? I don't owe you anything, Demon. What we had was good fun, and I enjoyed it and all that, but you were in Ilford and I was in here, right? You've got no rights over me!'

There was a long pause.

'What about your note?'

'Note?'

'"I'm going over the Wall, but for what it's worth – "'

'Yeh, yeh, yeh, I remember,' I said, cutting him short. I drew a deep breath. 'Well . . . it's what you wanted to hear, wasn't it? It made you happy, didn't it?'

'I see. It didn't cost anything.'

'No! It didn't cost anything! Satisfied? Look, Jim, you're a nice guy – I really mean it – but that's it, right?'

He looked up at me, and gave a watery smile. 'Yeh. I've got it.' There was another long pause.

'Let's get back to McCready,' he said. 'What you're saying is that your Henry set you up as a target just as much as he set up McCready.'

'Maybe. I'm not sure he realized what would happen. As far as Henry was concerned, he wanted to see if I'd contact McCready and tip him off that Henry was on to him.'

'But Jordan lied to you. He told you that McCready was in the Resistance. Now you know he was in fact part of the government – albeit a part of the government

277

opposed to Jordan. He just used you as an amateur killer, to eliminate an opponent.'

'It wasn't to eliminate an opponent. I didn't intend to kill the man, whoever he was. Anyway, even if you're right, so what?'

'Not much fun being used, is it?'

'Don't go feeling sorry for yourself, Demon. That's the way it is. Sure I used you, but you had a good time for your money. Maybe Jordan used me too, but I got what I wanted. I needed protection and I got it.'

'So, as far as you're concerned, you're sitting pretty.'

'Not quite. I'm officially dead, remember? I can't do a bloody thing. I suppose I'll have to wait till they can find me a new name. I can't go back and I can't go forward. Come on, I'm sick of thinking about it. Let's go and hear his Majesty speak to the masses.'

The hall was almost full by the time we arrived, and Jim and I slipped in at the back. As we sat down, the quiet murmur of voices hushed, and Henry entered from a door at the far end of the room, flanked by two of his personal guard. There was a sprinkling of applause from the new recruits which Henry stilled with a wave of his hand.

'Those of you who have been with us for a while know that I don't go in for any of that. I'm no more or less important than any one of you. Indeed Nigel would tell you somewhat less important.' He joined in the laughter that followed.

'The purpose of this meeting is to greet the newcomers, and explain what it is we're trying to achieve. I also want to fill you in on recent events, particularly the success of our campaign to disrupt the routes through the Wall.'

Jim turned and whispered to me. 'Where *is* Knife? I expected him to be here.'

I shrugged.

'I'm going to find him,' he whispered, and stood up.

'What are you up to, Demon?' I called as he began to ease his way down the row.

A number of people around us were 'shooshing' us and telling Jim to sit down. The movement at the back of the hall seemed to distract Henry, and he stumbled in his delivery. He watched Jim's exit closely, his eyes boring into his back. As the door closed he turned to one of the two men with him, there was a hurried whispered conversation, and the man left the platform. Henry apologized to the audience and resumed his speech, but from then on he never retrieved his previous flow. He still appeared distracted, and frequently cast glances at the door.

40

The meeting broke up, and I waited at the back of the hall for Henry. He waved to me, but carried on talking to two of his aides. After a while one of them came over to me.

'Mr Jordan would like to know if you want to stay in the Sick Bay tonight, or to go back to your apartment.'

I was astonished at the change of plan. Only hours before I was a virtual prisoner. Maybe Knife had said something to him. Anyway, I wasn't going to argue.

'The apartment, please.'

'In which case, will you follow me? There's a transport laid on for you and your friend.'

'Friend? Oh, Demon. I don't know where he's got to.'

'I think he's waiting for you outside.'

'Oh. Fine. What about Mr Jordan? I'd like to have a word – '

'He says he'll speak to you tonight on the phone.'

As we went out to the lobby, Knife approached us.

'Have you seen Demon?' I asked. 'He was looking for you.'

'No, I've been rather busy. Tell him I'll speak to him tomorrow. I gather you're going home.'

'So it appears.'

'Fine. This lot are for you,' he said, handing me a sheaf of papers, 'the others are for Jim. They belonged to two people who were killed in the power station raid. Henry says that the personnel files won't be updated until Monday, so you should be all right till then. They're just to get you over the next two days. After that we'll sort something out permanently. I've put your photos on them, so you'll be all right for a spot-check, but you'll fail a computer verification, so don't wander off, eh? That applies to both of you.'

'What do you suggest we do for the next two days?'

'Stay in the apartment. I'm sure you'll find something to do.' He smiled briefly, and went into the hall. I was escorted to the transport. Demon was already inside. I got in and sat next to him. We sat in silence all the way to Bloomsbury.

'You're going to be a bundle of fun for the next couple of days,' I said, but he wouldn't rise to the bait.

The transport dropped us off and I let us into the apartment. Graham was already at work. I went straight into the kitchen to make some coffee. Jim stalked around the apartment like a cat establishing its territory, and finally settled in the lounge.

'What do you think of it?' I asked, trying to break the ice.

'What?' he said, looking up. 'Oh, the flat. Yeh, very nice.'

'Come on, Demon, cheer up. It's not the first time – '

I didn't get to finish the sentence as there was a knock on the front door. Jim and I looked at each other. He raised his eyebrows. I shook my head; I couldn't think of anyone who would be visiting at that hour.

'Resistance?' I mouthed. He shook his head. I motioned with my hand: 'Gun?' He shook his head again. Too risky. He was right; apart from the fact that he was unlawfully Inside, and I was officially dead, possession of firearms without a permit meant we could be shot on sight. He slipped into the kitchen and returned with a knife, by which time I had slipped out of most of my clothes. The knock was repeated.

'Open up!' called a male voice. I took Jim into the main

281

bedroom, collected a bathrobe, turned out the light, and went into the hall, leaving the door to the bedroom slightly open.

'Who is it?'

'Police. Open up!'

'Why should I? How do I know who you are?' I stalled.

'Open this door before we break it down!'

I put the chain on and opened the door. Three men in Snorter's uniforms faced me – in black leather uniforms, which meant they were from Outside, not the Ceepee. The one in front handed me his ID. What were they doing Inside?

'An Outsider broke through the Wall this afternoon and we have reason to believe he's in this area,' he said, as if reading my mind. 'We're searching the whole building.'

I couldn't think of any good reason to refuse them entry. The ID looked genuine, so I closed the door, took off the chain, and opened the door wide.

'You won't find him here, but you're welcome to look,' I said. The three men entered.

'May I see your papers, miss?' said the first. The others began searching the apartment.

'Certainly. This way.' I led him into the kitchen where I had left my bag. As I reached for my papers I heard voices from the bedroom. The Snorter grabbed my wrist and yanked me with him towards the bedroom.

'Hey! What the hell – ' I complained.

'Shut up!' he said, retaining hold of my wrist.

Jim was in bed, looking as if he'd just woken up. I couldn't see the knife. One of the other Snorters was rummaging through Jim's jeans on the chair next to the bed. He came up with the false card and handed it to his superior. He barely looked at it. He shook his head and smiled nastily.

'Oh dear, sir. It appears we have a little problem.'

'What's that?' asked Jim, apparently not too concerned.

'You said your name was Roper? John Roper?'

'What of it?'

'Well, that's the name on this card all right, and it could even be your photo. But I must admit you're looking a lot healthier than you were a few hours ago. Wonderful thing, modern science.' He was obviously enjoying himself immensely. 'When I saw you last, you were stretched out on a slab at St Pancras mortuary. Now, get up, before I put a bullet in you.' He drew his gun from its holster and pointed it at Jim's head.

Before I could move, the others came behind me and took my arms.

'Up against the wall! Put your hands on it. Higher!' Jim did as he was told. 'And you, Miss Mason.' The one who held me forced me against the wall next to Jim and then backed away from us. Fuck me, I thought, this is it!

'Get those hands up where I can see them,' he commanded. I heard the sound of a magazine being slipped into a gun.

'You're making a mistake . . .' said Jim, half turning towards them.

'Not me, pal – ' began the Snorter. He didn't finish the sentence. I turned to see a frenzy of action. The bedroom was suddenly full of pink swirling robes. The Snorter with the gun was lying motionless, half across the bed. Another was thrashing about on the floor, a Pinkie astride his chest. The third was still fumbling with his gun when Jim reached him. I saw Jim's hand move sharply up and down. The Snorter and he seemed to embrace for a moment, and then the Snorter slid down Jim's body and on to the floor. It was all over. A Pinkie pushed past me and bent over Jim who was sitting on the edge of the bed, nursing a wound in his shoulder. In his hand was the kitchen knife. There was blood smeared on it up to the hilt.

'He's all right,' said the Pinkie, apparently to his colleague.

There was a light rhythmic tapping on the outside door and a third Pinkie entered.

'I've secured the outside. There were two more waiting in a transport.'

'What the hell's going on?' I demanded.

'Get him into the kitchen,' said one of them, ignoring me. They picked Jim up and carried him into the kitchen. They sat him in the same chair as the one to which I had tied Graham. One went off while the others looked at the wound, and I heard the sound of cloth tearing. He returned with strips of what had been Graham's best sheets. One of them produced a syringe.

'Just a sec,' said Jim. 'What is it?'

'Will someone please tell me what's happening?' I asked.

'Morphine – for the pain.'

'Will it make me sleepy?'

'Probably.'

'What the fuck is going on?' I shouted.

'Then I don't want it,' said Jim, but still wincing with pain. The Pinkies looked at each other.

'Excuse me? Remember me?' I said.

'Look, Demon, you've been shot – ' said the Pinkie.

'I haven't. I've been stabbed, and it was my own stupid fault.'

I decided that no one was going to answer me. I looked at Jim's ashen face and realized that he had been quite badly wounded.

'Look, Demon, either way, don't you think you should have it?'

'She's right,' said one of the Pinkies. 'It's a nasty

284

wound. We've got to get you back to the Annex. We've got some medics there.'

'Just a minute,' said Jim, 'before we go any further, perhaps you'll tell me how you happened just to be passing – not that I'm not grateful, you understand.'

'My name's Caplin,' said the one who came in last, as he cleaned Jim's wound and began to bandage him. 'This is Fuzz, and this is Strad.' He indicated his two companions. 'You saw us talking to Knife in the refectory. He told us to keep an eye on you.'

'And that means following us home?'

'He told us to stick with you whatever happened. We picked up the Snorters almost as soon as we left the Annex. They seemed to have been waiting,' said Caplin.

'I know,' said Jim.

'You know!' I interrupted. 'You mean you knew they were coming after us?'

'It all fell into place on the way back. I didn't know it would be them, and I didn't know it would be so soon, but I knew something like this would happen.' Even with his white and drawn face he managed to look smug. 'Are you finished?' he asked Caplin.

'Just about. I think you'd be better with your arm in a sling. Too much movement and you'll start bleeding again.'

'Whatever you say, doc,' said Jim. He was remarkably cheerful. I should have known he was up to something.

'Get me clothes, will you?' asked Jim. Strad went into the bedroom and returned with Jim's things.

'The "Leather Boys" don't do internal work, do they?' I continued. 'They're used Outside, and on the Wall.'

'That's right,' said Strad. 'I'll bet they weren't Snorters at all.'

'Maybe. It's not all that important. The question is how they got to be here,' said Jim, struggling into his shirt.

'Agreed,' said Fuzz.

I suddenly felt very cold. 'They were after me. Henry said I'd still be at risk. They must have been with McCready.'

'Possibly,' said Jim, 'but I don't think so. Got a J, love?'

'Yes, they're . . . er . . . in the bedroom.' I got him a joint and returned to the kitchen.

'But – ' I began.

'Your orders are to go wherever I go, right?' Jim asked Caplin, ignoring me.

'Yes.'

'What else?'

'To trust you implicitly. And to guard your life like it was our own.' He smiled grimly. 'We were a bit slow. We didn't expect them just to come up the stairs like that.'

'Never mind that now.' Jim paused, screwed up his face as if he were trying to recall something important, and then stood up. 'Kate, what's Jordan's phone number?'

'What? What do you want it for?'

Jim shook his head. 'I . . . I can't tell you,' he said slowly.

'Then you can hardly expect me to give it to you.'

'Listen, girl. I wouldn't ask for it unless this was an emergency. Someone has just tried to kill us, right? Why do you think you were allowed to go home? This is just the beginning. And believe me, it's not only our lives that are at stake.'

I shook my head. There was no way I was going to tell him without knowing why he wanted it. There was a long silence.

'435 2232,' said Caplin. 'But Demon . . . if this isn't an emergency . . .' Jim grinned.

'Thanks, Caplin. Now, I've got some business to attend to.'

'Where are we going?' I asked in astonishment.

286

'*We* aren't going anywhere. Caplin: she's not to leave here until you hear from me, right?'

Caplin looked hard at Jim. 'You're not keeping me prisoner!' I cried.

'Okay, Demon. I hope you know what you're doing,' said Caplin.

'Me too.'

'If you go out of that door, Jim Demon – ' but it was too late. The front door slammed behind him.

Part Five

41

'Is that you, Henry?'

'Who is this?'

'Demon. Jim Demon. Remember me? I'm the geezer who tried to kill you yesterday.'

'I remember. Where the hell did you get my number? Do you know what time it is?'

'We're quits now, aren't we?'

'What are you talking about?'

'We're even. I tried to do you in, and now you've tried it on me.'

'Listen, Demon, or whatever your name is: it's late, I'm tired, and I've still got work to do. If you've got something sensible to say, say it, or I'm going to hang up.'

'Henry, I have *lots* to say, but I ain't saying it over the phone.'

'Goodnight, Mr Demon.'

'Before you go, you'd better know that the second you hang up, I'm going to phone the Ministry of Information. I have a bit of *information* for them. About your predecessor, the late lamented Ms Fowler.'

'What about her?'

'Like I said, Henry, I'm not prepared to discuss it on the phone. Let's just say that my information is for sale and I'm giving you first refusal on it. If you don't want to buy, I'm sure your friends at the other Ministries would be delighted to do so. That might be a bit costly to you, of course. Your public image might get a bit tarnished, know what I mean?'

There was a long pause at the other end of the line.

'Okay. Where and when?'

'There's no time like the present. Come to St Paul's Cathedral. Go in, and go down the right-hand aisle. You'll find a staircase that leads to the Whispering Gallery. You'll come out through a door underneath a statue of St Jerome. Wait there. You got that?'

'I've got it.'

'And Jordan: come alone. I'll be watching you all the way in. If there's anyone with you, you won't meet me.'

'I understand.' I hung up.

I didn't know exactly where Jordan lived, but I'd skimmed through one of the directories in the booth, and the 435 exchange seemed to be somewhere in the northwest of the city, at a place called Hampstead. I reckoned it would take him at least half an hour to get to St Paul's, but I didn't want to take any chances, so I went straight back into the Cathedral.

Since leaving Kate's, I'd been racking my brains for somewhere safe to meet Jordan. I wanted to do it that night; every hour I left it meant Kate and I were at risk, and anyway, I felt safer in the dark. I'd spent most of my life in the shadows whereas Jordan wouldn't be used to it. That gave me an advantage. But where? Couldn't be out in the open – he'd just pick me off. It had to be inside, somewhere that was quiet, but big enough to give me some space to move. Then I remembered the Cathedral. It had been open the night Knife and I broke in, and that was after midnight. So I went down there. Sure enough, it was open all night.

When I got there and scouted round a bit, I realized it was perfect! There were a few people in the main part of the building, praying and that, but while I was looking for somewhere quiet, I found this passage which led to a staircase. I climbed the stairs – I lost count after two hundred – and came out into this circular gallery around the base of the dome. Incredible it was. There were eight doors leading on to it, each one under a statue. They were lit up with spotlights, so as you came out of a door, the light struck you full on, and you could be seen from any part of the gallery. Once you moved out of the light, you were completely invisible. It was really eerie, what with the whole dome being lit up with alternate strips of light and dark. But the best bit was the sound! I stood on one side of the gallery, and this old foreign geezer was standing on the other side, mumbling about something – probably all the stairs he'd had to climb – and I could hear every word he said! The sound seemed to come from all around me. I guess that's why the place was called the Whispering Gallery.

I took up a position just to the left of St Basil, right opposite where Jordan would appear. If anything went wrong, there was a door behind me and it would take him a minute or two to get round there. I knew that there was no way of guaranteeing that he would come on his own. I'd just have to take a chance that he'd believed me when I said I'd be watching.

I settled down to wait. Way down below the marble slabs were laid out in black and white diagonal lines like a chess board. Again I had the idea that Jordan and I were two players, each trying to out-guess the other. I checked Kate's gun. I had taken it while she was out of the kitchen getting me a J and I had hidden it in the sling. The magazine was half-empty. Or half-full, depending on how you looked at it.

I'd only been waiting twenty minutes when I heard faint footsteps approaching from opposite me. They were light, and hesitant, and although I couldn't be sure, I thought they were made by one person. There was a pause as the footsteps stopped, and for a moment I panicked. Had I missed him? Had he gone through the spotlight without me seeing? Then the sound resumed. A figure stepped full into the light; it was Jordan. I could see him clear as day, his slender, almost graceful frame, and that sharp face, like a bird of prey. I even thought I could see his eyes glinting from where I crouched.

I spoke softly, but as clearly as I could. 'Stay exactly where you are, Jordan. If you move an inch I shall shoot you.'

He raised his hand to shield his eyes from the glare. 'Where are you?' he asked, speaking too loudly. His words reverberated around the gallery, repeating themselves, overlapping, becoming indistinct. It sounded like a choir of ghosts whispering in my ears. I waited for the echoes to stop before answering.

'Speak softly, my friend. We don't want everyone to hear, do we? It doesn't matter where I am. We're here to talk, not to look at one another.'

'You have an unnecessary taste for melodrama, Demon. Couldn't you have picked somewhere more sensible?' he whispered.

'We're both here now. Let's get on with it.' I had a suspicion he was stalling for time, and I didn't want to remain there for a moment longer than was necessary.

'The ball's in your court. What's this information you're selling?' he asked.

'You set me up tonight.'

'Did I?'

'You did. Me and Kate. Only three people knew for certain where I was going after the briefing, you, your driver, and Knife.'

'So?'

'Of those people, only you and Knife knew that my papers were false, and it would have taken a computer check to prove it. But someone tipped off the Snorters.

That was you.' He didn't answer. I couldn't see it, but I'd have put money on the fact that he was smiling.

'That was silly, Henry. Clever sending Snorters and not the Ceepee, but silly doing it in the first place. I knew something wasn't right, what with your personal guard following me all over the Annex during the briefing. But I might never have been sure if those Snorters hadn't turned up. You set me thinking, see? What did I know without realizing it?' I paused. I wanted Jordan's interest. I wanted him taking part in the conversation, and, sure enough, he rose to the bait.

'Well, did you work it out?'

'Oh yes. You killed Marie Fowler. I mean, maybe you didn't actually shoot her or whatever yourself, but you betrayed her. You told McCready she was the head of the Resistance. Remember how we were at cross-purposes when you interrogated me? You said you thought there were two of us, meaning two people from McCready's Ministry. I never even knew what Ministry that was . . .'

'Information.'

'Yeh? Well, that makes sense. Anyway, that question was reasonable – after all, I *could* have been gunning for you for the same reasons as McCready. But then you asked me where I thought McCready had got "the Minister's name". It took a while before I remembered it. You blew it, didn't you? No wonder you were furious when you found out I was just an avenging lover!'

'Is that it? Is that what you have to sell? I'm not impressed, Mr Demon. Firstly, you'll never prove it. And secondly, how long do you think you can survive now? Inside or Out, where are you going to go? What are you going to do?'

'Do? That's simple, Jordan. I'm going to kill you.'

He laughed, a short, hard laugh like a hyena's. I was suddenly aware of a noise. There was someone on the stairs just behind me! I leapt away from the door, ran a few metres along the gallery to my left, and pressed myself into the shadows against the wall of the dome. I looked up again. Jordan was gone! I looked back at the doorway through which I had come. I wasn't far enough round to see it. I leant out slightly. The door was closed! I knew then that I'd made a mistake, a bad mistake.

I stayed where I was and listened. There was still no sign of Jordan. Think, Demon, think! I hadn't heard footsteps going down the far staircase; that meant that Jordan was still there, waiting for me. I was trapped! There were three doors between me and Jordan, but to get to any of them meant stepping into the light. Would he have covered all of them? Only one way to find out. I took a deep breath and launched myself further along the gallery. The whole dome came alive with the sound of running feet. I dived into the next beam of light and an explosion thundered around me. I hit the floor and felt something sharp strike my cheek. I rolled over once into the darkness on the far side and looked back. Masonry dust danced around in the beam of light, making it look as though it was solid. I looked at the door I had just passed. It too was shut. I suppose if you've got to die, a cathedral is as good a place as any, I thought. Like being run down by an ambulance.

'He's coming towards you, sir!' came a shout from behind me. There was a movement on the far side where I'd last seen Jordan. Jordan jumped into the light, running in my direction. I rolled on to my stomach, pointed the gun through the railings, and fired into the light. He changed direction and retreated into the darkness. Okay! If I could keep him there I might get a chance to try the two remaining doors between us. The echoes slowly faded away. We were all waiting for the next move.

'Radford, listen carefully,' hissed Jordan. 'When I give

the command we'll run towards each other. He can't shoot at us both.'

There was a pause. Another mistake, Jordan, I thought; now I know there are only two of you.

'Did you hear me, Radford?'

'Yes, sir,' came the very hesitant reply. Radford was no fool.

'Ready . . . Go!'

If I can take only one of them, it's got to be Jordan, I thought. I remained where I was and aimed into the beam that Jordan would hit first. The clatter of footsteps was deafening. I realized too late: he'd conned both me and Radford; he wasn't going to run anywhere. I swivelled round, but my arm caught in the railings. A shot rang out, but from the small gallery *above* us!

'Back up, Demon! Go the other way! I've got Jordan's doorway covered!' It was Caplin! I scrambled to my feet and ran like hell. I saw Radford's body just in time to leap over it, and kept going. I passed the door through which I'd come, through the next beam of light and on to the next door. Shut! As I looked to my left I saw Jordan sprinting towards me. He'd changed direction and was heading for the same exit. And he was going to get there before me. I passed the next door and looked up again. Jordan had stopped, facing me, haloed in the light of the last doorway, his arms raised in front of him. I knew he was going to fire, but there was nothing I could do about it. I charged at him. I was aware of another explosion, whether from Caplin or Jordan I didn't know, but I was still on my feet. Jordan turned and disappeared through the doorway. I was about to follow when Caplin called from above.

'I've barred the door! He can't get out at the bottom!'

I had him!

'Be careful, Demon!'

I stood at the top of the spiral staircase, trying to catch my breath. I could hear Jordan scampering down the stairs in the darkness ahead of me. I called after him.

'You're wasting your time, Jordan. It's locked at the bottom.' The footsteps slowed, and stopped. After a short pause they continued. He didn't believe me. I wasn't surprised; I wouldn't have believed *him*.

I started down the steps, counting them carefully. I kept close to the outside wall of the spiral where the steps were widest. The staircase was unlit, but every now and then I passed a window which shed just enough light to see. I had counted one hundred and twenty steps when the footfalls ahead of me stopped. I waited. Jordan rattled the door at the bottom, at first gently, and then with increasing force. Then silence. I continued my descent as quietly as I could. I kicked against something and it fell down a couple of steps ahead of me. I picked it up. It was Jordan's gun. It was still warm. He must have dropped it as he ran. I pulled out the magazine. Empty. I started down again, still counting, until I reached step two hundred and ten. Jordan should have been just around the corner. There was an alcove set in the wall and I sat on its ledge.

'You there, Jordan?' I asked softly.

'I'm here.' Jordan's voice came out of the darkness. It was very close and he sounded very calm.

'You dropped your gun.'

'It was empty anyway. Still got yours?' he asked wryly.

'Yeh.'

'Any bullets left?'

'Don't know. We'll find out in a minute.'

'Why don't you come down and get it over with?' he asked.

'I want to talk to you.'

There was a long pause. I could hear him breathing.

'Well?' he asked.

298

'You know I'm going to kill you?'

'So you keep saying. You said the same yesterday, but I'm still alive.'

'Things have changed. *I* have changed.'

'In one day?'

'In one day.'

'Because of Marie?'

'No, not really.'

'Why then? Why is it worth it today when it wasn't worth it yesterday?'

I shrugged. 'You really want to hear?' There was no answer. 'Okay.'

I wondered where to start. I hadn't really thought it out myself yet.

'I used to sit there in Ilford Public Library, admiring you. Honest, I really admired you. You predicted that the Technocratic Revolution would come, all that stuff about the "Haves" and the "Have-Nots", those with and those without the knowledge. And when I found out that not only had you predicted it, but you had *designed* it, in a way that was even better. I mean, I'm not saying you're a nice bloke, Jordan, 'cos you're not. You're a user. Even then, I understood it, you know? You'd warned everyone, fair and square.'

'Then what's changed?'

'I found you out. You're a fraud. Your system's a fraud. Expo's a fraud. Exit visas are a fraud. Usurping's a fraud. That's the worst. One hundred and fifty people a month are slaughtered trying to get into your false paradise. I used to think that, immoral though it was, all you were doing was legalizing what happened anyway, but I've realized that that's bollocks. You created the demand for Work Permits by telling everyone how great it was Inside. By lying about Exit Visas. You needed the Usurpers to give you an excuse to tighten up on security, to keep the pressure on your opponents.'

'No. You're wrong. I needed the Usurpers, but not for that reason. Don't you realize that in the twenty years before the Wall was built, science, art, all forms of human endeavour, took an immense leap forward? A new Renaissance! But the Wall ended it. It provided safety, wealth, comfort. The best minds in England gathered together within a few square kilometres, and they just . . . went to sleep! There was no struggle any more, everything was too easy. We started to stagnate. I just provided society with a threat, a predator.'

I thought about that for a while.

'It didn't work though, did it?' I said. 'The Usurpers were never a real threat 'cos so few succeeded. Even when they did, the important jobs were protected anyway.'

'The whole thing began to fall apart. I was faced with opposition even among my own supporters. Yet I *knew* I'd been right – that it could work – if I could only find the right stimulus.'

'So you formed the Resistance. That was far more effective. You could attack from Inside. I guess that Marie Fowler really believed in it, eh? She was merrily trying to destroy the monster she'd help to create, whereas all *you* were doing was giving it a kick in the pants.'

'So, now you've worked it all out.' He sounded bored, almost irritated. 'That doesn't explain why you say you're going to kill me.'

'Maybe not, but it's all I've got. I always thought that nothing was important enough to kill someone for. Sure, I wanted what I thought was on offer on the Inside as much as anyone – you'd have to be mad not to, after living in Ilford – but I wouldn't kill for a job. Yesterday I was out of my head for a while, but even then, revenge wasn't a good enough reason to kill someone, even a

300

bastard like you. In the last analysis, nothing would change. But now I know that if I kill you, something will change. Funny thing is, you've only yourself to blame, Jordan, 'cos you're the one who taught me the lesson: violence works. You've been using violence to prop up your Technological Revolution for years. I'm prepared to use violence to end it. And at least I'll have the satisfaction of knowing that the blokes in the Resistance will have an even chance from now on.'

'Do you really think that by killing me, everything will change?'

'I don't know,' I admitted. 'But, if you'll forgive the pun, I reckon it's worth a shot.'

I slipped off my ledge and prepared to descend the last few steps.

'Are you ready?' I asked.

'You won't do it, Demon. You won't shoot me in cold blood.'

He was wrong there too.

42

Ilford hadn't changed, but then, although it felt like months, I'd only been away a few days. Mum and Dad were pleased to see me. Well, Mum was. Dad hadn't noticed that I'd been anywhere, but like I told you, nothing much touches him any more. Apparently, after my interrogation, Jordan sent two Ceepee out to them to confirm who I was. Dad thought they were Console repair men. Still, Mum said they'd been very nice, and had had a cup of tea.

Mum asked me what I was going to do now. I told her I didn't really know. I asked Knife whether the Resistance was just going to carry on blowing things up. He looked wistful for a minute, and said that he supposed not, but that it was something to do in the meantime.

Jordan's death created much less of a stir than I had anticipated. Officially, it was announced that he had been lured to his death, presumably by the Resistance. Knife told me that, unofficially, many members of the government had heaved a sigh of relief. Jordan was quickly replaced by some rising star from the Ministry of Information, and the word was that the Security of Employment Act was to be reviewed in the next parliament. But most significantly, I happened to catch the Nooz at Noon a few days after I got back. There was this item on the crime figures inside the Wall. I'll tell you, there's more mugging and murder Inside than in Ilford! Thing is, they never used to give out that sort of information. I mean, who wants to Usurp into the middle of a crime wave? It struck me that, although it wasn't a big thing, that was the most optimistic bit of news I'd heard in years.

I expect you're wondering about Kate and me. That makes two of us. Mum says that Gina rang almost every day after I left. That girl's brighter than I realized, 'cos she'd worked out where I'd gone. Still, I don't think I'll be seeing her.

Kate's pretty pissed off with life Inside. Blowing up buildings is a bit too public-spirited for her – social reform never was her strong suit – and I think she's realized that even if she gets a new identity, life Inside isn't going to be that much fun from now on. I overheard her talking to Paul Rossi, and she asked him if as well as a new name she could get a new Social Security number, which means she's thinking of coming back Outside.

I asked the old lady if she would mind if Kate stayed with us every now and then. And you know, she was dead pleased! Said it would give her someone to talk to while I was down the Library. I sort of mentioned to Kate that there was a spare bed round our place if she ever needed it. She grinned, said I was all right, and affectionately punched my chest.

Anyway, I'm off down the Library. The way I see it, it's high time someone wrote the sequel to 'The Impact of Technology etc.', just to put the record straight, so to speak. And I figure I'm as good a man for the job as any, right? I mean, let's face it, I've seen it from both sides of the fence now. And I've already got the title: 'Dead Men's Shoes'.

What do you think?